BREAKAWAY

Also by Kat Spears
Sway

BREAKAWAY

KAT SPEARS

St. Martin's Griffin ⚏ New York

BREAKAWAY. Copyright © 2015 by Kat Spears. All rights reserved. Printed in the United States of America. For information, address St. Martin's Press, 175 Fifth Avenue, New York, N.Y. 10010.

www.stmartins.com

Designed by Omar Chapa

Library of Congress Cataloging-in-Publication Data

Spears, Katarina M.
    Breakaway : a novel / Kat Spears. — First edition.
        pages ; cm
    ISBN 978-1-250-06551-3 (hardcover)
    ISBN 978-1-4668-7247-9 (e-book)
    I. Title.
    PS3619.P4343B74 2015
    813'.6—dc23
                                        2015019024

Our books may be purchased in bulk for promotional, educational, or business use. Please contact your local bookseller or the Macmillan Corporate and Premium Sales Department at (800) 221-7945, extension 5442, or by e-mail at MacmillanSpecialMarkets@macmillan.com.

First Edition: September 2015

10 9 8 7 6 5 4 3 2 1

*For Harant "Harry" Soghigian, father and
best friend, a king among men*

ACKNOWLEDGMENTS

As ever, a million thanks to my editor, Sara Goodman, for the way she deeply loves my characters and pushes me to write the best story possible. She has so much faith in my books it makes me wish I were a better writer. And endless thanks to my agent, Barbara Poelle, for always telling me I'm great, even when I'm not.

This is a very personal book for me, reflecting the people I knew in high school, their very real struggles and life situations. I must acknowledge the funny and amazing boys and girls, now amazing men and women, I knew in high school who made up my South A family of friends. Every "your mama" joke in this book was inspired by them.

This book also reflects the personalities and clever dialogue spoken by the people who populate my life at the Lucky Bar. People who work in the service industry, especially those at the Lucky Bar, are the funniest and smartest people I know.

Thanks to Maile for allowing me to use her Jay Z/DMX

joke. I couldn't, in good conscience, ever take credit for that bit of brilliance.

Jason's personality and internal monologue were inspired by one very exceptional person. A person I love and cherish. And even though he will go unrecognized in these pages by anyone who knows him, he's the only reason I could write this book. I hope everyone who reads this book falls in love with Jason, because he truly deserves it.

BREAKAWAY

CHAPTER ONE

I sat on the stoop, a small concrete step outside the door to our apartment, hoping I could avoid going back inside until everyone was gone. We lived in what the rental office called a "garden apartment" because we had a door that opened directly to the outside instead of into the central stairwell, though there was nothing even remotely like a garden on the grounds of our apartment complex. The hard-packed earth and gravel yard sustained only a few scrubby patches of grass, and the trees were wilted and sad, their knobby roots exposed.

As I sat there Chick came walking up the slope from the parking lot, rubbing his nose on the sleeve of his jacket. He was wearing something that resembled a suit. A dark jacket that was two sizes too big for him, and a pair of gray slacks that were held up with a beat-up, brown leather belt. The knot of his tie was almost as big as his head.

"Hey, Jaz," he said as he approached me. "Sorry I couldn't make it to the funeral. Jordie and his mom couldn't pick me up and I didn't have another ride. You doing okay, buddy?"

Chick was panting slightly and the small pink scars on his face stood out in stark relief to his chalky complexion.

"Nice suit," I said as I ran my finger under the collar of my shirt to relieve the pressure on my neck. "Did you beat up an old man on the street to steal that?"

"You're hilarious," Chick said with a tilt of his head. "And an asshole. But somehow, I still care whether or not you're doing okay."

No, I wasn't okay, but I didn't say that. Actually, at that moment I had been thinking about how much I was dying to get out of my tie, but figured I should keep it on until everyone was gone. "I'm doing all right," I said grudgingly. The way Chick's eyes were probing my face, I knew he wanted more of an answer, but he wasn't going to get it.

Chick's real name was Walter Fitzgerald Gunderson, but a really bad case of the chicken pox when he was a little kid had forever marked him for the nickname Chick. He was small and thin and took more sick days than any other kid in school. The scars on his face were a daily reminder of just what a sickly little kid he had been. At seventeen he still looked like he was twelve. I was the one who had started calling him Chick when he returned to third grade after a long absence for his illness. Maybe it had started out me calling him that because I was being a prick, but he had taken it as a show of friendship. I had made it to my senior year only because Chick did the homework I didn't have the patience to do myself, and I was the only thing that stood between him and the regular mistreatment he would have taken from bullies. Freshman year alone I got at-home suspension three times for fighting, just because I was sticking up for Chick.

"Is Mario here?" Chick asked as he peered through the window of the apartment.

"Yeah," I said. "Jordie too."

"Everything go okay at the funeral?"

I hesitated as I tried to think what I could tell him about the funeral. Nothing. There was nothing I could say, but I knew what everyone would be talking about at school. My little freak-out, which, I was trying to convince myself, maybe not everyone had noticed. Still, I didn't know how I was going to go to school on Monday, since it was all anyone would be talking about.

There had been plenty of people from school at the church for the funeral service, even a few teachers, but the sea of faces had been just a blur. The only faces there that meant anything to me were Jordie's and Mario's, the only people there who were real. Everyone else was just a confusion of insincere tears and empty condolences.

At the church, Mario and Jordie had both come to sit in the front pew, the space reserved for family, without being asked. They were the only family I had besides Mom and Aunt Gladys and Uncle Dan. At least, the only family that mattered.

I was supposed to have been a pallbearer, along with Aunt Gladys's husband, my uncle Dan, and the two men who were serving as ushers during the service. But when it came time and I sat there contemplating the white casket smothered in pink lilies sitting at the base of the altar, I felt a sick feeling rising in my gut. All I could think about was that only a few inches of lacquered wood separated me from Sylvia's body, and it creeped me out so much, I couldn't move, as if my feet were glued to the floor. There was no way I could put my hand on that coffin. No way I could lift it knowing the weight I carried was the dead body of my sister.

I had just stood there like an idiot for a minute, then turned and looked back at Mario as everyone in the church waited for me to join the other three men at the casket, their hands poised above the handles. Though it felt as if an eternity passed while Mario read my face, in reality it was only a few seconds. Mario stood and, without another glance at me, took my place at the fourth handle. I hung back near the altar while everyone else filed out of the church behind the casket.

"How was the service?" Chick asked, bringing me back to the present.

"I don't know. Okay, I guess," I said, wishing he would drop it. Chick had a terrible habit of talking about his feelings, and expecting other people to do the same. That, and his weak body, had permanently relegated him to the friend zone with girls.

"You know, I've never been to a funeral before," Chick said thoughtfully. "Least not one that I remember, since I was a baby and all when my mom died. But it's good for you, you know? Gives you a chance to be sad. You really need that."

"Mm," I murmured as that was all the encouragement Chick usually needed to keep talking.

Mario and Jordie came spilling out the door then, eager to get away from the crush of strangers. Mario had been tugging on his tie and the knot was twisted to one side, his shaggy black hair lapping over the collar of his shirt. He had forgone his usual fauxhawk, at his mom's insistence I was sure. She made him go to confession and Mass every week, though he always went to Saturday evening Mass so he didn't have to get up early on Sunday and spend half the day at church with his family. Over the years I had endured many sermons as I waited for Mario's release into the freedom of a Saturday night.

Mario's mom had come to the church but left before we went to the cemetery because she couldn't get the time off work to stay for the graveside service. She was a small woman who didn't speak very good English, though her chocolate brown eyes knew everything with a glance. She and Mario crossed themselves during the service since they were Catholic. Mario's mom usually attended Spanish Mass so I wasn't even sure she understood everything the priest said, but she knew instinctively when to stand, when to drop her head and pray, when to cross herself.

"Hey, Chick," Mario said. He worried the knot in his tie as he spoke. I had never seen Mario dressed in a suit, and the clothes looked almost as uncomfortable on him as he must have been in them.

Jordie wore a suit too, but with the comfort of long practice. His dad was a colonel in the army, and that was what we all called him, the Colonel. Even Jordie called him that. But Jordie's dad also came from money. Jordie's mom was Vietnamese, a fact he was always trying to forget, though she cooked the best Vietnamese food you'd ever taste. Her pho was legendary. Jordie was a strange blend of his parents—fair skinned with honey-brown hair, but with his mother's eyes.

"How you holding up, Jaz?" Mario asked.

I shrugged. "Okay, I guess."

"Jesus, so many people were at the funeral," Jordie said. "I couldn't believe it. You'd think Sylvia was Miley Cyrus."

"You keep mentioning Miley Cyrus, man," Mario said with

an accusing glance at Jordie as he dug a crumpled cigarette out of his pocket and straightened it with care. "Why are you so into Miley Cyrus?"

"I'm not *into* Miley Cyrus," Jordie said, taking Mario's bait. I was immune to it. Mario could never suck me into a defensive conversation anymore. I knew him too well. But Jordie, even after knowing Mario and me for five years, almost a third of our lives at that point, was still an easy mark. "I'm just using it as a comparison," Jordie said, giving way too much explanation. He never was good with a comeback. "Miley Cyrus is famous. So, I'm saying it's like Sylvia is famous."

God, Jordie couldn't just let it go. Mario had gotten what he wanted, a rise out of Jordie, so he would soon lose interest.

"I'm just saying you mention Miley Cyrus a lot," Mario said to Jordie, changing tack as he lit his cigarette, then took it away from his lips to blow at the ember. "If that's what you're into, that's cool."

"Watch out," I said with a nod toward the parking lot. "Your mama just got here, Mario."

Mario's cigarette was already on the ground, his foot hovering just above it as he spun to look over his shoulder in a panic. Jordie and Chick laughed in appreciation as Mario cussed at me.

"*Pendejo* motherfucker," Mario said. He scowled in my direction as he bent over to retrieve his cigarette, now flattened, the tip still barely smoking. He straightened the cigarette again and relit it, then kicked my shoe.

"Mama's boy," I said, the worst insult we could throw at each other short of talking shit about someone's mom. Maybe I was immune to Mario, but I could still get him just about anytime I wanted.

"So, Jordie," Mario said, "that girl Cheryl. I saw you talking to her at the funeral."

"Seriously?" I asked, giving Jordie a pained look. "You were hitting on girls at my sister's funeral? Damn, man," I said with a shake of my head.

If fucking with Jordie were an Olympic-qualifying event, Mario and I would have gold and silver medals. We never messed with Chick. He was too sensitive and was always the first to come to the defense of whoever was being singled out for mistreatment. Even though most people knew never to fuck with Chick because of me, he still got picked on and bullied when I wasn't around. But Jordie was fair game. Since he had gotten a car for his seventeenth birthday and was waiting to hear about early acceptance to Dartmouth Jordie had become almost impossible to be around. He was so consumed with his future, how every choice, every test grade, could have some devastating impact on his life plan. Jordie had so much going for him—money, good looks, supportive family—that I figured anytime Mario and I could give him some self-esteem-reduction therapy, it was just helping him out.

Jordie was stricken at my comment, like I was really upset he had been hitting on girls at Syl's funeral, and looked back and forth between Mario and me questioningly. "I wasn't hitting on her. I was just talking to her. She approached *me,*" he said defensively. "Why? Do you . . . I mean, you don't think she's into me, do you?"

"You mean, because of your looks?" Mario asked. "Absolutely not. But for your money? Yeah, maybe."

"You guys are dicks," Jordie said, finally catching on to the fact that we were messing with him. "Cheryl's family has plenty of money. She doesn't need mine."

"She does look expensive," Mario said.

"I'd be careful with that girl," I said. "She knows how to look out for number one."

"Yeah, well, nobody asked you, so stop talking," Jordie said. "Anyway, Jaz, you're the one who's going to be getting the serious strange. I must have had fifty girls asking me about you this past week, since Sylvia died."

"Me too." Chick, rejoining the conversation abruptly, had been lost in his own head for a bit, the way he got sometimes when his mind wandered to places most other people's didn't go. "Girls were asking me about Jaz. Wanting to know where he hangs out and whether he's dating anyone."

"Congratulations," Mario said then flicked his cigarette butt toward the parking lot. "You've hit the big time. You'll be like a celebrity until everyone remembers they only give a fuck about themselves."

"Hey, Jaz, you want us to stick around?" Jordie asked.

"Nah," I said. "You guys have suffered enough. You go ahead." Since I knew they would stay if I asked, I didn't really need them there.

"I can drop you guys off on my way home," Jordie said.

"You guys go ahead," Mario said as he settled onto the stoop beside me. "I'm going to hang for a bit."

Mario and I sat in silence and watched Jordie and Chick walk to Jordie's car. It wasn't until you saw Chick walking beside someone as healthy and athletic as Jordie that you really noticed how stunted and wilted he was. It was several minutes after Jordie's car had disappeared behind the next apartment building that I broke the silence.

"I couldn't touch that casket," I said. "I couldn't stop

thinking about her—I mean her actual body—being in that box. Creeped me the fuck out, man."

Mario just nodded in understanding as he tossed a pebble across the sidewalk.

"Everyone at the funeral probably thought I was a total freak," I said and rested my forearms on my knees, one hand grasping my opposite wrist. I squinted into the sun as it set over the roof of the neighboring building.

"Who gives a fuck what anybody thinks?" Mario asked. "She was your sister."

"Yeah, I know. I don't give a shit." And it was true. In that moment, I didn't really give a shit about anything.

CHAPTER TWO

I knew I couldn't avoid it forever, would eventually have to go interact with people who had come for Sylvia's funeral. Mario followed me back inside the apartment. I knew he would stick it out to the bitter end, even if he was dying to get out of his suit and tie as much as I was.

Though I knew it was spotlessly clean in our apartment, everything looked shabby and worn next to the neatly pressed outfits people wore. The sofa bed was put away but it was still kind of weird to have a bunch of people, who were really just strangers to me, sitting where I slept.

Aunt Gladys and some of Mom's friends from work had spent the day before the funeral cleaning the apartment and getting ready for company. Everybody had come back to our place to eat after the funeral. Neighbors had been coming by all week with food and Aunt Gladys had gotten some deli platters from the Safeway. That seemed weird to me too. People bring a whole bunch of food over to the house and then we have to feed them after the funeral, clean up their mess.

Mom was in rough shape, had been crying nonstop for the past week, and wasn't even really able to greet the guests who came to offer their condolences. Many times over the past week I had thought about touching her in some way, putting my arm around her or something to offer her comfort, but lately I had gotten the sense that she didn't really want me around. Like maybe she wished that it were me who had died instead of Sylvia.

We hardly ever had company. Sylvia never brought her friends home because she was too ashamed of our living conditions, and since the television was in Mom's room, we usually kept the sofa bed out. When Sylvia's dad still lived with us we had a four-bedroom apartment and I had my own room. Now I used the living room, so if we did have people over it made the situation kind of awkward, like now, when it would be obvious to anyone that there were only two bedroom doors. Maybe people would think Sylvia and I had shared a room.

At first people had just stood around the edges of the room, talking in whispers like we were still in church. No one wanted to dive straight for the food. Everyone held back, trying to be polite, but I could see them all looking at the spread. There were heaps of sandwich meat and cheese and some of those baby quiches. You'd have to eat two dozen of them just to get a decent mouthful so I left those alone.

Our little apartment was so crammed with people it was impossible to get to the bathroom, which was constantly in use anyway. I was standing there with Mario, thinking about how badly I had to piss when Alexis, Sylvia's best friend and a Wakefield cheerleader, showed up with her mom and dad. She looked like a doll dressed in a charcoal gray dress with her black hair pulled back in a severe bun, her face clear of any makeup.

Sylvia had been a cheerleader, and the members of the squad had kept a vigil at the hospital while Sylvia languished in her coma. The cheerleaders had gotten special permission to take turns missing school so that Sylvia was never alone. I had gone to the hospital a few times to visit Sylvia, but always at times when I knew I wouldn't run into any of her friends. As immediate family I was allowed to visit Sylvia after visiting hours, but I never could stay in the room with her very long. I spent most of the time I was at the hospital drinking really terrible coffee in the cafeteria.

"Hi, Jason," Alex said with a sniffle.

She looked older than I would have expected. Just a week ago she had seemed like a little kid to me, my kid sister's silly little friend. Now she looked like a young woman, and not a bad-looking one either. She startled me by leaning over to give me a hug, and she held on to me while her whole body shook with sobs.

"I miss her so much," Alex said, the words riding the crest of a sob. I didn't know what to say or do so I just rubbed her back with one hand while trying to hold the other one steady so I wouldn't spill my drink down the back of her dress.

Finally I got away from her and made it to the bathroom. I stayed in there for a while so people probably thought I was taking a dump. Actually I was sitting on the bathroom floor, my stomach aching with such sharp pains that I had to gasp for breath at times. I could feel the cool of the tile through my shirt, but beads of sweat still formed on my forehead and upper lip. After what seemed like forever I started to feel better and splashed cold water on my face.

I studied my reflection in the mirror to see if I needed to shave. It had been a few days but since Mom didn't say anything, I didn't bother shaving before the funeral. I didn't really like to let my beard grow in because even though my hair was dark brown, my beard grew in looking almost red. It looked stupid, dark brown hair with a reddish beard, so I never even tried to grow a goatee.

When I left the sanctuary of the bathroom the living room was so choked with people that I slipped into Sylvia's room just to avoid the crowd. In Sylvia's room, with her stuff scattered around, her clothes still hanging in the closet, it felt like she wasn't dead, just out with her friends or at cheerleading practice. Like any minute she'd come walking in the door and start yelling at me for being in her space.

The mattress groaned in protest as I sat on the edge of her twin bed. There was a jumble of trophies and ribbons on the dresser—swimming, cheerleading, gymnastics. Sylvia had been a cheerleader since she was in ninth grade, the only freshman accepted to the squad the previous year. I reached over to pick up a faux-bronze trophy with a miniature cheerleader on top. I wondered what kind of trophy you could get for cheerleading. Best pom-pom handling?

The inscribed plaque at its base was from Sylvia's cheer-leading camp—BEST TEAM SPIRIT, it said. The irony of that made me smile a little. It was a joke I could have shared with Sylvia, pointed out the irony to her and she would have gotten the humor in it right away. The only person, other than maybe Mario, who would have found it funny and not told me it was a sick joke. Thinking about that, that I would no longer have one of the two people who actually got me as a person, made my gut tighten again, and another wave of pain passed through my core.

"Jason?" Mom was standing in the doorway. She was swaying almost drunkenly from side to side. She hadn't been

drinking, had just been a little unsteady since Sylvia died, as if
one of her limbs had been amputated and it had ruined her balance. I almost wished she *would* start drinking. Maybe it would
make her sleep more, instead of staying up crying all night,
every night.

Her long auburn hair had started to unravel from its braid.
She was only thirty-six, young to have a son who was a senior
in high school, and I had gotten used to the fact that men looked
at her the way men shouldn't look at a mother with two
kids. But now she was so disheveled, her face drawn with
lines of worry and fatigue, she bore almost no resemblance
to the woman I knew.

After steadying herself with the wall she tottered over to
rest her hand on my shoulder. She gripped my shoulder with
a strength I didn't know she had, her body weight straining
the muscles in my neck.

Fresh tears spilled down her cheeks and she reached to
take the trophy from my hands. "She was such a beautiful girl,
Jason."

"I know, Ma."

"There are some people from school who just got here. You
should go and talk to them," she said.

"I don't really feel like talking," I said.

"I know. I know." She bent her head close to mine and
hiccoughed a little sob as she put her arms around my shoulders. My skin itched with discomfort. I waited for as long as I
could, until I thought the hug had lasted long enough, before
I shrugged my shoulders gently to break the embrace.

"I guess I'll go see who's here," I mumbled, and left her sitting
on the bed, holding Sylvia's trophy, tears dripping into her lap.

CHAPTER THREE

Aunt Gladys tried to talk me out of going to school the next day. I didn't tell her that if I were going to miss school, it definitely wouldn't be so I could sit home with Mom and watch her cry more.

"Your mother's very fragile right now, Jason," Aunt Gladys said.

Yeah, no kidding.

"But maybe it would be better for you to get things back to normal as soon as possible." She smiled encouragingly, as if she understood me. As if there was anything to understand.

I have always been amazed by how far saying nothing can get me. If I just shut my mouth, usually people find their own way to agree with me and I don't have to do any work at all.

I knew I would have to endure unwanted attention at school because of Sylvia. She had been a cheerleader and a total brainiac, so it wasn't as if she could die and people wouldn't take any notice. I think they had plans to plant a tree or something and put a plaque next to it with her name on it. It was

hard for me to imagine a gesture that could be any more meaningless.

Alexis was waiting by my locker when I got to school. Her
long hair was loose and it hung around her shoulders in shiny
blue-black curls. She was hugging her books against her chest
and staring up at the ceiling while she waited.

"Hey, Jaz," she said as I dumped my backpack on the
floor.

"Hey, yourself," I said.

"You doing okay?" she asked.

"I think so." I said it real smart-like but she didn't even
notice. As if she would be the one I would talk to if I needed a
shoulder to cry on.

"Good. Listen, I didn't get much of a chance to talk to you
yesterday. I was wondering if maybe you wanted to get together
after school?"

"What for?" I asked.

She shrugged and leaned her head against my locker. "To
talk. I don't know. You could come over to my place and we
could just hang out or something."

"I've got practice."

Alex shook her head. "No, they canceled all the extracur-
ricular activities today out of respect for—well, you know.
There's going to be a memorial in the auditorium during last
period to talk about Sylvia."

"Are you joking?" I asked. Jesus, the funeral had been bad
enough and now I was going to be expected to sit through
another service, sit there trying not to lose my shit in front of
the entire school. I thought about ditching right then, just
walking out of school and never looking back. Sylvia would
understand if I didn't go. If it had been me who died, Sylvia

would do the same thing. She would say, screw all of them, they never really knew Jason anyway.

Alexis was still talking but I wasn't really listening to her. My heart had started to bang around crazily in my chest just thinking about listening to people say Sylvia's name out loud, a fresh punch to my gut every time I had to hear someone talk about her.

"Gosh, Jaz, everyone is really broken up about it. All the teachers and the squad and all the varsity players . . . everyone." She sniffled and I could see a tear threatening to fall from her lower lash. "I can't believe you didn't know about it. So, meet me after the assembly, okay? Outside the auditorium."

I gave her a noncommittal grunt that she seemed to take for agreement before leaving me at my locker to freak out on my own.

When I got to second-period gym class I was still trying to decide if I should just find Mario and get him to ditch the rest of the day with me. There was only one other person in the locker room when I got there because I was running late. Eli, who played as a forward on the varsity soccer team, was just lacing up his Chuck Taylor's.

Eli was a quiet kid so I never paid him much mind off the pitch. He was an excellent striker, maybe our best, but he never acted smug about it and I respected him for that. Eli wasn't the strongest or the fastest but he was a clever and nimble player—Ghost we called him on the field because of his pale hair and almost colorless eyes and his ability to slip through defenders like a puff of smoke.

Sometimes I'd see him in the locker room when he thought he was alone. He always had at least one nasty-looking bruise or welt on his body and I recognized the marks on him for what they were—a band of purple around the upper arm from the squeeze of a rough hand, red and swollen skin along the cheekbone from a backhanded slap, shiny pink scars on his knuckles from defending himself.

Sylvia's dad had been an angry son of a bitch, pissed off about the crap he was fed by life, and he liked to take it out on me. Never Sylvia. Sometimes my mom. Always me. Until he finally split for good when I was eleven, I had been his daily reminder that life hadn't worked out the way he wanted it to. And he made sure I paid for it.

Sylvia hated her dad. Even though he had never raised a hand to her, she hated him for the way he treated me, treated Mom. She always said she wished my dad were her dad too. Not that my dad was much better. For most of my childhood my dad had been like vapor to me. More of an idea than a physical presence, and when he *was* around he was usually high or drunk. Somehow he managed to not really be there even when he was with me. He wasn't mean though, was actually a pretty laid-back guy. Just not much of a dad. And that was how I thought of it, like I didn't really have a dad. Just some guy who had been with my mom when she was really young. Too young.

Eli kept the beatings he took at home a secret and I never brought it up. Why would I? If he didn't want anyone to know, it was none of my business. He always hung back and got dressed last so no one could see him with his shirt off. I understood that, remembered when I was a kid how I thought it was so critical to keep the beatings I took at home a secret from the rest of the world. It's like if other people know that you get hit at home, they'll know something's wrong with you, think you're a freak, so you keep it hidden . . . no matter what.

But that day I was running late for class, so Eli and I were in the locker room at the same time. I pulled my shirt on and when my head popped out of the neck hole, Eli was just standing there eyeing me. Like I said, he's a real quiet kid and I hadn't even heard him approach.

"Hey, Jaz," he said, looking me right in the eye. His eyes were an almost colorless gray, which always gave me the impression his soul was empty. Today he seemed even more somber than usual, and the way he looked at me made me want to look away.

"What's shakin', Eli?"

"I'm sorry about your sister," he said. "She was a real nice kid."

"You think so?"

He lifted one shoulder uncertainly, his head dipping apologetically. "Yeah, sure. I didn't know her all that well. We had a couple classes together, AP English and Physics."

"Right," I said with a nod. "I forgot you're in all the smart-kid classes."

Eli's face shifted into one of his rare, lopsided grins. "Yeah, well. I don't know what I'd do if I lost my brother. I hope you're doing okay."

"Yeah, thanks," I said as he started to turn away and walk back to his own locker. "Hey, did you hear about this memorial assembly they're having at the end of the day?" I asked. "The thing for Sylvia?"

"Yeah, sure. They were announcing it all last week," he said. "We don't have seventh-period class today so everyone can go."

"Huh."

He waited to see what else I would say, maybe like he was wondering if I had lost my mind or something. "I guess I just missed the announcement," I said finally. "I didn't know about it. What do you think they're going to do? All hold hands and sing and shit?"

Eli chuckled at that. "I don't know. Maybe."

"I think I'm going to skip seventh period today," I said. "Maybe I'd better skip sixth too, just to be on the safe side."

"Don't let the cheerleaders hear you say that," Eli said in warning. "I think they're the ones who organized the whole thing. Singing and all."

"Yeah, thanks for the heads-up," I said thoughtfully. Eli drifted away while I stared off into space, trying to picture this whole ridiculous thing in my mind. Would the cheerleaders wear their uniforms? Did they have a special mourning cheer? Sylvia, being the smallest one on the squad, had always been the top of the pyramid. Maybe they would do a pyramid with no top—a symbolic metaphor for the significance of Sylvia's short life.

Maybe I would go after all. Out of curiosity if nothing else.

CHAPTER FOUR

As I entered the auditorium after sixth period I felt everyone's eyes on me. I sensed their anticipation, waiting to see how I would react to Sylvia's memorial. Mr. Hudson, the principal, had pulled me out of fifth period to see how I was holding up and asked me if I wanted to get up and say something about Sylvia at the memorial service. I just looked at him like he was crazy, and he seemed to take that for an answer. Chick and Mario were sitting together near the back, Jordie in the row in front of them with a seat held for me. I fell in beside Jordie, giving him just a shake of my head. Mario put his foot up on my seat, his smelly shoe near my neck. I pushed his foot away and Chick cried out as Mario's foot landed on his shin.

Usually during an assembly the teachers are just struggling to keep everything under control, trying to keep everyone from shouting and goofing off, but not today. Once the assembly started, most people avoided looking in my direction. And it was really quiet—like church quiet.

Just as I had feared, there was singing. At first I didn't

recognize the song but when I realized they were actually singing Kelly Clarkson's "My Life Would Suck Without You," I almost lost my shit. Fucking jazz choir.

I realized then that this memorial assembly was going to be a cakewalk compared to Sylvia's actual funeral. Nothing about it was real. Standing beside Sylvia's casket at the cemetery, that was as real as it got. The worst was when they lowered her casket into the ground. The box had trembled as the electric winch started with a small jerk and I had imagined Sylvia's body rocking against the plush satin lining. I had wondered if they put some kind of strap around the body—a seat belt or something—to keep it from shifting around in the coffin. Later, even now, this idea still bothered me, wondering if her body had shifted into some awkward, uncomfortable position as she tried to find some rest in her grave.

And when it was time to leave the cemetery, I'd had a hard time walking away. It felt weird to take Sylvia to that place and just . . . leave her there. Like somehow we should have been bringing her with us when we left. Maybe that's why some people get cremated and scatter their ashes. That way you don't just get left behind.

I was a little disappointed that the cheerleaders didn't turn out in uniform for the memorial assembly, but a couple of them got up to say nice things about Sylvia, Alex being one of them. Since Sylvia was only fifteen when she died there wasn't a whole lot to say. It's not like she had been on the verge of curing cancer. And Sylvia had done a good job of keeping most of herself hidden from people at school. Like an iceberg, the only part of her that broke the surface was the pretty, outgoing cheerleader. Kept submerged was everything of substance about her, the things that made her who she was—resentment of an asshole father, shame about our poverty, hatred of her diabetes.

They mentioned Sylvia being in Model UN and all the fun memories of her from cheerleading camp. Then there didn't really seem to be much else to say, so the chorus sang another song and Mr. Hudson released us after a moment of silence.

During the moment of silence, most people dropped their heads and closed their eyes while I squirmed in my seat. Jordie slapped the back of his hand into my gut. His chin was pressed to his chest and his eyes squeezed shut. I wasn't sure if he was trying to comfort me or was telling me I should drop my head too so I would look like I was praying.

Sitting there thinking about how all the people in that auditorium—the ones up onstage saying all the right things about Sylvia but who didn't know shit about her—my stomach started to ache again. The pain was so intense that I was unconsciously holding my breath and gripping the armrests of my seat. My knuckles were white and the muscles in my forearms trembled from the exertion. By degrees I started to relax as the pain subsided a bit, but then I was left with the feeling that I had to go to the bathroom really bad.

When the memorial assembly was finally over, Alex came to find me and asked me to go back to her house to hang out for a while. I waved off Jordie's offer of a ride home and followed Alex for the short walk to her house.

Her family lived in a two-story brick house with a screened-in porch and a deck with a gas grill. They weren't rich, but comfortable. Alex was an only child and both her parents worked, so the house was deserted when we got there.

I followed her inside and into the kitchen and watched her

black curls against the green of her sweater as she got glasses down from the cupboard and poured us both a drink.

"Want to go up to my room?" she asked, her brown eyes wide open—trusting, maybe hopeful.

"Sure," I said as I took the sweaty glass from her.

There were dolls and stuffed animals watching me from the window seat as I sat on her bed, the one chair in the room taken by a pile of clean laundry. I looked for a place to set my glass and finally set it on a book that lay open facedown on the bedside table.

Alex put on some music, then came to sit beside me, her leg touching mine.

"Sylvia's favorite band, huh?" she said.

The music she chose had been Syl's favorite, Maroon 5, which made me wince just to hear it. Sylvia was always listening to whatever crap pop artist was churning out hits on the radio. It was something I had always teased her about, her shitty taste in music. I had tried to turn her on to some of the bands that I really liked. But it was no use. After a minute I said, "Jesus, she really had terrible taste in music."

Alex laughed and it startled me. I had almost forgotten she was there. She was looking up into my face, her eyes wet with new tears. I kept silent after that, knowing that if I did, this would only go one way. I had seen it in her eyes when she asked me to come over.

At first I hesitated because all I could think about was what Sylvia would think if she could see us together. Since Sylvia had died I couldn't shake this creepy feeling, the idea of her watching me, able to see me no matter where I was or what I was doing. I could almost feel her there, in Alex's room with us, like some Jedi Force ghost, wanting to tell me that this was a terrible idea.

Despite Sylvia's ghost, Alex and I did end up making out, and she was really into it. She even had a new pack of condoms, still in a CVS bag, that she dug out from the top drawer of her dresser. Like maybe this plan had been in the works for a while. Even though she had invited me over and I knew she would let it go all the way, when the time came to go for it, I backed off.

With most of our clothes off, my weight on top of her, we had reached the point when the only logical next step would be for us to have sex. That was when I stopped and pulled away. She asked if something was wrong and I said no, just closed my eyes and lay back on the bed, engaging in the necessary internal dialogue to convince myself that I really didn't want to sleep with Alex.

In case you don't know, talking yourself out of having sex when there's a mostly naked girl lying in your arms is virtually impossible. The amount of willpower I was mustering practically made me a candidate for the priesthood, though Mario had told me priests weren't even allowed to jack off. Which is crazy.

Mario was the only person who knew I was a virgin. My life had started as an accident, someone else's mistake. I could just as easily have been an abortion, unwanted by both my parents from the minute I was conceived. If I ever had a kid, he would know it was on purpose, that I wanted him around and would give him more than just my name.

My dad was the one who always told me, don't sleep with a girl unless you're willing to have a kid with her. Reminding

me every time he said it that he thought having a kid by accident was the worst possible thing that could happen to a guy.
He never told me not to do drugs or to mind a curfew or get
good grades. Just don't end up with an unwanted kid.

Asshole. It's not like I asked to be born.

Mom had such terrible taste in guys. She was always going
out on dates with the worst kind of losers. Sylvia and I used to
talk about that, how it seemed like Mom was only attracted to
guys who were assholes. The guys at school mostly left Sylvia
alone because everyone knew if I got wind of a guy trying to
sleep with her, he would be dead. But she never got all crazy
about guys anyway, probably because of all the creeps she saw
Mom hanging around.

Alex was quiet, lying beside me with her head tucked in
the crook of my arm. I may have dozed for a minute but I
wanted to be long gone before her dad got home from work. At
the funeral I had seen him standing behind Alex as she wept
openly, his jaw set and his hands clasped tightly in front of
him. Proper mourning posture, but he didn't do anything
to comfort his little girl in front of a group of strangers, even
though you could see it eating him up inside. He was the kind
of guy who would swing a fist, ask questions later.

As I sat on the edge of the bed pulling on my shoes, Alex
stood at her dresser in a fluffy pink robe brushing her hair.
"Jason?" she said, as if I might not hear her from only six feet
away.

"Yeah?"

"I was . . . you know, I thought we would go all the way."

I wasn't sure what she wanted from me. An apology?

After a minute her voice again, this time quieter. "Jason?"

She came to sit beside me on the end of the bed and put

her hand on my leg, then seemed to think better of it and put her hand in her lap.

"I—I really care about you, Jason," she said without looking at me.

"Thanks," I said since there didn't seem to be anything else appropriate to say.

"I was thinking," Alex said as she nervously plucked at the ends of her hair, "with Sylvia gone, maybe we should spend more time together. You know, since we're both upset about her being gone. We could be there for each other."

"I think I probably need some time to myself," I said, giving her the first line that came to mind.

I didn't wait for her to show me out.

CHAPTER FIVE

On my way home from Alex's house I stopped off at Bad Habits, a sports bar and nightclub that was on the Pike, the main drag through town. During the past two summers I had worked in the kitchen at Bad Habits, washing dishes, running food, and helping out the bar-backs to keep the bars stocked when the place was busy. That afternoon when I got there it was only five o'clock, so the place was empty. It didn't usually fill up until six or seven, when people drifted in for happy hour.

I entered through the kitchen door and waved to the bar-backs who were washing dishes and setting up for the night. Bad Habits did enough evening business, they didn't even bother opening during the day, except on weekends when the games were on television. Chris, the owner, was behind the main bar reading *The City Paper* when I strolled in. The Internet jukebox mounted on the wall was playing at a subdued volume—"Drain You" by Nirvana, which I knew without asking Chris had used his own money to play. The interior of the bar was much darker than the outdoors and it took my eyes a minute to adjust to the gloom.

"Well, looky who it is," Chris said by way of greeting but didn't look up from reading the paper. He was big—well over six feet and broad through the shoulders—with dark brown hair and green eyes. He had tattoos on both arms, almost a full sleeve of artwork on his right arm. His nose looked like it had been broken at least once, but that didn't stop the women who sat at his bar from passing him their phone numbers on cocktail napkins. "How've you been, kid?" he asked as he set aside his paper. "Shouldn't you be in school?"

"It's five o'clock. School's been out for hours," I said as I slid onto one of the vinyl stools, a split seam on the side of it held together by duct tape. I rested my elbows gingerly on the smooth polish of the bar top, expecting to find it sticky to the touch.

"Right," Chris said with a nod. "Hard to tell the time in this place. Noon might as well be midnight. What do you want?"

"I'll take a beer, I guess."

"Oh, a beer you guess?" Chris said, his voice a low growl from so many years of smoking and shouting at drunks while working behind the bar.

"Just one."

He gave me a long look before pulling out a bottle and removing the top with a flick of his wrist. "Your mom would die if she knew I fed you this stuff."

"She wouldn't care. I drink at home all the time," I lied easily.

"Mmph."

"What are you, my dad now?"

He chuckled, a rich throaty sound that made him seem older than his late thirties. "How's your mom?"

I shrugged and didn't look at him, traced my finger through the condensation on the beer bottle. "I don't know. Since Sylvia died we haven't really spoken much. I'm not sure she knows I'm still alive."

He didn't say anything, just watched my face while I kept my expression neutral.

I told him about Sylvia's memorial assembly at school, about how awkward it had made me feel. Mentioned how Alexis and other girls showed so much interest in being around me since Sylvia's death, like they wanted some of the tragedy to rub off on them.

That was the thing about Chris—I could tell him things I wouldn't tell other people. It was like he had seen and done so much in his life that he was beyond judging other people.

After I had talked myself out he said, "I'm getting ready to open for happy hour. Finish up and get your skinny ass out of here before I get busted for serving a kid in my bar."

"Whatever, man," I said. "How about giving me some quarters and I'll shoot a game of pool?"

"Why don't you get a job?" he asked as he popped the drawer to the cash register and slapped four quarters on the bar, then grabbed my half-empty bottle of beer and tossed it into a trash bin in one fluid motion. "Matter of fact, I could use someone to help in the early evenings and on the weekends—you could come back to working part-time. Eight bucks an hour."

"Yeah, which is exactly seventy-five cents over minimum wage," I said. "You're a real humanitarian."

"And you've got a smart fucking mouth that someday is going to get your ass kicked for you," he said, but Chris was all bark and I didn't pay him any mind. "You know, that's how I started out in this business. Worked as a bar-back in a place like this right out of high school. Started bartending once I was legal and saved up to open my own place."

I had to fight to keep my eyeballs from rolling back in my head. This story had been recited for me before.

"I was a punk, like you, when I was your age," Chris said, his insult rolling off me without causing injury. "Of course, I didn't have any choice but to get my shit together. Maybe if you got a job after school it would keep you out of trouble."

"I never get in trouble," I said.

"Maybe you never get caught, but that doesn't mean you don't get into trouble," he said, needing to have the last word, which is just his way. We could have kept it up like that for hours, but I let it go.

I took the quarters and went to the back room, where a full-size pool table stood under a low-hanging light fixture with a green shade. Just as Chris had said, the place started to fill up within a half hour and the music was good and loud when I made my exit the way I had come in.

CHAPTER SIX

The same week of Sylvia's memorial assembly the soccer coach, Arturo, approached me to ask how I was holding up and whether I would be ready for our Friday game against crosstown rival Yorktown High School.

"Mr. Hudson thought maybe you should sit out a few games. That you needed some time," Arturo said in his heavily accented English.

"Bullshit," I said.

"I'm just telling you what he said to me," Arturo said without even raising an eyebrow about my cussing.

I knew Arturo didn't want me to sit out the game against Yorktown. They almost always clobbered us at soccer. No surprise. The north-side school was in an exclusive neighborhood of broad tree-lined streets and palatial homes that sat back on large wooded lots. Their team members had all been playing since they were in kindergarten and they had the best equipment, best coaches, and moms with the leisure time to keep them playing year-round in the community leagues.

The day of the game our team stood silently as the York-town players filed out onto the field. They were all white, tall, broad shouldered, and carried themselves with the kind of confidence that only money can buy. In contrast, at least half the boys on the Wakefield team were brown skinned or of some mixed pedigree, and more than half of us qualified financially for the free breakfast program at school. At our school, football still ruled, soccer was for the castoffs of the high school athletic program. Our players looked scrawny and small next to the Yorktown goliaths. I was the biggest guy on our team by several inches.

Most of the time I don't care that much about soccer. It isn't like I obsess about it or watch it on television. Every once in a while Mario's dad would take Mario and me to a D.C. United game. But when I'm out there on the field and an offensive player from the other team is charging toward me, pushing the ball toward my home goal, all I can think about is how much I want to stop him, want to lay him out on the pitch and claim the ball for myself.

I drew more yellow and red cards from the refs than any other player on our team. Maybe I have a reputation for play-ing dirty, tripping up players but making it look like I was just trying to get my foot on the ball, throwing an elbow here and there when I'm running the block. Sometimes, if the other guy is really aggressive, I end up in a shoving match or a fight. Usu-ally I start the fight.

Arturo mostly turned a blind eye, though he wasn't stupid. He knew as well as I did that I earned every foul that got called against me. But I like to win, and so did Arturo, so he played dumb and always started me at center midfield.

Which is why, when we were thirty minutes into play and

I was still sitting on the bench, I was cussing Arturo under my breath. He hadn't even glanced in my direction since kickoff and it looked like he was planning to keep me on the bench for the whole game, maybe under Mr. Hudson's orders. Chick, who was on the team only because Mario and I would refuse to play unless Arturo kept him on, was warming the bench beside me, would maybe get ten minutes of play at the end of the game and only if we were already up by a couple of goals.

At halftime we were down by two goals. Mario and Jordie were breathing hard when they sat down on the bench beside Chick and me. They had been playing rough defense for most of the game, our forward players left with little to do since they rarely got the ball.

"They're killing us," Jordie said as he spit on the ground between us.

Mario was silent. His brown skin glistened with sweat and his black fauxhawk had wilted in the heat.

"Why isn't Arturo putting you in, Jaz?" Jordie asked angrily.

"Ask him," I said.

"I will," Jordie said, and stalked off to talk to Arturo.

"That girl Cheryl's here," Mario said dully as he rubbed at his face and neck with a threadbare towel. "That's why he's so pissed about losing. He can't stand the thought of losing in front of her."

"Oh yeah?" I asked without much interest but glanced around the bleachers until I spotted Cheryl sitting with a couple of her girlfriends. They were perched on the bleachers, knees pressed tightly together to hide what their short skirts were designed to reveal.

"Don't ask me what he sees in that girl," Mario said. "She's totally plastic."

Jordie returned then and said, "He's putting you in."

"'Bout damn time." I skinned out of my sweat jacket and jogged out onto the field with the team.

I took the center midfield without thought, though Mario had been working that field position for the first half of the game. Mario fell back to sweep the goal, a turf that he ruled with his quiet grace.

Ten minutes after I took the field, we got our first chance. One of our midfielders took the ball and was pushing it toward the goal with such speed and determination, the entire Yorktown team was caught up in watching him. That gave Eli the chance to slip into position near the goal, pushing the line of the penalty box but careful to remain on side. He was the Ghost now, all speed and stealth.

At the last second, when it looked like the midfielder was going to take a wild shot with a hard kick, he faked out all the Yorktown defenders by slowing the momentum of his leg and sending the ball in a soft lob toward the left of the goal box. Eli was waiting, ready, and headed the ball into the goal. The goalkeeper dived, too late, and caught only air.

We were still down by a goal, so our celebration of Eli's strike was quick and quiet, everyone all business. Yorktown had the ball, and their center was moving swiftly, his imposing size scattering our defenders as he came toward me. I had one defender to contend with, who stayed on me like stink on shit. He was all arms and legs, blocking me so I had to fight the urge to just shove him out of the way and leave him behind me on the ground.

The big center player was going for it, wasn't even looking to see if his forwards were set up to take the ball home to the goal. He was the tallest member of their team, taller than me even.

Mario slipped into position and I could see the hard set of his eyes, his brow wrinkled against the low angle of the sun, as he was determined not to let them get a third goal. The center was much taller and thicker than Mario, who was lean and slender and only about five-nine. But Mario wasn't afraid of getting hurt—he would take a beating and get up to ask for more, even if he couldn't give it back. Mario rushed out from the goal, our keeper shouting something unintelligible at him, but Mario had eyes only for the ball, and as he moved up the field, he seemed to float rather than run.

In the next minute, the big Yorktown center was down, a tangle of limbs with Mario, who had also taken a tumble. It all happened so fast, the refs couldn't even determine if a foul had been made or not.

The Yorktown player jumped to his feet shouting, "Goddamn spic! What the hell was that?"

"Who're you calling a spic?" Mario asked, giving him a shove that didn't even upset the guy's balance.

The Yorktown player towered over Mario so I stepped in between them and bumped the guy with my chest. "Say it again," I said as I shoved him. He took a stumbling step back, one arm windmilling to keep his balance. I repeated myself, my voice quiet and level. "Say it again."

"Fuck you," the guy said, but he was starting to look worried.

"I want to hear you say it," I said as I slapped him on the side of the head, the blow meant to humiliate more than hurt.

"Jaz, let it go, man," Mario said, hands on his hips as he squinted into the sun.

By now Arturo and the ref were there, Arturo calling my name with a warning. I ignored them, grabbed the guy by the collar, and shook him. His hands went to my wrists as he tried to relieve the pressure of the twisted collar on this throat. "I want to hear you call him a spic again, you fucking pussy," I said.

The ref was pulling at the Yorktown kid while Arturo was pulling at me.

The Yorktown player punched me then, hard to the cheekbone, and I saw stars.

My vision was blurred from anger and the blow to the head and there was a confusion of shouts from the people around us. Gathering a surge of strength from adrenaline, I threw Arturo's hand off and got the guy by the hair. I pounded his face with my right fist, two punches that cut his lip on his teeth. Though I felt nothing in my hand at the time, later my knuckles would be sore for a few days.

He drove his elbow up into my chin, and my teeth clacked together loudly in my head. The taste of hot blood filled my mouth and he punched me again as I turned my head to spit blood onto the grass.

I got in one last punch, a solid blow to his jaw that knocked him back on his ass, before someone grabbed me by the arm and yanked me back, hard, so that I was forced to let go of the guy. He scrambled away from me crab fashion on his butt as I turned my anger on the person who was pulling my arm. By the time I realized it was Mario pulling me, I had already given him a shove and sent him reeling.

"Goddamnit, Jaz!" Mario shouted at me. "Chill the fuck out!"

Arturo was there and the coach from the Yorktown team along with the ref blowing his whistle and waving a red card, everyone shouting and carrying on. The guy I had been fighting was still on the ground, one hand covering his mouth as blood seeped through his fingers.

"You're like a fucking ape," Mario said as he followed me off the field.

"Shut up, you goddamn spic," I muttered under my breath.

Mario laughed. "Oh, man," was all he said.

That was how I ended up spending the last ten minutes of the game on the bench. The Yorktown player I had been fighting was thrown out of the game too after Mario explained the reason for the fight.

We ended up losing to Yorktown 2–1. I was pissed at myself for letting it happen. If I hadn't been on the bench for most of the game, we might have had a chance. Jordie was pissed too and made a big show of it for his audience, Cheryl and her friends Raine and Madison.

If there was such a thing as the popular crowd at school, Cheryl and Madison were its royalty. Their families had enough money and connections that they could afford to blow off schoolwork and spend all their time partying and would still have all the options of college and a bright future open to them. Mario was right about Cheryl being plastic, but it didn't surprise me that Jordie had taken an interest in her. Being popular had always been more important to him than it was to the rest of us. His family had money, real money, with a vacation house at the beach and a membership to the country club, though Jordie had never invited Mario or Chick or me to see either one.

Madison and I hooked up at a party once, made out when

we were both drunk. She never spoke to me again after, so maybe she didn't remember. More likely she woke up the next day and realized she had swapped spit with some white trash guy at a party and would spend the rest of high school regretting it.

Raine Blair was of indeterminate social clique, equally at home with the Goths and the drama club freaks, but she came from a rich family so she orbited the popular clique as well. She was in my Civics class and was always piping up about current events and political issues. Her hair was a violent shade of blond with bright pink streaks throughout, and her clothes were an amalgam of '80s punk and '90s grunge. I also knew from locker room talk that she had a reputation as a girl who slept around, but that mostly struck me as wishful thinking on the part of the guys doing the talking.

Jordie called me over as I was walking to the locker room to change back into my street clothes. I wasn't in the mood to talk to anyone.

"Hey, Jaz, you know Cheryl and Madison and Raine, right?" Jordie asked.

"Yeah, sure," I said with a nod at all of them. "How you doin'?"

"You look terrible," Cheryl said with a giggle. "That guy really messed up your face."

"It's not so bad," I said, wishing I could tell her to fuck off.

"Is it true that guy called Mario a spic?" Madison asked, cracking her gum with a series of small clicking sounds.

"Something like that," I said.

"That is messed up," Madison said, her eyebrows raised as she studied her phone and quickly lost interest in our conversation.

"Are you okay?" Raine asked. The way she asked it was like she actually gave a crap and my head swiveled to look at her curiously. Her cheeks went pink with a blush.

"Yeah, I'm fine—" I said, but Jordie cut me off then, drawing Cheryl's attention away from me and back to him.

"So, are we going to go get something to eat?" he asked Cheryl.

"Sure," Cheryl said with a bright smile though Raine remained silent.

"You gonna roll with us, Jaz?" Jordie asked me. "We're headed to the diner."

"I'll catch up with you later," I said, knowing I had no intention of going anywhere with them. My face had started to ache and I wasn't in a mood to be civil. Jordie would be pissed if I blew his chance with Cheryl.

CHAPTER SEVEN

Mario and Chick were waiting for me when I emerged from the locker room thirty minutes later, my hair still wet and my cheek aching. "You ready, princess?" Mario asked.

We headed down to the park near the apartment complex where Mario and I lived. The park was huge and included a network of trails and bike paths that stretched between two major residential areas. A picnic pavilion of raw wood was perched on the bank of the stream that meandered through the woods, a small footbridge the only access point to the pavilion from the bike trail.

A small path, barely noticeable unless you knew it was there, ran along the edge of the stream at the point where it flowed into the thickest part of the woods. Under the canopy of tree limbs, a collection of large boulders split the ribbon of water into two smaller streams. We'd sit on the rocks drinking beers or, when we were lucky, would bring girls to this place under the cover of darkness. Since only the pavilion area was accessible by car, the cops rarely bothered coming this far into the park.

Usually we kept a stash of beer hidden in a hollow space under one of the trees that grew along the bank of the stream, the dirt below it cut away from the moving water. Buried under a pile of damp leaves I found a six-pack of Natty Light and a single bottle of Miller. I left the Miller and carried the six-pack to the large rock in the middle of the stream where Mario and Chick already sat. It was close to dusk, dinnertime, when the park quieted and we saw only the occasional person walking over the footbridge with a dog or a baby stroller. Sometimes we would see other people our age, usually people we knew. Once the sun went down, the park was ruled by people our age, the only place we could always go to get away from our parents and the cops.

Sometimes the cops did come into the park, especially late on Friday and Saturday nights, to catch us out partying. We knew the park so well that as long as we made it into the woods we could get away easily. The cops didn't care enough about us to risk twisting an ankle or getting jumped by some delinquents, so they stayed out of the woods. It was only in the pavilion or along the trails that we had to worry about getting busted.

As we sat sipping on our beers, Mario pulled a bowl out of his pocket and loaded it with something. I bit the inside of my cheek to keep from saying anything about it. Sometimes I smoked pot, but not often since it didn't seem to do much besides make me paranoid and sometimes, like a bonus, would give me a headache. Mario had been doing much more than smoking pot lately, and doing it a lot, sometimes during school. He would disappear during lunch and return glassy eyed and stupid for fifth period.

"What's that, Mario?" Chick asked.

"Shit," I said before Mario could answer, and then leaned over and spit over the edge of the boulder.

"It's just weed," Mario said with a pointed look at me. "It's not laced with anything, though I wish it was. Want some?"

"Maybe," Chick said as he stood and came to crouch beside Mario, watching him as he hit the bowl, like Chick was watching some kind of tutorial.

"No, he doesn't want any," I said, and Mario shot me an ugly look. We stared at each other in a battle of silent will but then I decided I wasn't going to give him the satisfaction and looked away. "Leave that shit alone, Chick," I said. "It will make you stupid."

"What do you know about it?" Mario asked. "It's just plain old weed. Never hurt anybody." He turned his attention back to his bowl, lit it, and took a long drag, then held the smoke in for a minute before blowing out a thin blue cloud.

"You ever tried Molly?" Chick asked.

"Yeah, Molly's good," Mario said with a nod, trying to sound like a fucking expert about something, "but you don't smoke it. Smoking it is a waste."

"Yeah?" Chick asked, intently focused on Mario, and I covertly rolled my eyes with annoyance.

"Molly you take in a capsule," Mario continued, aware of my annoyance but ignoring it. "Or if you only have a crystal, you can roll it in toilet paper or rolling papers or something and then swallow it. It's called parachuting."

"It's *called* being a fucking idiot," I said, then shook my head. "Jesus, what kind of an idiot eats toilet paper?"

"*¡Nadie está hablando contigo!*" Mario said, his voice raised in anger.

"*¡Cállate!*" I shouted in return. Without thinking, I grabbed

the bowl out of Mario's hand and, before he could utter a word
of protest, threw the thing into the stream.

"Hey!" Mario shouted. "What the fuck, Jaz!"

"Keep that shit away from Chick," I said, gritting my teeth
to keep from raising my voice again.

"Oh, man," Mario said in almost a whine. "That wasn't even
mine. That was Travis's bowl. Man, now I have to go downtown
to the head shop to replace that. You gonna pay for it?"

"No. Fuck off," I said as I took a swallow of my beer to
smother my anger. "Chick doesn't need to be messing with that.
You keep that shit away from him. Keep it away from me too."

"Since when did you become such a straight edge?" Mario
asked me sullenly.

"Are you really asking me that question?" I asked, incredulous, but he wouldn't even look at me. Mario knew exactly
why I hated the drug scene. I don't mean smoking a joint at a
party or anything like that, but the hard stuff. The stuff that
turned people into strangers. My dad's whole life had been
one big party when I was a little kid. Ecstasy and mushrooms
and LSD. He partied so much, he forgot to give a shit about
what happened to me. Forgot soccer games and birthdays and
weekend visitations.

Chick shifted in his seat and the sound of his sneaker
scraping against the rock was loud in the silence that hung
between us.

Mario stood and moved to the edge of the boulder, leaned
over as he tried to locate the bowl in the boil of water around
the rocks. Chick and I just sat there, waiting to see if he was
actually going to go diving for the bowl. I sure as hell wasn't
going to help him. If Chick even offered, I was going to tell him
to mind his own business.

After a minute Mario gave up on finding the bowl and said, "I'm taking off. I'll see you around."

I didn't watch him go. Just finished my beer as I listened to the sound of his retreat across the rocks, a small splash and a muttered curse as his foot slipped off the rock closest to the bank of the stream. Then he was gone.

"He's just mad," Chick said quietly. "He'll get over it."

"Yeah, sure," I said indifferently. "I'm hungry. Let's head over to Bad Habits, see if Chris will hook us up with a couple of burgers."

CHAPTER EIGHT

Though it bothered Chick to see Mario and me argue, the truth was Mario and I had been arguing like that since first grade. We had traded bloody noses and black eyes, insulted each other's mothers, and made comments about the inferior size of each other's dicks for a long time now. Sometimes I thought about apologizing after the fact or, if we had a particularly bad fight, it might occur to me to bring it up again to talk about it, though I never did. But usually, the insult or injury was forgotten within a few hours.

So it didn't surprise me the next day when Mario showed up at my door with a soccer ball tucked under one arm, an unlit cigarette behind his ear. "You up?" he called through the screen of the open window above the sofa bed.

Mom had left early that morning to open the store. She was the assistant manager of the Dollar General, a thirty-minute commute by bus. I was lying in bed, staring at the ceiling, trying to decide if there was any reason to get up and start the day.

"Yeah," I said, then sat up and shifted to the end of the bed where I could reach the lock to let Mario in.

"Mama sent this," Mario said as he tossed a package wrapped in tinfoil at the end of my bed.

I knew without opening it what it was. The package was warm in my hands, heavy for its size, and smelled of cornmeal and braised pork. Mario's mom's version of the breakfast burrito, with a homemade corn tortilla, beans, and pork. My mouth started to water just thinking about it.

Mario sat at the small table Mom and I used sometimes for eating, but mostly used to hold piles of crap we didn't have anywhere else to store. Since our apartment was small, most of the clutter generated by life didn't get saved and would end up in the trash eventually. Things just sat on the table until we came to terms with the idea of discarding them for good.

Since Syl died we had been unable to throw out anything that bore some relationship to her. Mail, even junk mail, that had her name on it, items from her locker at school, like the tattered paperback copy of *Lord of the Flies* she had been reading when she died, and extra copies of the church program from her funeral service, were all arranged in an uncertain heap on the round table. I couldn't look at them, but couldn't throw them in the trash either. So, instead of joining Mario at the table, I sat on the end of my bed in just my underwear and unwrapped the gift of a breakfast that would keep me going most of the day.

Mario's eyes passed over the collection of items on the table with some interest, but he just absently rolled the soccer ball under his foot as if he didn't notice the accidental shrine to Sylvia. "Jordie's going to pick up Chick and meet us at the Metro. Head down to the Mall and try to find a good pickup game."

Mario was referring to the National Mall, the open green space between the Lincoln Memorial and the U.S. Capitol where, on any given weekend, you could find twenty pickup games of soccer if you knew the right places to look. Some of the players were young guys like us, but more often they were aged-out athletes who were just looking to stay in shape. Sometimes we played alongside Hispanic or African guys who spoke almost no English.

When Mario and I arrived at the Metro, the subway system that could get us from our Virginia suburban neighborhood into D.C. in less than ten minutes, Chick and Jordie were already waiting for us.

We stood in the subway car even though there were seats available, the kid in us still able to enjoy the thrill of standing in the moving train. We talked loudly, joking around and oblivious of the people around us. We got off at the Smithsonian station and walked toward the Washington Monument, gravel crunching under our shoes. Jordie and I both carried our rubber cleats slung over one shoulder, but Mario only had his street shoes. Jordie mentioned it as we strolled along.

"You're going to be playing like shit in those Chuck Taylors," Jordie said to Mario. "Where are your cleats?"

"I left them under your mama's bed last night," Mario said.

"Fuck you," Jordie said but with a smile in appreciation of Mario's joke.

Chick was the only one not laughing. "Why do you guys do that?" Chick asked. "Talk shit about each other's moms."

"Because it's hilarious," Mario said.

"You never talk shit about my mom," Chick said almost

defensively, as if he wished we would say shit to imply his mother was a whore too.

"Of course not," Mario said. "You can't talk shit about somebody's mom if their mom is dead or really sick or something. That would be twisted."

"What?" Chick asked. "Like you're showing some kind of respect for my mom? Just because she's dead?"

"It's an unspoken rule," Jordie said with a nod. "A dead mom is off-limits."

"Bro code," Mario said in agreement.

"That's ridiculous," Chick said, his voice rising with exasperation as he stopped in the middle of the gravel path. "None of you ever even met my mom. Shit, *I* never even met her. But you know each other's moms. See them all the time. Christ, they cook for you. How is it okay for you to talk shit about each other's moms but not someone you've never met?" When he finished this little tirade, Chick was breathing heavily, his chest rising and falling quickly. Genuinely upset.

The three of us just stood watching him for a minute, unsure what he was so worked up about. Mario's comment about Jordie's mom was actually pretty mild compared to some of the ringers we had used in the past. I reacted first, putting my hand on Chick's shoulder and giving him a squeeze. The muscle was tight under my hand, trembling. "Chick, man, calm down," I said. "It's just a joke. Nobody means anything by it."

"It's just fucked up is what I'm saying," Chick said as he rubbed at his eyes with irritation, as if trying to keep from crying.

"We won't do it anymore," I said as I turned to look back

over my shoulder at Jordie and Mario, asking for their agreement. "Okay?" I asked. "No more jokes about anybody's mom."

"In front of Chick," Mario amended.

I stepped away from Chick so I could slap Mario on the
back of the head.

"Ow!" Mario said with a scowl as he rubbed at his head,
then smoothed his hair.

"Or unless somebody sets it up perfectly in conversation,
in which case you have to do it,'" Jordie said. "You gotta give us
that. Right, Chick? If it's a perfect setup then we still get to go
straight for the 'your mama.' Okay?"

"You guys are such assholes," I said in a growl. "Can you
be serious for two minutes?"

"Yeah, sure," Chick said with a shrug. "If it's the perfect
setup, you can't just leave it hanging there. Of course." I could
tell he was trying to make light of the situation, blow it off as
Mario and Jordie made jokes, but he still seemed bothered by
the whole thing. It was weird, this sudden problem he had with
the way we spoke to each other, had always spoken to each
other.

"Come on," I said, and put a hand at the base of Chick's
neck to move him along.

"I was just thinking," Chick said as he dragged his feet and
kicked at the gravel, stirring dust up with his already filthy
high-tops. "What with Sylvia dying and all. We should be more
careful. About saying things you can't take back later."

"Sure, Chick. I get it," I said. From the angle of Mario's
head I knew he was listening to our conversation, had heard
what Chick said about Sylvia, but he didn't give any other in-
dication he was listening.

We walked in awkward silence after that. Maybe afraid

that anything we said might set Chick off again. Maybe thinking about Sylvia for a minute like I was. Maybe all of us unsure
what to say to each other if we couldn't talk shit about each
other's moms.

CHAPTER NINE

I was walking to school the next week when Jordie pulled up to the curb and honked at me. Since Jordie lived on the opposite side of town, I wondered why he had gone out of his way to pick me up. As I slid into the shotgun seat, I winced at the sound of "Bangarang" pumping out of the car speakers. Sometimes I couldn't even figure how I got to be friends with a person who had such terrible taste in music. When Jordie got his iPhone, he gave me his old iPod since he didn't need it anymore. I had to delete just about every playlist and start over, the music was all so awful.

Jordie had finally mustered the balls to call Cheryl and ask her to go out with him Saturday night—told me all about it on the drive to school. Actually, he had texted her to ask her, which was kind of a chickenshit way to ask a girl out. I didn't have a cell phone. If I wanted to ask a girl out, I had to actually talk to her.

"Cheryl and I are going to go to the movies on Saturday night," Jordie said.

"Good for you."

"I need you to go with me," he said.

"What do you mean, go with you? On your date?" I asked in disbelief.

"Well, she wants me to bring someone for her friend so we can all go together. . . ."

"Oh no. Uh-uh," I said. "I'm not taking out her ugly friend so you can get your freak on."

"Come on, Jaz, you know I would do it for you," Jordie whined.

"I don't know any such thing," I said and Jordie grinned. "Who's her friend, anyway?"

"You know that girl Raine, the one who was at the game last week?"

"Are you kidding me?" I asked. I wondered if Raine knew Jordie and Cheryl's intent. It didn't seem possible that Raine would have agreed to go on a double date if she knew I was the friend Jordie was bringing.

"I think she's hot," he said, misunderstanding my surprise. "I mean, except for her hair and her clothes, of course. Besides, you don't have to marry her. Just go to the movies with us and once I have a chance to work my charm on Cheryl you and Raine can get lost for all I care."

I gave him my patented look of disgust, then sighed. "Just a movie?"

"Just a movie."

"And you're buying," I said. Statement, not a question.

He hesitated for a beat and I thought I had him—Jordie could be a cheap son of a bitch, cheap in the way only rich people know how to be—but then he agreed. "Yeah, all right.

But if I'm financing the whole thing, the least you can do is go for pizza before the movie."

"Man, how good of a friend do you think I am?" I said with a scowl. "There's nothing in this deal for me. I'm only doing this out of the goodness of my heart, you know?"

"Yeah, you're a regular Nelson Mandela," he said with all apparent sincerity. "Saturday night at seven, okay? And try to look presentable."

On Saturday evening Jordie picked up the girls first since they all lived in the same neighborhood. I sat on the stoop outside of my apartment in the fading sunlight and waited for them.

I could hear the television in the apartment and the clink of glass as Mom washed dishes. Mom and I hadn't spoken in a few days. She kept the television on almost full-time to fill the house with noise and stayed up watching all night while I was sleeping. It didn't bother me, since I could sleep through just about anything.

My stomach was aching again, the pain still intense, but I was getting used to it now, learning to manage it by slowing my breath as I waited for the pain to subside.

Jordie walked up to meet me, approaching from the side of the building. "You ready?" he asked.

"You're early," I said as I dropped the twig I had been peeling.

"Yeah, well, if you're ready," he said with a critical look at the jeans and T-shirt I wore with a flannel, arguably none of them really clean, "the girls are in the car."

"You're not going to bring them in?" I asked.

He eyed me for a minute trying to judge if I was kidding, but said nothing and just shoved his hands into his pants pockets, a gesture that was so familiar to me, I no longer thought about the uncertainty it meant he was feeling. "Well, you know," he said. "Your mom's been a little . . . well, just . . . . lately."

"Yeah," I said, cutting him some slack because I didn't want to talk about it. "Let's go then."

Cheryl was in the shotgun seat, Raine leaned forward between the front seats of the car talking to her, but when they noticed our approach Raine scooted back in her seat and adjusted her skirt around her knees.

As I climbed into the backseat beside her she shifted her legs away from me and smoothed her short skirt over her legs again. Tonight she was dressed somewhat conservatively, for her—black miniskirt with high black boots and a Hello Kitty sweatshirt under a black biker-style jacket with an anarchy symbol painted on the sleeve in white paint. The jacket was ripped in places and I wondered if she had bought it used, or bought it new and made the rips herself.

"Hey," I said to Cheryl, and gave Raine a nod. I took a moment to give her legs a look where they were bare above her boots and below her skirt. She caught my look and seemed a little miffed as she shifted again in her seat and stared hard out the window.

Jordie drove us to the strip mall where there were a bunch of restaurants and a multiplex. He and Cheryl kept up the conversation while Raine and I sat in silence. We got a table at the pizza place near the theater. It was packed with people at this time on a Saturday night and the waitress looked irritated to have to serve us, a group of kids.

Raine hesitated before sliding into the booth, as if she was hoping she could sit on the same bench as her friend instead of next to me.

"I can sit somewhere else if it will make you more comfortable," I said to her.

"I'm not uncomfortable," she said as she tossed her hair and slid into the inside seat.

"Jaz is just kidding," Jordie said, giving me a look that told me to shut my mouth.

Raine ignored Jordie and instead of getting annoyed said, "Jaz—why do people call you that?"

"Why do people call *you* Raine?" I asked.

"My name is Lorraine," she said as she crossed her arms on the table, "which is a horrible effing name, so I go by Raine. Why do people call you Jaz?"

"My dad was the one that called me that," I said with a shrug. "Guess it just stuck."

"What happened to him?" Raine asked.

"What do you mean?" I asked. "Nothing happened to him."

"Well, you referred to him in the past tense," she said. "Did he pass away?"

"He's just not around," I said, letting impatience register in my voice.

"Oh," she said with a nod and a look of understanding that made me want to tell her to piss off. "I think I'll just call you Jason," she said, her eyes still on me, watching for a reaction.

"Suit yourself," I said, distracted by four guys who sat in a booth near the back by the jukebox. They were a group of heads, with greasy hair and grungy clothes, two of them in knit caps even though it wasn't that cold outside. It suddenly occurred to me that I recognized one of them, the set of Mario's shoulders as familiar to me as my own face. Mario had been spending more and more time around his stoner friends lately.

"Hey," I said as I nudged Jordie's foot with mine under the table and nodded toward Mario. Jordie looked around and saw who I was pointing to but didn't show any interest in Mario or his friends.

"I'm going to go say hi," I said as I started to slide out of the booth.

"What if the waitress comes?" Raine asked.

"Just get me a Coke," I said.

"Don't you want anything to eat?"

"It's a pizza place. I figure we're ordering a pizza, right?" I asked. "Just get whatever. I don't care."

I walked over to Mario's table, and the guys he was with all looked up at me expectantly. "Hey, man," I said to Mario. "Where's Chick?"

"I don't know, man," Mario said with a shrug, his eyes hooded. "It wasn't my night to watch him, was it?"

I studied the guys Mario was with more closely. They all looked a little out of it—one of the guys was rocking slightly in his seat, like he had to go to the bathroom and was trying hard to hold it.

"What kind of shit are you on?" I asked Mario. We hadn't spoken about our argument after the last soccer game, had just let it go, but now, somehow, it was still there between us.

"What are you? A narc or something?" one of the guys asked me before Mario could respond. The guy was tall and skinny, his blond hair cut close to his scalp, his Adam's apple prominent in his throat. His eyes were an icy blue, hard and without empathy.

"Yeah, man, I'm a narc," I said. "Figured anyone stupid enough to eat toilet paper wouldn't be able to tell."

Mario laughed and for a second I caught a glimpse of my oldest friend in his expression. "Jaz is just being a dick," Mario said. "Jaz, this is Travis," Mario said with a lazy gesture toward the guy with the icy eyes. "Man, Jaz is a friend of mine. He's not a narc. What are you up to?" Mario asked me.

"Nothin'," I said with a glance back over my shoulder at Jordie and the girls. "Playing wingman for Jordie with his crush."

"Oh shit," Mario said as he looked back at our table and recognized Cheryl, "he finally got the balls to ask her out, huh?"

"Yeah," I said. "She brought along her friend Raine."

"I know Raine," Mario said. "She was my lab partner last year. She's pretty cool. I should have asked her out."

"You're welcome to her," I said. "She hates my ass. I'd better get back before Jordie sends out a search party. I'll see you, man." I didn't bother saying good-bye to Mario's buddies. They didn't pay me any notice anyway.

Raine was cold toward me when I returned to the table, didn't even look at me while we ate. She and Cheryl kept up their own conversation while Jordie shot me pleading looks when the girls weren't paying attention.

"We should go if we want to catch that movie," Jordie said finally.

"Why don't we forget the movie?" Cheryl said. "Maybe we

could go down to the park and have a few drinks. Can you guys get some beer or something?"

Jordie turned to me, his expression hopeful. I just gave him a nod, figuring if the night was going to suck this much, I might as well be drunk for it.

CHAPTER TEN

Jordie drove to Bad Habits and pulled around to the back entrance, in the alley near the Dumpsters. "Wait here," I said as I got out and went to the kitchen door. Chris's muscle car, a 1969 GTO, was parked in the alley so I knew he was there. Chris was a cagey fucker and if I ran into him he'd be on me in a second, but no one else would much care. I just had to hope he was too busy at the front of the house to notice me.

Javier, one of the bar-backs, stood at the sink washing a pot, a cloud of steam rising into his face and making beads of sweat pop out on his forehead.

"Hey, kid," he said when I walked in.

"Hey, Javier. *¿Qué tal?*" I said. He answered me but I didn't really pay attention, then I was past him and on my way down the hall toward Chris's office. I took the key from its hiding place above one of the exposed pipes in the ceiling then slipped into the office and closed the door behind me. The liquor was lined up in rows on a deep wooden shelf along the far wall. I quickly grabbed a bottle of vodka and tucked it into my fleece jacket and used my arm, bent at the elbow, hand in my pocket, to hold it pressed to my side where it wouldn't be noticeable.

I locked the office door and put the key back exactly the way I had found it, then walked back through the kitchen.

"I tried to tell you," Javier said, "let you know Chris is behind the bar, not in his office."

"That's cool," I said. "I'll catch him later."

"I'll let him know you stopped by," Javier said as I slipped out the kitchen door.

You do that, I thought, but just gave him a wave of acknowledgment.

Cheryl turned around in her seat to look at me as I got back into the car and put the bottle of vodka between my feet. She gripped the seat back and rested her chin on the back of her hand. "Jordie says you work there," she said. "At that bar."

"Used to," I said. "Over the summer."

"And what?" Cheryl asked. "They just let you stop by and take a bottle of liquor whenever you feel like it?"

"Something like that," I said.

Raine snorted quietly and I cut my eyes toward her. She was looking at me with judgment, like I had just met every expectation she had for me. "You stole it. Isn't that right?" she asked.

"Who cares if he stole it?" Cheryl asked before I could say anything. "Let's go."

Jordie stopped at the Get & Zip to get bottles of juice and soda and then we went to the park pavilion, buried in a dark nest of trees, a sole streetlight lighting the parking lot. We sat at a picnic table passing the bottle of vodka around until we drank our mixers down far enough to just add the vodka to our own bottles.

Cheryl started to act drunk almost right away, but Raine mostly kept quiet, her hands tucked between her legs for warmth. My leg brushed against hers under the table and she pulled away as if I had touched her in some private place.

After a little while Jordie stood and pulled Cheryl to her feet. "We'll see you guys in a bit," he said, then drained his bottle of vodka and orange juice. "Cheryl and I have some stuff to talk about."

Cheryl giggled as she stumbled against Jordie's chest and he put a steadying arm around her waist. "Jaz, you take good care of my girl," Cheryl said with a meaningful look.

"Cheryl," Raine said with a warning in her voice, though I couldn't tell if she was warning Cheryl not to head off into the seclusion of the woods with Jordie, or if she was worried about being left alone with me. But Cheryl ignored Raine's warning as she and Jordie turned to walk off into the dark together, and left Raine and me steeped in an awkward silence.

Crickets.

Raine and I sat mutely as the sounds of the night rose around us. I almost jumped when she said, "I'm sorry about your sister."

"Yeah?"

"I didn't really know her since she was just a sophomore, but she seemed nice."

"She was an okay kid, I guess," I said, refusing to give anything away. I had been slowly adjusting, each day getting used to the idea a little bit more that Sylvia was really gone. Gone for good. I didn't like to talk about her. Every time I did, it put me right back at the starting line, had to work to start forgetting again.

"Was she your half sister?" Raine asked.

I gave her an affirmative grunt, now wanting to tell her to drop the subject.

"I figured that, since you had different last names," Raine said, almost apologetically. "So, what, your mom and dad are divorced?"

"They were never married, but yeah, they split up."

"When you were how old?"

"Uh . . . when I was just a baby," I said, wondering why she cared.

"What about Sylvia's dad?"

"He split," I said. "About six years ago."

"Geez," Raine said breathily. "Things must be tough for your mom."

"I guess," I said, and took another swig of vodka. "Though you'd think she'd be used to people leaving her by now."

"It's hard to tell—are you really an insensitive jerk, or is it all an act?" Raine leaned her head on her fist as she stared up into my face, waiting for an answer.

"You're very funny," I said, turning to look at her.

"I wasn't trying to be."

Another long silence followed. My soda was almost gone, so I hit the vodka bottle a few times without a chaser. It burned on its way down but felt good somehow—like without the burn of the vodka there was nothing to feel. My stomach started to knot again and I hoped the waves of pain wouldn't hit me now, not when I was alone with Raine.

"This is usually the part in the scary movie when the kids who are stupid enough to party in the pitch-black woods get slaughtered," Raine said. She glanced over her shoulder at the dark stand of trees around us and I felt it through the seat we shared when a shudder passed down her spine.

"Yeah, you're right," I agreed with a nod. "But a serial killer would take out Jordie and Cheryl first since they're getting it on," I said. "We'd hear their screams and have plenty of time to run."

She laughed at that, which surprised me. It was the first thing I'd said all night that had elicited something besides an eye roll.

"I hope Jordan's not the kind of guy who would take advantage of Cheryl because she's drunk," Raine said, her voice tight, as if she never expected anything good to come from a guy.

"It took him two months to work up the nerve to ask her out. By text," I added pointedly. "I'm pretty sure Cheryl is safe with Jordie. Besides, she doesn't seem to mind the attention. She was the one who wanted to get the booze and come down to the park."

"So what?" Raine shot back, our brief moment of fun quickly forgotten. "You think that means she's asking for it?"

"Asking for what?" I asked with a frown.

"To get taken advantage of." Raine's voice was rising in pitch as she grew upset.

"What the hell are you talking about?" I asked.

Raine tossed her hair with a twitch, like she was annoyed. "I suppose you think that if I'm down here drinking that I'm easy too."

"It never occurred to me to wonder about it," I said honestly. "I'm just here as a favor to Jordie. He wanted to go out with Cheryl but she didn't want to go solo."

Raine gave a sharp intake of breath and said, "Oh, so—what? You're giving me a sympathy date? Is that how you see this?"

"Why are you so mad?" I asked. "Aren't you just doing this as a favor for your friend too?"

She didn't answer, instead got up from her seat and dug around under the table for her purse. "You're a real creep, you know that?" she huffed.

"Where are you going?" I asked, now completely confused.

"I don't know," she said, her voice strangled, like she might cry. "Home. Away from here."

"What are you going to do?" I asked. "Walk out of here alone? In the dark?"

"What do you care?" she asked.

"I guess I don't," I said because now she was making me mad by coming at me on the offensive when I hadn't done anything to her. "But it isn't exactly safe to go walking around down here by yourself at night."

"You know what?" she asked hotly. "I'd rather be murdered than spend another minute alone with you!" And with that she stormed off, walking toward the small bridge that led to the main path that would eventually end up at the Pike.

In the almost complete darkness I could only see her for a minute before she faded into the black and the sound of her footsteps blended into the sound of the rushing stream.

With her gone the night sounds seemed amplified—the crickets and frogs as they sang to the night, the rustle of dried leaves as small animals moved through the forest, the sighing of the wind through the trees.

"Shit," I said to myself in disgust, then stood and followed in the direction Raine had stormed away. I jogged along the asphalt path and after a minute overtook her and almost mowed her down.

She screamed when I pounded up behind her and bumped into her in the dark.

"You're crazy, you know that?" I asked her. "You trying to get yourself killed?"

I jerked back reflexively as she turned and slapped me, hard, across the face.

Startled, I laughed as I put up a hand to block a second slap because she really could hit pretty hard. "Are you some kind of lunatic or something?" I asked as I rubbed at my stinging cheek with one hand, the other still holding her wrist.

"You're a complete jerk."

"Okay, yeah. I'm a jerk."

"You are," she said, not letting me tell her what she wanted to hear.

I tried to put an arm around her shoulders to guide her back with me, but she pushed me away and said, "You can forget it," then started walking back toward the pavilion. With nothing better to do, I followed her.

Cheryl and Jordie were sitting at the picnic table again when we returned, Jordie's arm around Cheryl's waist and one of her legs across his lap. Raine was composed now, the evidence of her crying hidden by the dark.

"Hey, you two," Cheryl called out in a singsong voice. "Having a good time?"

At the end of the night, Jordie dropped Raine off first and I walked her to the door. The porch light was on, burning a couple hundred watts, and I prayed that her parents wouldn't come out to see who was bringing Raine home.

"Nice house," I said as I took in the three-car garage and the wraparound front porch.

"Thanks," she said without even a hint of sincerity.

"Well," I said, "that was . . . awful."

"Yeah. I kind of hope I never see you again," she said as she crossed her arms over her chest.

"You want a kiss good night?" I asked.

"I'd rather eat vomit."

I chuckled at that. "Good night, Lorraine."

"Drop dead," she groaned as she turned and let herself into the house.

CHAPTER ELEVEN

When I got home that night I was hungry and went to see if there was anything worth eating in the fridge. Mom's attention to domestic duties was erratic at best lately and I didn't expect to find much in the way of groceries. Sometimes Aunt Gladys would stop by with a casserole or something, which was what I'd hoped to find, but didn't. As I pulled the milk carton out of the fridge one of Sylvia's bottles of insulin toppled over and rolled off the shelf and onto the floor. The small vial didn't break and I picked it up and rolled it between my thumb and forefinger while I studied the label. After a minute I gathered up the vials from the shelf and dumped them all in the trash. I was sick of seeing it. Sick of the daily reminder of Sylvia.

"What are you doing?" Mom's voice at the door made me jump.

She was leaning against the doorjamb as if it were all that was holding her up, her robe tied loosely and her hair matted on one side and sticking out in several places. Every time I saw her, she seemed to look more tired, more disheveled.

"Looking for something to eat," I said.

"What was that you threw away?"

"All of that leftover insulin."

"Who told you that you could throw it away?" she asked, her voice high and tight.

"No one told me," I said. "I just did it."

She pushed me out of the way and snatched up the trash can. I watched her, mildly surprised, as she dug around to find all the bottles I had just tossed.

She lined them up on the counter and dropped the trash can back at my feet. "In the future don't throw away things that don't belong to you," she said, glowering at me.

"Ma, what the hell do we need insulin for? Sylvia's dead."

She slapped me hard across the face, and her body shuddered as her eyes filled with angry tears. "Don't talk about your sister like that."

"Like what?" I asked, ignoring the sting of my face. It was the second time in one night I had been slapped on the same cheek, and Raine, completely uninvited, wandered through my mind. "All I said was she's dead. What's wrong with that?"

"How can you be so heartless, Jason? You act as if you don't even care about Sylvia. About anyone."

"How would you know what I care about?" I asked her. "We barely even talk to each other."

"You're just like your father," she hissed as she pushed her hair back from the wetness of her cheeks.

She always did that. Threw the fact that I was just like my dad in my face, like it was the worst insult she could lob at me. I knew I looked a lot like him, because people who knew him always said that, said I looked just like him when he was my age. But if my mom really knew me, she would know I spent most of my time trying not to be anything like him.

I didn't say it to her, didn't want to keep the argument going, but when Sylvia died, it was like losing the only family I'd ever had. She wasn't even my full sister, but she was more family to me than my mom or dad had ever been. Sylvia was the only person who understood Mom's crazy, the only person I could really talk to about anything like that. But usually I didn't have to talk, didn't have to tell her what she already knew.

I walked out of the kitchen and left Mom to have one of her breakdowns on her own. They were starting to get on my nerves. She wasn't the only person who'd lost something, but the way she acted it was like she was the only one who had a right to be upset about Sylvia.

CHAPTER TWELVE

Once a week Arturo made us all hit the weight room in the gym to do strength training. The rest of the week he had us doing laps and playing scrimmages, so the time we spent in the weight room was like a vacation from all the running.

"Where the hell is Mario?" Jordie asked for the tenth time since we had started working out.

I didn't answer since (1) I didn't know, and (2) I was sick of hearing him ask the question. Mario had missed two other practices in the past two weeks and technically Arturo shouldn't even let him play in the next game, but he was so hot to finally beat St. Andrew's in soccer that he would probably let Mario play anyway. We smoked St. Andrew's in just about every other sport, but they had held out against our varsity soccer team, undefeated for four years.

Jordie was angry because he believed we didn't stand a chance against St. Andrew's without Mario playing the sweep. And he was right.

Mario had been blowing off practice and playing like shit

lately and Arturo was so pissed off about it, we were all curious to see what his punishment would be.

We were all in the weight room when Mario showed up thirty
minutes late for practice. Though it wouldn't have been obvious to anyone else, I knew immediately that he was high.

I was sitting on the weight bench, taking a rest between sets
when Mario finally rolled in. Just the fact that he purposely
avoided looking in my direction was evidence enough that he
was on something, even if his eyes hadn't also been glazed and
red rimmed. Arturo was in his office, the room next door to the
gym but with a glass wall so he could see us. Arturo was tipped
back in his chair, feet on his desk, and glanced up when Mario
walked in but didn't bother to come yell about Mario being late.

Chick stood at the end of the bench behind me, waiting
for me to lie down under the weight bar and start another set.
He had offered to spot me, and I said okay just to humor him,
but there was no way Chick could lift the amount of weight I
had on the bar. I could bench-press more than he could dead-
lift.

"Hey, Mario, where've you been?" Chick asked as Jordie and
I exchanged a look. Jordie's expression held a judgment against
Mario that I refused to share so I kept my mouth shut.

"I've been busy," Mario said.

"Well, thanks for taking the time out of your busy schedule
to show up for practice," Jordie said, looking for a fight.

I lay back on the weight bench so I didn't have to partici-
pate in the argument Jordie was inviting. I gripped the collars
that held the weight disks in place, my arms wide to take the
pressure in my chest instead of my arms. For the next two minutes, while I went through a series of reps—full range and half

lifts—my mind was completely focused on not dropping the bar on my neck, and the burn of tired muscle. When I sat up for another rest, Jordie and Mario were still bickering.

"You know we might have had a shot at regionals this year if you would actually show up for practice," Jordie said.

"Take it easy, Jordie," Chick said, but both Mario and Jordie just ignored him, Mario snapping back at Jordie harshly.

"Why do you care so much about what I do anyway?" Mario said as he settled into the first of the circuit machines.

"I don't give a shit what you do," Jordie said. "I care about the fact that we're going to lose the game against St. Andrew's if you don't get your shit together. What's Arturo supposed to do, put Chick in the sweep?" Jordie asked, his voice so snide that if he had been talking to me, I would have smacked him in the mouth to shut it.

"Hey," I said, interrupting Jordie's little tirade. Jordie stopped and turned to me as I jerked my head discreetly in Chick's direction. Maybe Chick wouldn't really take offense at what Jordie had said. It wasn't any big secret that Chick couldn't really play. But it was a wasted effort to point it out anyway since Jordie didn't even get what I was talking about, was oblivious to anyone's feelings but his own.

Even though I understood why Jordie was pissed at Mario, I was still getting a little sick of Jordie's attitude. Lately all he seemed to care about was his image—his clothes, his car, spending time at the country club. Part of it was because of Cheryl. She was so shallow, she made Justin Bieber seem like a humanitarian. Jordie spent so much effort lately trying to impress Cheryl, it didn't leave much time for anything else.

It surprised me that Mario was arguing so much with Jordie. In the past Mario had always been the mediator, the one who

stepped in to stop a fight, to calm everyone down. He hated it
when I got into fights—would always try to talk me down
before my temper was too far gone. But now Mario was angry,
sick of Jordie and his bullshit.

Mario blew Jordie off and made like he was really into
doing reps on the weight machines. Jordie turned to me. "Are
you going to say something?" he asked.

"Like what?" I asked impatiently. "I'm not his dad."

"He listens to you."

I laughed at that and shook my head. "You're wrong," I
said.

"Yeah. He does," Jordie said. "You guys are besties. You're
the only one he listens to."

"You say that like you're jealous," Mario said, his eyebrows
twisted with a question. "Are you jealous of my relationship
with Jaz?"

But Jordie wasn't taking the bait this time, was sick of
Mario's shit the same way I was. "Shut up, Mario," Jordie said.
"You're not as funny as you think you are."

"I wish you would both shut up," I said, putting an end to
the conversation.

As I lay back down on the weight bench, I noticed Chick
was muttering to himself, talking under his breath so
I couldn't hear what he was saying. This wasn't the first time I
had noticed him talking to himself in a way that could attract
curious stares from others. As long as he was with us he
seemed okay, but when he was by himself and didn't know
other people were watching I would notice him carrying on,
talking to himself while seemingly unaware of everyone else
around him.

It wasn't like he was talking to an imaginary person.

Maybe this was just how he worked things out, having a conversation with himself about things. It was normal . . . for Chick, and I didn't usually pay it any mind. Most people are a little bit crazy. Some are just better at hiding it than others.

"Chick," I said to snap him out of it.

"Yeah, Jaz?" he said, taking a few seconds to surface from his daze.

"You okay to spot me?" I asked.

"Yeah, sure. Of course." He straightened his shoulders as he turned back to the weight bar above me. "Jordie's so mad," he said.

"He'll get over it," I said. Chick didn't look convinced, still looked stressed out and like he might start crying. "Hey, you got me?" I asked. "This thing's heavy. I don't want to drop it on my face."

"Yeah," Chick said. "Yeah, I got you."

"Stop worrying about Jordie and Mario," I said.

"I'm not worried." I knew Chick was lying, that he was still really bothered by their fight, but I let it go, figuring it was like clouds passing over the sun—we just had to wait it out. And even though I would turn out to be wrong about that, when I looked back later I didn't see how I could have known.

CHAPTER THIRTEEN

Thursday after practice I had to go to the library to finish an assignment for school. Normally I would have used Jordie's computer, but since he had started hanging out with Cheryl, I didn't see much of him outside of school and soccer. The Colonel hated it when I went over anyway, had always hated Jordie hanging out with Mario and me. Maybe he was afraid our poverty would rub off on Jordie, somehow make him less eligible for the Ivy League. Jordie's life plan was already mapped out, and it didn't include hanging out with Mario or Chick or me after high school.

As I was leaving the library, I noticed a distinctive head of pink and blond hair bent over one of the tables in the quiet study area. Raine and I hadn't said a word to each other since the night we were drinking down at the park with Jordie and Cheryl. If I made the mistake of looking her way in class, she would give me the finger, but other than that we didn't communicate.

When I saw her in the library, I didn't really make up my mind to go and talk to her so much as my feet just led me there.

"Hello, Lorraine," I said as I helped myself to the seat across from her. When she looked up at me, in that instant before recognition set in, her face was set in a mask of unreadable emotion, almost like mentally she was someplace else completely. Today she was wearing a black sweatshirt with the neck cut so large her bra straps were visible. Usually I wouldn't notice much about what a girl was wearing but with those bra straps staring me right in the face it was hard not to pay attention. Her lipstick was an alarming shade of red and she wore a dozen or more thin silver bracelets on one arm. I was struck by the fact that she really was pretty once you overlooked the hair and clothes.

She didn't say hello, just studied me for a minute, taking in the cut at the corner of my eye, my split and swollen lip, before saying, "What happened to your face?"

"Nothing," I said innocently. "I was born this way."

"Very funny," she said with a look that told me she didn't think I was funny *at all*. "Were you in a fight?"

"Yes, but it was against four guys and they look worse than I do."

"You mean they're uglier than you are?" she asked wryly. "Because I find that very hard to believe."

"You're hilarious," I said and nudged her foot with mine.

"What are you listening to?" I asked as she removed her earbuds.

"Foals," she said as she tucked a lock of pink hair behind her ear. "Do you like them?"

"No," I said with a slow shake of my head. "I don't like them. . . . I love them."

She found that mildly amusing, the corner of her mouth twitching upward in a brief smile, but still played it cool. "Did you come here with someone?" she asked.

"Are you asking if I came with a date?" I asked her, intentionally giving her grief because I liked watching her lose patience with me. When she got angry her lower lip pouted out in a way that was kind of sexy. In fact, it made me want to bite her lip—not hard, just gently, to feel the meat of it between my teeth. "You think I would bring a date to the library?" I asked, my eyes still on the small wet patch at the inside of her lower lip.

"I know the concept is completely foreign to you," she said with a patronizing tilt of her head, "but I'm just making polite conversation."

"You're still mad at me," I said.

She eyed me coolly, letting the silence hang between us as she considered my question. I was thinking about her lower lip again when she spoke. "Don't flatter yourself. I have better things to do than sit around being mad at you."

Sometimes it was hard to tell if she was trying to be funny, and I liked that. Her hair was a color unknown in nature, but her eyes were a clear blue, unusual because the blue irises were outlined with a pronounced black edge. Her skin was sun kissed and luminous, completely unblemished. The way she looked at me gave me the impression she could read my thoughts. As I thought about her I realized she was maybe more than pretty, maybe beautiful.

"What kinds of things?" I asked.

"What?" she asked, her brow wrinkling in confusion.

"You said you had better things to do," I said to remind her. "What kinds of things?"

"Are you still trying to be funny?" she asked.

"I don't really have to try," I said with mock humility. "I'm just naturally funny."

The look she gave me was meant to sting but it just gave me a silent thrill because I had gotten a rise out of her again. I bit the corner of my lip to keep my mouth from spreading into a grin.

"Who were you fighting with this time?" she asked.

"Just some D-bags who were messing with Chick," I said. "They were following him around, calling him a retard and stuff."

"Chick—he's that little guy on the soccer team, right?" she asked. "Why do you call him Chick?"

"His scars," I said as I gestured at my own cheeks and jaw. "The ones on his face. They're left over from when he had chicken pox. He was so sick, it almost killed him."

"Isn't it kind of mean that you call him that?" she asked earnestly, like she was really concerned about Chick's feelings. "It's like you're making fun of him by calling him that."

"Nah," I said as I drummed my fingers lightly on the table. "He likes it. Makes him feel like the original gangsta."

She shifted her legs under the table and her leg bumped mine. She pulled her leg back quickly, as if scorched by touching me. "You get in a lot of fights," she said, narrowing her eyes as she assessed my injuries more critically. "You just got in a fight three weeks ago at the soccer game."

I leaned in toward her and placed my elbows on the table, my head resting against my hand. She held my gaze as I spoke, looking at me in a way that made me want to know what she was thinking. "I like fights," I said. "When you're fighting, it's the only time you're not thinking about something else, you know? What's right there in front of you is the whole world, the only thing that matters. It feels good. Not to think. Just to . . . be."

We watched each other for a long minute, me expecting her to pull away any second, to sink behind the ice-queen exterior again. The air between us was charged with some kind of electric current, and my heart was beating so loudly in my ears, I wondered if she could hear it too. Then she said, "You should try getting laid instead."

I laughed so suddenly that my split lip opened up painfully, the salty tang of blood flooding my tongue. The librarian at the reference desk shot an ugly look in our direction but I lowered my voice again when I spoke. "You offering?" I asked as I nudged her hand with mine to let her know I was joking.

She smiled, not shining me on, but not giving away too much. "I'm surprised to see you at the library," she said. "I didn't get the impression you were a big reader."

"I'm pretty sure I don't want to know what you think of me," I said. "Unless it's some kind of weird fantasy involving fetish stuff. In which case, I want to know all about it."

"In your dreams, Jason. Only in your dreams." She was blushing like crazy now, her cheeks so red that it made her eyes stand out in vivid contrast. I liked it. So much, in fact, that I thought I could sit there all night just saying stuff to make her blush if she would let me. "So, what are you doing here?" she asked as she cleared her throat, trying to cover her embarrassment as she glanced around the room to see if anyone had overheard our conversation.

"I was just using the computer," I said. "We had an online assignment for Calc."

"Is your Internet down at home?" she asked, the color

ebbing from her cheeks now that we were talking about a safe topic.

"We don't have Internet at my house. We don't own a computer."

"Really?" she asked in surprise.

"I didn't mean to upset you, princess," I said, not intending to be snide but hearing it come out that way anyway. "I suppose before now you thought that everyone had an iPhone and drove a Lexus."

She cut her eyes away from me, looking at some imaginary point in the distance, and her expression turned sad. "Of course not," she said in almost a whisper. "That was a mean thing to say," she said. "Take it back."

"Take it back?" I asked with surprise. "Like a do-over?" I was being a total smart-ass but she just nodded, waiting for my apology. "Okay, fine," I said, feeling ridiculous as I did. "I take it back."

She nodded her head once, her eyes shut, as if earnest in her acceptance of my apology. It was strange, the feeling that came over me, like a sense of relief that the tension between us had passed.

It was right on the tip of my tongue to ask Raine if she wanted to get together sometime. I wasn't really sure what kind of expectation a girl like Raine had, what kind of place a guy usually took her on a date. All I wanted was to sit and talk to her without interruption, without worrying about who was watching or listening.

I had just decided that I would casually suggest we get together one day that week for coffee or to go off campus for lunch when a guy walked up to the table and interrupted. He stood right next to Raine's chair, his hip touching her shoulder, and his expression told me he hadn't expected to find her talking to another guy.

Raine's face relaxed into an easy smile as she looked up at him and I took a minute to envy him for that. I felt stupid suddenly, for thinking that there could have been anything between Raine and me.

The guy was dressed in a button-down shirt, ironed, with khaki pants and, I guessed without looking, some kind of loafers for shoes. He was clean-cut and carried himself confidently, with the swagger of an athlete. Though his face was familiar to me, he didn't go to our school.

"Hey," the guy said in my direction because it would have been awkward if he just ignored me, but he didn't wait for a response, just turned to Raine and said, "You ready?"

"Sure," she said. "You're finished with what you needed to do?"

"Yeah," he said as he stepped aside, his hand on the back of her chair as if to pull it out for her.

"Brian, this is Jason," Raine said. "We have Civics together."

"How you doing?" Brian asked without much interest and with a chin thrust at me.

I nodded at him, unsure where to rest my gaze but not wanting to just look at the table like I was some kind of pathetic whelp. At least he had walked up before I had a chance to make a fool out of myself, asking Raine out when she clearly set her standards a little higher than a guy like me.

"Jason plays soccer too," Raine said, and as she did I realized why the guy looked familiar. I had played against him before. He played for W & L, a high school on the north side of town. The north and south sides of our town were separated by four lanes of traffic, but it might as well have been an ocean. South of the main highway that divided the town in half was where most of the immigrant and working-class families lived, though there were a few neighborhoods, like Jordie's, where people had money. On the north side, the two high schools were full of kids who came from rich families.

"Yeah?" Brian asked. "What position?"

"Center midfield, usually," I said. "You?"

"Forward," he said.

Of course, you do, I thought. Nothing less than a glory position for this guy. He probably drove a BMW convertible and already had his last name waiting on the side of a law firm.

"Jason is an old friend of Jordan's," Raine said, determined to drag the awkwardness out.

"Really?" Brian asked with some surprise. "Jordan and I play tennis at the club sometimes. He's never mentioned you."

No surprise there. Jordie was good about keeping his two lives separate. "He's never mentioned you, either," I said. "Guess he can't admit to fraternizing with the enemy." The way I said it was friendly, like I was just making a light joke about our soccer rivalry, but he took it the way it was meant. I could tell by the hard set of his eyes, but he wasn't going to take the bait in front of Raine.

"Well, I guess I'll see you on the field next Friday," Brian said.

"I guess you will," I said with a nod. Challenge delivered, and received. I had never wanted to beat W & L so badly in the years I had played against them.

"Yeah, well, I'll see you around, Jason," Raine said as

Brian took her backpack from her and slung it over his own shoulder.

"Yeah, I'll see you," I said as she turned away, Brian's hand on her lower back in a possessive way. He didn't even bother to acknowledge me as they left.

CHAPTER FOURTEEN

That weekend, Chick asked me to go to the movies with him. There was some new horror movie out and he really wanted to go. I didn't go in for movies much, didn't like to sit still for that long, but he sounded so pathetic when he asked me that I couldn't really say no.

We took the bus to the theater, which took almost an hour because we had to wait first for the bus by my house and then for a transfer. Ever since Jordie got his car at the beginning of junior year we had all gotten used to riding everywhere. Since he started dating Cheryl I had barely seen the inside of Jordie's car. Cheryl had taken the shotgun seat for herself and wouldn't give it up for anything.

From the bus stop we had to run across six lanes of traffic to get to the theater. It was two blocks out of the way to cross at the light, so we never bothered even though it was a busy road with lots of traffic. A low hedge ran around the theater parking lot and I jumped across it but Chick had to walk through it, cussing under his breath as the sharp branches snagged his clothes.

The strip mall that housed the theater included a pizza place and a coffee shop, places where kids from school congregated on the weekends. Even if people who attended the local high schools weren't going to a movie or eating out, they tended to gather there. The back corner of the parking lot, far away from any of the businesses, was crowded with cars, music pumping out the windows of some of them. There were lots of kids just hanging around, goofing off, riding skateboards. Nobody had anyplace to go, but even a parking lot was better than just being at home.

We stopped to talk to a few of the guys from the soccer team since we had missed the early show and were going to have to wait around for the late movie. While we were hanging around talking, Alexis and a few of her friends pulled up in a minivan.

"Hi, Jason," Alexis said as she sidled up to me and put a hand on my hip. Whenever I saw Alexis she always put her hands on me in a familiar way, like there was something between us. "What are you doing tonight?"

"Chick and I are going to see a movie."

"You should come with us instead," Alexis said. "There's a big skate rally down at the waterfront. There will be bands and food and everything."

"Sounds cool," I said noncommittally.

"So, you'll come?" she asked.

"Maybe."

"Oh, come on. Please." She dragged out the word "please," her voice high pitched and whiny.

"I don't know. Chick really wants to see this movie."

"So?" she asked, her brow creasing with disdain. "He can go see the movie. You don't have to go with him."

"I'll see if he wants to go to the waterfront," I said. "We can catch the movie another night."

Her expression shifted to distaste and she wrinkled her nose. "No offense, Jason, but I don't really want him to come along. He's so creepy."

"He's not creepy," I said. As I said this I glanced around to locate Chick, make sure he wasn't within earshot. He was loitering at the edge of a group of guys from the soccer team I had just been talking to. Chick never said much but he had perfected the art of looking like he was part of a group, even if no one really noticed he was there. "He's just . . . a little socially awkward."

"You can say that again," Alexis said. "And he *is* creepy. I see him talking to himself at school sometimes. He's totally weird."

She had a point. But Chick was completely harmless.

"Just tell him you're going to go with us," she said, tugging at my sleeve and stepping in closer to me.

"Nah. I'll catch you next time," I said.

Alexis acted like she was really disappointed and for a few minutes kept trying to talk me into going with them. It's not as if I really wanted to see the movie, or that I hated the idea of making out with Alexis again, which she was clearly offering with her body language and the look in her eyes, but it had been weeks since the four of us had hung out—Jordie, Mario, Chick, and me. In fact, other than soccer practice, the four of us hadn't seen each other much since Syl's funeral. I could tell it was worrying Chick, and I felt too guilty to leave him.

Alexis's friends were talking to some of the guys hanging

out in the parking lot, but after a few minutes most of them piled into their cars and drove off. I collected Chick and we started walking toward the theater, still thirty minutes early for the show.

"You could have gone," Chick said.

"What are you talking about?" I asked, playing dumb.

"With Alexis. I heard her asking you to go to the skate rally." The way he said it, I knew he had heard more than just her asking me to go.

"She's kind of whiny," I said. "If I'd gone, I would have been stuck with her all night."

"You think there's a girl out there who will ever want to be with me?" Chick asked, looking up at me, the hurt in his eyes so clear that I had to look away. "I mean, not because of my looks or anything. I know no one would ever be into me because of my looks. But maybe I could find someone who's . . . into me."

"Of course," I said, but it sounded so weak and uncertain that I knew I was failing Chick. As his friend I should have been able to think of a dozen reasons why someone would want to be with him.

"You remember that time Jordie had a party when his parents were out of town?" Chick asked but didn't wait for any response before saying, "That girl Crystal was there. Man, she was fucking beautiful. You got wasted. Drank a shit ton of Four Loko and you ended up puking on her shoes."

I smiled to myself, remembering. "Shit. Yeah. I had forgotten about that. She was wearing a practically brand-new pair of designer shoes and I destroyed them. Who knew puke could come out that color, huh?"

He didn't laugh at my joke and said, "The next day, you saw

her at the pool and she totally hooked up with you. Even though you threw up all over her, ruined her shoes and everything."

"I saw her the next day," I said, filling in the blanks of the story. "Went up to apologize to her about her shoes. Offered to pay to replace them. Thank God she said it was okay, that she had been able to clean them. There was no way I could have paid to replace them anyway."

"You puked all over her shoes and she hooked up with you anyway. Just because of the way you look. Because girls think you're hot."

"Whatever, man," I said, unsure where this conversation was going. "She liked that I apologized, offered to pay to replace her shoes. All we did was make out."

"You think if I had puked on a girl's shoes at a party and went to apologize the next day, she would end up making out with me?" Chick asked, like a challenge.

He had me there. I wasn't sure what to say. "Maybe not," I said, and he snorted in agreement.

"I know most people think I'm a total freak," Chick said, hurting himself with his own words and I tried to think of a way to end the conversation.

"I don't think most people give enough of a shit about anyone to spend much time thinking about it either way," I said, hearing the bitterness creep into my voice. "And anyone who thinks that about you is a fucking asshole anyway, so don't worry about it."

"It's true. I'm a freak." He shrugged one shoulder in an effort to show indifference, but it just came across as awkward and sad. "Freakishly small, freakishly ugly, freakishly freak-ish." He smiled at that but it wasn't a happy smile. More like a smile of miserable acceptance.

"Don't say that," I snapped at him. "Who gives a fuck what other people think anyway?"

"Mm," he murmured, and the silence that settled between us was thick with tension. I didn't want to ask if he had overheard Alexis's comments about him being creepy. And anyway, even if he had, I wouldn't know what to say about it. It's not like any of it was untrue, that Chick was small for his age, that he was socially awkward, especially around girls.

I was a virgin by choice, but it's not like I had never been with a girl, like I couldn't get laid if I wanted to. With Chick, there was no choice, though he had never confided any feelings he had about himself to me before now. What was there to say?

An hour later I was wishing I had ditched Chick and left with Alexis and her friends to go to the skate rally. Not because of our awkward conversation about his physical and social shortcomings, but because of the movie he had chosen for us to see. I had never given horror movies much thought before—could sit through all the gore and violence and parts that were supposed to make you jump, and it had never bothered me.

The first part of the movie was okay. But once the zombies started to show up, I couldn't keep my mind off Sylvia, her actual physical person, the way she must look by now, in her grave on the other side of town. I would never have thought about how Sylvia being dead could affect so many things in my life—like how I couldn't even watch a movie with zombies or dead people in it without getting sick about it.

I spent the whole time with my stomach aching and sweat beading on my forehead while I kept thinking, *Jesus, that's what Sylvia looks like now.* A fucking zombie corpse. And I had to go to the bathroom until I could calm the fuck down and get my mind to stop racing. The whole time I kept wondering how long this was going to last, how long before I would start to feel normal again, start to feel like everything I said or did wasn't some potential land mine for being miserable.

CHAPTER FIFTEEN

When Jordie called me that Saturday morning to see if I wanted to go to the National Mall to find a pickup soccer game, I had just assumed he would call Mario and Chick too, but it was just the two of us who ended up going. It occurred to me that recently I had seen all three of my friends, just never at the same time. Jordie I saw out at parties and at soccer but he was never available anymore to go to the movies or just hang out and have a few beers down at the park.

I hadn't seen much of Mario, who now spent most of his time out with Travis and his other tree thugger friends. Mario's hair had gotten longer and shaggier and now he wore crystals around his neck and every other fashion choice that offered clear evidence he was smoking a lot of pot and listening to bad electronic music. We used to make fun of people who listened to Disco Biscuits, and now he was one of those douche bags.

It was early when Jordie picked me up and drove us toward the north side of town to catch the Metro.

"I don't know what I should do, Jaz," Jordie was saying as he drove. "I mean, we have been going out almost every night for three weeks, so it isn't as if it would be weird if I asked her not to see other people. But it's not like you ask a girl to *go* with you after junior high school. How are we supposed to become a couple?"

"I think people just start to assume when you are together that much that you are a couple. For God's sake don't ask her to go steady or anything lame like that," I said. My mind wasn't really on Jordie's problem. I didn't think much of his relationship with Cheryl and didn't expect for it to last very long anyway.

"I saw you eating lunch with Alexis in the cafeteria the other day," Jordie said. "Man, to hear her tell it, you guys are like boyfriend and girlfriend now."

"What the hell are you talking about?" I asked with a frown. "I'm not into Alexis at all."

"You're telling me you aren't sleeping with her?" he asked skeptically.

"I'd sleep with your mom before I slept with Alexis."

"Piss off," he said as he shoved my shoulder. "Anyway, your mom is the one who's a MILF."

"You need your head examined," I said.

"What?" Jordie asked in all innocence. "Your mom's young. What is she, like thirty-five? She's hot, man."

"Stop talking or I'm going to bust your lip," I said. We rode in silence for a while as I tried to think of a casual way to ask about Raine. Jordie hadn't mentioned her lately, hadn't said anything about our failed double date. When I did mention her, it came across as just idle conversation. "I ran into Raine the other night at the library."

"Yeah, she mentioned it," Jordie said. I wanted to ask him what she had said, why she had mentioned it, but I didn't want to seem too interested.

"She was there with some guy. Brian. You know him?" My question was casual but Jordie raised an eyebrow before answering.

"Yeah, from the club. He goes to W and L," he said.

"They a couple?" I asked, now realizing that no matter how casual my tone was, it was still obvious I was showing way too much interest in Raine.

"I don't think so," Jordie said. "Brian's had a thing for her since we were all in middle school but I'm not sure she feels the same. Besides, she's got a thing for you."

"For me?" I asked in surprise. "Are you joking? She hates my ass."

"Why do you think Cheryl made me set it up so we went on a double date for our first date?" Jordie asked. "That was because Raine wanted to get with you."

"You're crazy," I said dismissively, but my mind was working overtime.

"If you say so," Jordie said with a shrug.

Just about every girl at school had shown an interest in me since Sylvia died. Mostly I figured they just wanted some of the glory of the spotlight, to be noticed. Maybe Raine wasn't any different, but since she was already beautiful and rich, she didn't really need any help from me to be popular.

Jordie parked near the Metro station and then we rode the train downtown. That day we ended up finding two pickup games on the Mall—one with a group of older South American guys I had played with before when I was with Mario, the other with a group of guys our age who were all really good.

After the games we stopped for empanadas and sat on the patio in the sun to eat them before catching the Metro back home.

"You talked to Mario?" Jordie asked me as we stood in the train car for the ride home.

"Not really. He's buzzing all the time lately."

"What the hell is he thinking?" Jordie asked.

"I guess he's not," I said.

"He's got the rest of his fucking life to be off chops," Jordie said with disgust. "Why the hell is he messing with that shit now? Right in the middle of season?"

My tongue burned with a sharp retort. Jordie wasn't really concerned about Mario or his health. He was only worried about how Mario's using would impact our soccer record. When it was just Mario and me, Mario would often complain about Jordie in the same way—thought Jordie was stuck up and a narcissist. Which maybe was true, though it wasn't really Jordie's fault. He had just been raised privileged, an only child, used to the idea that everyone should give a fuck about how his life turned out. He would never understand where Mario was coming from, and I wasn't going to be the one to explain it to him.

When I got home that afternoon, Ma and Aunt Gladys were sitting at the rickety dining room table, a pot of coffee and two mugs between them. Aunt Gladys's hand was on Mom's arm, but she pulled away as I came into the room. I kicked off my shoes and went to get a glass of water from the tap.

"Hi, Jason," Aunt Gladys said when it became obvious Mom and I had nothing to say to each other. "I'm glad you're home."

I leaned one shoulder against the kitchen doorway and

waited for her to continue. "I was thinking," Aunt Gladys said, her voice softening as she spoke to Mom, "that if you aren't feeling up to it, Jason and I could clean out Sylvia's things. Box up some of the clothes. Maybe move some of Jason's things into the room so he could have the space."

Ma lifted her bloodshot eyes to look at me and I looked at the tops of my feet.

"Box up her things?" Ma asked.

"Well, not everything, of course," Aunt Gladys said quietly. "Just . . . I thought a little change might do you some good. Maybe do you both some good."

"Is that what you want, Jason?" Mom asked me, her voice hard and tight. "To throw out your sister's things?"

Aunt Gladys jumped in before I could answer, "Of course he doesn't, Claire. No one's talking about throwing out her things. But you have to . . . you have to accept that Sylvia is gone. You have to move on with your life."

Mom started to cry and covered her mouth with her hand, as if to hold the grief inside her head. She didn't want to let it go, wanted to just go on being miserable forever. In the weeks since Sylvia died, things hadn't changed at all. Mom's sadness never got any better, only worse.

"Why don't you just drop it?" I said to Aunt Gladys, more harshly than I had meant.

"I'm just trying to help," Aunt Gladys said as she held her hands wide in supplication.

"How?" Mom asked. "By telling me to forget about my daughter? She was *my daughter* for Christ's sake. I never did one thing to make her life better. And now she's gone. Because of me. You can't possibly understand. You don't understand what Jason and I are going through."

"Don't drag me into this," I said with a sigh as I gave up on the idea of being able to relax in my own house.

"I didn't come over here to start a fight, Claire," Aunt Gladys said, losing patience.

I felt trapped, stuck there listening to them argue. The only two places I could go to get away from them was the bathroom, though there were limits to how long I could reasonably stay in there, or Sylvia's room, where all I could do was hang out with Syl's ghost.

Sometimes I thought about it that way, Syl following me from room to room, watching over my shoulder. I tried not to let my mind think that way because if she could see me any-time she wanted that meant she could also see me when I jerked off in the shower. And there is nothing creepier in this world than the thought of your sister's ghost seeing you jerk off in the shower. Just like how I couldn't even think about going to a horror movie like the one I had seen with Chick. Maybe I would never be able to see a horror movie again without think-ing about Sylvia.

I tried to populate my mind with some kind of happy memory about Sylvia so I wouldn't get caught up in dwelling on her watching over my shoulder or thinking about her as just a dead body, but it was hard. There weren't many happy mem-ories to conjure from my childhood. Instead I would try to picture Sylvia the way she looked when I would see her around school—laughing with her friends in the hallways or the cafeteria, something like that.

Aunt Gladys didn't know, didn't understand what it was like to have someone in your mind all the time, someone you couldn't apologize to or share your regrets with. I figured Mom thought about Sylvia in the same way I did. Like if she ever thought about being able to hug Syl one more time her mind would immediately wander to thinking about Syl's body the way it was now, resting in its coffin in the cemetery, where we had left her to rot.

Mom and Aunt Gladys were still bickering when I banged out of the house and headed for Bad Habits to see if I could beg a free meal for dinner. There was no place else to run.

CHAPTER SIXTEEN

When I left my apartment I was headed for Bad Habits but then decided I didn't feel like asking for a free meal and, as payment, have to explain why I couldn't just eat at home. So I decided to stop by Chick's instead and see if he was around.

I walked out to the Pike, only a few blocks from my house, at the intersection where the Goodwill backed up against the Laundromat, and crossed at the light. From there I could cut through the park to a large apartment building that rose up from behind the discount grocery store. It was an older building, in need of paint, and the lobby always smelled like either stale urine or pine cleaner, sometimes the two different smells fighting it out for dominance in the enclosed space.

Chick's dad had been a recovering alcoholic for a long time. When he was still drinking he had a few serious falls, enough that it gave him some brain damage and he wasn't really right in the head. He wasn't mean and, in fact, was always grateful for company if I stopped by to see Chick. Chick's mom had died when Chick was just a baby. I didn't know the whole story but she had been a drinker too, part of the reason why Chick was born with most of his health problems I always assumed, though you would never hear Chick say that. Sometimes Chick's dad would talk about his dead wife, and the way he talked about her it was like he thought Chick and I knew her, would remember what she looked like or how she acted. It was almost as if he didn't realize how long she had been dead, as if she had died just a few months ago instead of when Chick was too small to even remember her.

The two of them, Chick and his dad, lived together in a small apartment. I was never really sure where they got their money since Chick's dad couldn't hold down a job. I guess they survived on the disability check Chick's dad got from the government. Chick had an EBT card he used for groceries. My family had never qualified for food stamps, because my dad sent us money every month, though sometimes I wondered if we would have been better off with government assistance than we were with my dad's check. Sometimes he gave me a little extra money for myself, like for clothes at the beginning of the school year or an envelope of cash at Christmastime.

If I did have extra money, from working over the summer or Christmas money from my dad, I always felt like I had to turn it over to Mom to use for household expenses. It wasn't just because I wanted to help out. When I gave her money it would make her stop complaining about my dad being a deadbeat and an insensitive jerk, if only for a little while. Not that I cared so much about protecting him or his reputation, I just didn't like hearing Mom complain about him. I always felt like I had to choose a side, and to be honest, I thought they were evenly matched in a competition for the shittiest parent award.

When I got to the apartment, Chick was playing video

games, his dad working on one of his Civil War models at the kitchen table. He created elaborate battle scenes, each soldier and weapon hand-painted, complete with bridges and trees and other landmarks. Each scene he created was based on a real battle, and his knowledge about troop movements and weather and other details about each battle seemed to be endless. He couldn't get his act together enough to keep groceries in the house or keep the place clean, but he could remember everything he read in one of his history books.

"Hey, Jaz," Chick's dad said as he opened the door to my knock. He was one of the few adults who used my nickname. Most everyone over the age of eighteen called me Jason. I preferred Jaz since it was one of the only things my dad had ever given me.

"Hey, Mr. G," I said as I stepped into the apartment. "How've you been?"

"I'm okay. Working on the Second Battle of Bull Run."

"Cool," I said, since there was nothing else polite to say about it. I fell into the sagging couch beside Chick, who was intently focused on one of his video games.

"Hey, Jaz," Chick said without looking away from the screen. "What are you up to?"

"Nothing. I just had to get out of the apartment."

"Yeah? Why?"

I could tell Mario just about anything, though usually I didn't have to. He just knew everything. Like his mom, he could size up any situation or person with a glance and his first impressions were almost always right. Jordie was too self-interested to be very perceptive about the feelings of other people. There was never much point in telling Jordie anything because he would just find a way to relate the conversation back to his own feelings or problems. Chick genuinely cared about all of us—you can't get handed such a crappy deal for life the way Chick had been and not be sensitive to other people's feelings. But if I tried to explain to him the things I had been thinking or the way my mom was acting, it would just make it worse for me. He would ask impossible questions that I couldn't answer, or make me keep talking about it long after I had gotten tired of the subject.

"No reason," I said, an easy out. "I just don't feel like being at home. I was thinking about going to get something to eat. Want to roll?"

Chick's dad gave him some money as we were leaving. Twenty bucks. Enough to get us both a chicken-fried steak with potatoes at the diner. My mouth watered just thinking about it.

The diner was a popular after-school hangout. It was open twenty-four hours and was a destination for late-night or early-morning breakfast for just about everyone in town. The club kids came here when they had the munchies at three in the morning, and on Sundays there was a line down the street of people waiting to get into one of the dozen or so booths that lined large plate-glass windows overlooking the busy street.

Stacie was working, serving both the lunch counter and the booths by herself. I knew Stacie because she used to hang around Bad Habits a lot. She and Chris had an on-again, off-again thing. Mostly off. She was crazy beautiful and completely chill. I thought Chris was an idiot for letting her go, but he never asked my opinion. She was at the register when Chick and I walked in and I stopped to say hello. When she saw me she let out a squeal of delight. "Hey, darlin'," she said, giving me half her attention as she counted change from the cash drawer.

She handed the customer his change then came to present her cheek to me for a kiss. Stacie was in her early thirties, tall and statuesque, her hair cut short and dyed a dark purple. She had high, prominent cheekbones and full lips stained ruby red, tattoos on both arms, beautiful images of half-naked women in pinup poses. Her low-rise jeans and cropped shirt revealed a muffin top, and her breasts were large and filled out her T-shirt in an impressive way. I felt how much substance she had when she leaned in to hug me and I couldn't stop my mind from wandering where it shouldn't go.

"I'll bet the girls are falling all over themselves to get with you," Stacie said. "Please tell me you're at least a gentleman about it. Not breaking hearts all over town."

"How could I be interested in any girl but you, Stace?" I asked innocently.

Her eyes widened as she said, "You *are* breaking hearts all over town. Speaking of which, how's Chris doing?" Now she was ignoring a customer at the other end of the bar who was trying to get her attention.

I shrugged. "The same. You know how he is."

"Oh, I know," she said with a meaningful roll of her eyes. "Tell him I said hi. Or, actually, don't. Tell him you saw me and I looked great but forgot to ask about him."

"Sure thing," I said and she waved Chick and me toward an empty booth along the wall.

As we sat waiting for Stacie to come and take our order I glanced around at the crowd of kids hanging at the tables. There was a group of girls sitting in a booth near the jukebox and I gave them only a passing glance at first. Then my heart stuttered and my mouth went dry when I noticed her. Raine was fidgeting with the straw of her drink, laughing at something one of her friends was saying. Her eyes crinkled a little at the corners and there was a dimple in her right cheek. She caught me noticing her and I looked back to Chick quickly, relieved when Stacie stopped at our table to drop us a couple of Cokes and to take our food order.

I was fighting to keep my attention on Chick and what he was saying. He was talking about some video game he liked to play, something completely foreign to me. My mind was distracted as I wanted to look at Raine again, but didn't.

I still didn't believe what Jordie had said about Raine being into me, but you could probably call our interactions lately some kind of flirting. Sometimes when I passed her in the hallway at school I would wink at her and she would roll her eyes in return—not in a way like she was really irritated, but kind of playful. Or in Civics if I turned to look at her she would discreetly flip me the finger. Even if she was in the middle of talking up in class, she would hide her hand under the desk, giving me the finger while the rest of the class was listening to her spout off about land mines in Cambodia or the AIDS epidemic in Africa. Then I would have to fight to keep from laughing out loud.

Just to have something to do I went to use the bathroom and on my way back passed the Internet jukebox hanging on the wall, the same kind Chris had at Bad Habits. Raine was standing at the jukebox tapping on the screen as Radiohead's "There There" started to play from the speakers mounted near the ceiling throughout the room.

"You play this song?" I asked as I stopped by the jukebox.

"Yes," she said. "Just seemed like the right song for the moment, though I don't love Radiohead."

"No one should love Radiohead," I said. "What else are you playing?"

"I haven't decided yet. You want to put in a request for One Direction or something?" I could tell she was trying not to smile as she said it.

"You're hilarious."

"I know," she said, deadpan. "So? Request?"

"Haim."

Her mouth opened as she drew in a breath of surprise. "I love them. Which song?"

"Play 'Don't Save Me.'"

"Sure," she said with a nod. "Good song."

Chick and I ate and I managed to keep my eyes off Raine for the rest of the time we were there. A small miracle. As Chick was paying the check at the register I noticed the people at her table getting up to leave. Since I was unsure if I should wave to her or say good-bye I kept my head down, my eyes fixed on my iPod as I scrolled randomly through the playlists.

When Chick and I left the diner Raine was standing in the parking lot talking to one of her friends. Just the sight of her made me respond physically, the now familiar racing of my heart, my breath hitching in my chest.

She was leaning against the door of her car as Chick and I walked down the steps to the parking lot. We turned onto the sidewalk and started the long trek back home.

As we turned into the alley to take a shortcut, a silver Acura slid up alongside us and the passenger-side window rolled down. The sunroof was open and the strains of Thievery Corporation's "Sound the Alarm" drifted out onto the late afternoon breeze. Raine leaned over from the driver's side and said, "You guys want a ride?"

"How much?" I asked.

She laughed. "No charge."

"We live all the way down the Pike," I said, giving her the opportunity to back out. "By the park. You going that far?"

"Whatever," she said with a shrug.

Chick took the backseat and me the front without consultation or comment. I did it without conscious thought, but the fact that Chick would always defer the front seat without question was just part of who he was, the gesture usually unnoticed.

We were all quiet for the ride to Chick's house except for the occasional directions I gave, telling Raine when to turn. Each of us was lost in our own thoughts and Raine kept the music turned up, her playlist now on The 1975. Chick music, but they had a few catchy songs.

We were only a few blocks from Chick's apartment when Chick spoke up. "Hey, Raine," he said, "you know that girl Felicia?" asking Raine about a girl who was part of the drama crowd.

"Sure," Raine said. "We've been in drama together the past couple of years."

"She seems nice," Chick said, his head turned to watch the world passing by the window.

Raine was watching his face in the rearview when she said, "Yeah, she is nice."

"I always see her with that Garrett guy. Are they a couple?" Chick asked.

"Garrett's gay," Raine said. "They're just good friends."

"You should ask her out, Chick," I said. "Just for coffee or something. No big thing."

"No," Chick said quickly. "I don't think she would be into me."

"Some girls are into nice, quiet guys, Chick," Raine said, and my heart swelled with gratitude that she was being so nice to him.

"You think?" Chick asked. "Most girls only talk to me because they want to ask me about Jaz. You know, since Syl died. Sorry, Jaz," he added quickly.

"It's okay, Chick," I said as I raised my hand to rub the hair at the nape of my neck, a nervous habit I had never really noticed until recently, now that I had so much more shit making me nervous.

Raine pulled up outside Chick's building and he climbed out and gave us a wave before trotting away, his shoulders hunched under his oversized hoodie, a hand-me-down from Jordie. Even if my clothes weren't four sizes too big for Chick, they were beyond usefulness by the time I was done with them.

"Thanks for taking Chick home," I said once we were alone in the car.

"It's no problem," Raine said as she backed the car out into the road.

"You remember where I live?" I asked, figuring our date had probably been one of the more forgettable things that had ever happened to her.

She didn't answer me right away but after a minute blurted suddenly, "You want to go get a coffee or something?"

I hesitated because I didn't think I had more than a dollar

or two in my pocket. Maybe I could agree to go and then just say I didn't really want anything to drink once we were there.

"If you don't—" she started to say.

"No," I said, cutting her off. "I mean, I do. I want to. I'd rather go just about anywhere than home right now."

"I feel ya," she said.

"My mom's been kind of hard to live with lately," I said. Massive understatement. "What are you up to tonight?" I asked to change the subject so things didn't slide into awkward territory again.

"I'm grounded this weekend," she said and bit her lower lip as her expression turned worried. "I got out of the house today by saying I was going to the library to study. My mom flipped out after she saw my progress report from school. I haven't been doing so well in some of my classes. I'm getting tutored in math, which is super lame and embarrassing."

"What math are you in?" I asked.

"Algebra Two. Also lame. What about you?" she asked.

"I'm in Calculus."

"You're in Calc?" she asked, like it was the most amazing news she had ever heard.

"Yeah, I'm not as stupid as you think I am," I said, wishing as soon as the words had left my mouth that I could take them back.

"I didn't mean it like that and you know it," she said, glancing away from the road to study my expression. "Anyway, I'm practically flunking half my classes at this point, so I get help with my homework a couple of days a week."

"I've always been good at math. Only one right answer, you know? Simple."

"That's what makes it hard," she said. "You can't fake your

way through math. I've always had to fake my way through school, be the bullshit artist. I have a hard time staying on top of my classes."

"Yeah?" I asked. "Why's that?"

She cut her eyes toward me but didn't answer right away, seemed to be thinking about what to say. "I don't know."

"You don't know, or you don't want to say?"

She blew out a small laugh and said, "I don't want to say."

"Fair enough," I said.

"Being an underachiever is *un*acceptable in the Blair household," Raine said, making a joke out of it now. "The Blairs are winners, and winners never quit." Jordie talked the same way a lot of the time, like life was so hard because he always had his parents placing expectations on him. Though I kept my mouth shut about it, sometimes I thought maybe that wasn't such a terrible thing, to have parents who actually gave a shit when or if you came home, wanted you to do well in school, to be good at something. But then, no one had ever expected much from me, so maybe it was more of a burden than I realized.

A minute later Raine pulled the car into the parking lot at the Starbucks closest to school and put the car in park.

"You want to go here?" I asked, surprised that she had chosen a place so close to campus where other people from school might be hanging out.

"Yeah. Why not?" she asked.

"Aren't you afraid of being seen with me in public?" I asked. "I thought you had a boyfriend."

"Did you think we were going to make out in a booth or something?" she asked. "We're just going for coffee."

I felt a twinge of longing when she mentioned making out

and I'll admit, my mind wandered down that path for a fleeting, fantastical mental visual. "So, *is* Brian your boyfriend?" I
asked, wanting to hear her say one way or the other.

"No," she said. "He just sometimes thinks he is. If you're
so worried about it—"

"I'm not," I said, cutting her off.

"Good, then drop it." She got out of the car and shut the
door, not waiting to see if I was following her.

I didn't want to check my pockets to see how much money
I had and then have to figure out what I could afford by looking
at the menu. Not in front of Raine. I just avoided the whole
thing and when we got in line I said I didn't really want a
coffee, would just sit and hang out while she drank hers.

"I'll take a latte with whole milk," she said to the cashier,
"and just a plain coffee for him." Before I could argue she handed
money over to the cashier and paid for both of us.

"You didn't have to buy me a coffee," I said as we moved
to the end of the counter to wait for our drinks.

"I know I didn't *have* to. Is that your way of saying thank
you?" she asked.

"No," I said. "I'll thank you later. In private."

She laughed and said, "Cut it out. I know you think you're
charming since you have girls throwing themselves at your feet
every day, but I am totally immune. Got that?" She arched one
eyebrow as she waited for my answer.

"Got it," I said.

We crossed the room to grab a small table near the window. As we slid into our seats Raine checked the display on
her phone and said, "I have to get the car home by six because
my stupid brother needs it."

"Your stupid brother?" I asked with a chuckle. "You sound like you're four."

"Eff you, okay? My brother is a total jerk."

"I know your brother," I said as I removed the lid from my coffee to drink. "He seems like an okay guy."

"Maybe to you he is," she said. "He wrecked his car so now we have to share mine. He's a pain in my ass." She rubbed the bridge of her nose, then said, "But I guess most people feel that way about their siblings."

I nodded but didn't say anything, just kept my gaze fixed on the window, watching a guy in a Jetta struggle to parallel park in a space big enough to fit two cars.

When I looked at her again her eyes were wide, her coffee cup poised halfway between the table and her lips. "I—I'm sorry," she said with a stammer.

"About what?" I asked.

"I didn't mean . . . I shouldn't have said that."

"Said what?" I asked.

"About my brother," she said, her eyes searching for something to look at, anything other than my face.

"You mean because of Sylvia?" I asked.

"Yes," she said as she took a deep breath and sat back in her seat, her hands balled in her lap. "I'm sorry."

"Don't worry about it. It doesn't bother me."

"What do you mean it doesn't bother you?" she asked. "It doesn't bother you that your sister died? You're full of shit."

"You just said you hated your brother."

"I know, but I didn't mean it. He can make me crazy, sure, but I would be devastated if . . . if something happened to him."

"Then I guess you shouldn't say things you don't mean," I said.

"Don't do that," she said.

"Do what?" I asked with a scowl.

"Get mad. You know, you don't have to act like you're too cool to be sad about it. That's your reaction to everything. You either treat it like a total joke or you get mad about it."

"You don't even know me," I said, my voice rising, but I was fighting back the emotions that lay coiled in my belly like a snake.

"You're right," she said. "Let's just forget it. I wasn't trying to make you mad."

"I'm not mad about it," I said and ducked my head, forcing her to meet my eye. "I like talking to you. Okay? I just . . . don't want to talk about Sylvia."

"Okay," she said quietly, and then she surprised me by putting her hand on my wrist and gently pinching the fleshy part of my hand at the base of my thumb. It was as if she was silently apologizing and my heart fluttered against my ribs like a bird with an injured wing. I wanted to grab her hand before she could pull away. It surprised me, this attraction I felt for her. I never would have pictured myself liking a girl like Raine, but there it was.

"Aren't you going to put anything in your coffee?" she asked to change the subject. She put her chin in her hand and rested her elbow on the table. "You're like a cowboy or a construction worker or something, drinking it without any cream or sugar. How can you drink it like that?"

"I like the taste of coffee," I said as I took another scalding sip. "If you don't like the taste, why do you drink it?"

•   •   •

We talked for almost an hour—about music, our friends, school—our conversation just flowing naturally from one topic to another. She had a way of making a joke that was so quick and smart that sometimes even she seemed surprised by her own sense of humor. Our knees accidentally touched a few times under the table, and sometimes she would interrupt me to ask a question or to make a comment, and when she did she would lean forward and put a hand on the side of my knee, as if to say, hold that thought while I tell you this. I would keep my eyes on her face while she was talking, but all I could think about was her hand on my knee, though she didn't seem the slightest bit uncomfortable about it.

Her brother texted her twice to ask where the hell she was and when she would be home. After she interrupted our conversation both times to look at the messages on her phone I took the phone from her.

Finally, when the sun had set and she was thirty minutes late leaving to get the car home, we left and she drove me home.

The more I got to know Raine, the more I realized that being just friends with her would not be easy. The problem was, as soon as I had started thinking of her as beautiful, I couldn't really unthink it. And the more I got to know her, the more I thought that maybe I didn't just like her. Maybe I was on my way to making playlists about her.

As she pulled off Four Mile Run to drop me off I was suddenly conscious of how run-down and dirty the neighborhood was. The upper apartments had balconies, but most only had laundry hanging on a line or were used to store bikes or other outdoor equipment. These weren't balconies where people sat to enjoy a sunset or a cup of tea.

The XM radio was on the alternative station and she

reached over to turn up the volume when a song I didn't recognize started to play. "Sorry, I love this song," she said.

"What is this band?" I asked.

"Why?" she asked. "You don't like it?"

"I didn't say I didn't like it. I've just never heard it before," I said.

"They're called Neutral Milk Hotel."

"Weird. They still around? It sounds really old but I've never heard it."

"It's just the way they record it, makes it sound like it was recorded in the '60s," she said as she turned down the volume a little so we could talk over the music. "They've been around for a while, maybe since 2000 or 2001. Do you like it?"

"I dig it okay. Reminds me of Bob Dylan a little bit."

She nodded. "Yeah, I could see that."

"My dad's really into Bob Dylan," I said absently as I stared out the window. "You know that song, 'Girl from the North Country'? Bob Dylan did a duet of it with Johnny Cash. My dad loves that song."

"I thought your dad wasn't around," she said, and I remembered I had told her that when we were out for pizza with Cheryl and Jordie.

"I see him sometimes," I said. "I've never lived with him, didn't see him much when I was growing up, that's all."

"Oh," was all she said.

"Well, thanks for the ride," I said as I gathered my jacket from my lap and opened the door. "I guess I'll see you around."

"Sure," she said.

I was out of the car and she started to put the gearshift in reverse when I reached into my pocket and said, "Don't forget your phone."

"Are you coming to Madison's party next weekend?" she asked.

"Maybe," I said, knowing I wouldn't.

"Okay. I guess I'll see you," she said, and she seemed to be waiting for something though I wasn't sure what, so I just gave her a wave and shut the car door.

CHAPTER SEVENTEEN

Friday we had our away game against W & L. The team rode across town on the activities bus, all of us silent, like we were getting ready to go in front of a firing squad. Everyone on that bus knew we were probably about to get clobbered. W & L was a good team. At least a few of their players would be headed to college on soccer scholarships the next fall. And we were playing on their turf. We could barely beat W & L at home, much less on their territory.

The home team was already milling around the sideline when we filed off the bus and onto the field. There were a few shouts at us from the bleachers, the W & L crowd a much bigger turnout than what we would get at Wakefield. The shouts weren't welcoming so we ignored them, but there were at least two friendly faces there as we took the field.

Cheryl and Raine stood by the fence that separated the field from the bleachers, waiting to say hi before they went to get seats. Jordie stopped to talk to Cheryl.

Raine smiled as I approached and I felt my face relaxing

into a smile in return. She was standing with her hands resting on the top of the fence, one foot tipped casually on toe point.

"You here to root for the other team?" I asked.

"Maybe," she said, lifting one shoulder in a shrug. "Depends on how much of a jerk you are to me."

"Your loyalties should be to your home team," I said, "regardless of whether you like who's playing."

"I didn't come here to cheer for a team," she said with a meaningful tilt of her head as she looked up at me through hooded eyes, "just one person in particular."

"Lucky guy," I said, my voice close to breaking. The tables were turned and she had finally managed to say something to make me blush.

"Maybe," she said.

"Jaz, let's go," Jordie was saying, maybe not for the first time, and I realized I had a goofy grin on my face. "Arturo's calling."

"I'm coming," I said without taking my eyes off Raine.

"Jaz!" Jordie was shouting now, and without another word, I turned to walk away from her.

As I sat on the sidelines stripping off my jacket and swinging my arms to limber up I noticed Raine's maybe-but-probably-not-boyfriend, Brian, jog over to talk to her while she still stood at the fence. He leaned in to give her a hug and she turned her face to let him kiss her on the cheek. Was it my imagination or did she intentionally take the kiss on her cheek that was meant for her lips? But she was smiling up at him, laughing at something he said. My face burned with heat again, this time from humiliation. Now I felt stupid, like maybe I had misread the signals. When Raine said she had come to cheer for just one person in particular, I thought she had been talking about me, flirting with me. But now I was thinking she was just covering up the fact that she was there to show support for the other guy.

I tried to keep my eyes off them, but I couldn't bring myself to turn away completely. I wanted to see if her smile was the same as it had been when she was talking to me.

Then I decided to forget it because the W & L team was lining up on the field and I had never been more determined to win a game in my life. I hoped Arturo wasn't going to pull some bullshit and yank me out of the game early.

"This is gonna suck," Mario muttered to me as we sat on the bench watching the W & L team and waiting for the ref to call us onto the field.

"We got this," I said with confidence I didn't really feel.

As soon as the whistle blew to start play I had two defenders on me like stink on shit. I was used to being a target. After all, I had a reputation for playing rough, drawing fouls, and getting thrown out of games. But the way they were playing didn't make any sense. Even when the ball was nowhere near me I still had two guys on me, getting in my space like they were trying to draw me into a fight. Maybe they thought I could get myself thrown out of the game early for unnecessary contact and we'd have to play the rest of the game a man down.

At first it was just an annoyance, the players crowding me, practically begging me to push them out of the way, or passing the ball tightly between two or three players trying to run me in circles. Eli caught on quickly to their game and fell back from his forward position to create a distraction. They were so busy with their defenders up near me, they weren't paying close attention to their goal and what our forwards were doing.

Finally I did manage to get my foot on the ball. The pass I sent to Eli was a sloppy one, the ball skidding along instead of rolling true, but he trapped the ball easily and changed direction in the same movement. As I watched Eli take the ball and run with it I forgot to pay attention to the W & L players who were still around me. My head was turned at an angle when one of them drove an elbow up into my eye. I went down like a brick, the pain so intense for a minute that I thought the hit might have blinded me. The refs didn't see the dirty play since their focus had been on the player with the ball.

I was on my knees with one hand on the ground to hold myself steady, the other holding my eye, when the ref finally saw what was going on and stopped play to come and see if I was okay. Jordie was standing over me and shouting curses at the W & L players near me, telling them to back off. I was still in too much pain to open my eyes, so it was just a confusion of voices around me.

"Can you get up?" the ref was asking me.

"What the hell does it look like?" Jordie asked hotly. "That guy just gave him a full elbow to the eye."

It was Chick who helped me to stand. "Blood?" I asked because if I was bleeding, I had no choice but to leave the game.

"No," Chick said, his gaze shifting from one of my eyes to the other, "but bloodshot. Can you see?"

"Out of my other eye. Sort of," I amended as my uninjured eye was watering so much, everything was an indistinct blur.

"You should sit," Jordie said.

"You want to call in a sub?" the ref was asking Arturo as he walked over to take a look at me.

Arturo didn't answer right away as he took a moment to assess my injury. "You okay?" Arturo asked me.

"Fine," I said.

"He can play," Arturo said with a wave at the ref as he turned and walked off the field.

There were only a few minutes to play until halftime and the W & L defenders backed off a little now that the ref was watching more closely.

At halftime I sat on the bench, catching my breath, ignoring the crowd and the W & L players. Chick got me an ice pack from Arturo's kit, and the cold plastic was a welcome relief to the heat of my injury. The heartbeat of pain behind my eye just reminded me to stay angry so I would go into the second half as determined to win as I had been in the first half.

Arturo came over to talk to me, his gaze on the middle distance as we spoke so no one would know we were having a serious conversation. "I don't know what you said or did, but these guys clearly have an interest in taking you out."

"It's nothing," I said.

"Well, you seem to be a good distraction so I'm going to keep you in," he said. "You got a problem with that?"

"No."

"Don't give the ref a reason to toss you. If anyone gets tossed I want it to be one of theirs."

I just nodded at that and he strolled away to have a quiet conversation with Eli.

The second half was worse. I was completely neutralized by the two midfielders, who wouldn't leave me alone, and if I did get my foot on the ball my defenders would do their best to trip me. They kept me running as I tried to control the middle of the field, but they were just running me down.

I was catching my breath at midfield when there was a

scuffle at the sideline and Eli emerged with the ball. He was on a breakaway, headed downfield with only one W & L defender and the goalkeeper between him and the goal. He was way out in front and no one was going to be able to catch him. I was running the block and the goal was all but a done deal. Eli was going at the W & L goalkeeper full speed and with a few quick fakes he was able to put the ball away. I was completely focused on the action at the goal and had almost forgotten about the defender just behind me. About a second after Eli scored the goal, I took a late hit from out of nowhere and was down for the count. I didn't know what hit me.

Later my teammates would tell me that one defender was so intent on neutralizing me that he didn't even pull up once the goal had gone in. He was coming at me full speed downfield and didn't try to keep from mowing me down. At the same time, one of the players I had been blocking decided to go through me instead of around me in a last-ditch effort to stop Eli. I got caught in between the two of them and got knocked into next week.

The next thing I knew, Arturo, the medic, and Mario were all looking down at me and I was staring up at the clouds drifting overhead in the late afternoon sky.

"Jason." Arturo was saying my name over the ringing in my ears.

"Yeah," I said. "I'm here."

"Hey, lie still," Arturo said. "You got knocked out so they going to take you off the field in a stretcher."

"No freaking way," I groaned. "I can get up." I rolled into a sitting position and when I did my head began to spin. For a minute I thought I might throw up.

"Seriously, Jason," Arturo said, sounding a little angry now, but I could tell he was worried. "You need to lie still. You could have a concussion."

Mario took a knee, then put a hand on my shoulder and leaned me back against his bent leg. *"¿Estás bien?"* he asked.

I nodded and then again thought I might puke so I closed my eyes until things stopped spinning.

"You want to stand up?" Mario asked.

"He needs to see a doctor," Arturo said. "He was unconscious for a few seconds at least."

Mario and Arturo spoke in Spanish for a minute. They spoke too quickly for me to catch all of it. Mostly them debating the fact that I was so stubborn it was less work to let me try to walk off and then collapse if I needed to rather than get me to see a doctor.

Then Arturo turned his anger on the ref, asked him why he was even on the field if he wasn't going to call fouls on the players who had been harassing me the whole game. By this time Arturo was completely worked up and he was dropping curses in Spanish and waving his arms around. Since I had been inside the penalty box when I was knocked out the ref had to give us a penalty shot on the goal, which Mario had to take for me since I was in no condition to walk, much less score a goal.

After a few minutes I was able to walk off the field unassisted, though pride was the only thing carrying me. As I limped to the sideline I saw Brian watching me, the smile playing at the corners of his mouth enough to tell me that the elbow I had taken to the eye and the bruised brain I was sporting were both thanks to him, even if he hadn't gotten his hands dirty. He didn't care that his team would be down two goals once Mario took my penalty shot, since Mario had never missed a penalty in his life. All Brian cared about was knocking me out of the game because he had seen me talking to Raine.

I sat on the bench, my forearms resting on my lap as I watched Mario line up to take the shot on goal that was rightfully mine. He stood with his hands on his hips and squinted up at the failing sun, as if determining the angle of light and the direction of the wind. In actual fact, he was giving the goalkeeper a minute to psych himself out and worry about which way the ball might fly.

Mario ran at the ball, his body leaned forward so that when his foot connected, the ball would fly hard and low into the goal. At the last second Mario reared back a little so the angle of the ball would fly higher. It was too late for the keeper to change his momentum. He was already on the ground, diving left as the ball sailed into the top right corner of the goal.

Mario didn't even celebrate. Just turned and walked away as the bleachers went quiet.

After the game, we had to ride the activities bus back to school. My teammates celebrated loudly on the bus. The pounding in my head was intense and my neck ached, so I rode with my head resting against the cool glass of the bus window. Every bump we hit was a painful reminder of my injuries. Jordie leaned over the back of my seat and gave my shoulder a shake as he whooped in excitement.

"Lay off, dumb-ass," Mario said as he slapped Jordie's hand away. "He just got knocked out."

"Sorry," Jordie said, not sounding sorry at all. He was too excited by the win to be put out by Mario's insult. "Let's hit the diner. A bunch of those guys from W and L said they were going to go eat and I want to rub it in that we beat their asses at home."

"Can't," Mario said. "I've got plans."

"What about you, Jaz?" Jordie asked.

"I don't have any money," I mumbled.

"I'll buy," Jordie said. "It will be worth every penny when those guys see you walk in the joint after they tried so hard to put you down."

When we got to school Mario didn't even go back into the locker room to change. His ride was waiting in the parking lot, the same group of guys I had seen him with the night Jordie and I went out with Cheryl and Raine. They were all standing around an old piece-of-shit silver Corolla, rust spots on both rear quarter panels. All of them were smoking cigarettes and laughing hysterically about something. The blond guy, Travis, was wearing skinny jeans and a brown cardigan. Fucking hipster.

My head was still hurting when I emerged from the locker room. The hot spray of the shower had helped somewhat but the dull ache at the top of my spine was still there, my eye still puffy and hot to the touch. I waved off Jordie's invitation to join him at the diner and started the long walk home by myself.

CHAPTER EIGHTEEN

I skipped practice the Monday after the W & L game because I still felt dizzy if I stood too quickly and the dull ache in my neck hadn't gone away. After school I was so tired I planned to just go home and sleep. It had been on my mind all day. I rode the bus home because I was too tired for the walk, though I couldn't remember the last time I had taken the bus home after school. The noise of the riders, the high whine of the engine, and the jostle of the vehicle over bumps in the road made my head start to pound for real.

As I trudged across the packed-earth grounds of my apartment building I heard shouting, the noise drifting out across the parking lot, but I didn't think much of it. Living in an apartment complex like ours we were all right on top of each other. I had gotten used to ignoring the drama of other people's lives—the fights, kids crying, loud parties.

But as I drew close to our door I realized the shouting was coming from my own apartment, the very living room where

I slept, in fact. I ran the last fifty feet and hit the door hard, then stopped to pull the screen open. The sound of me hitting the door startled whoever was inside, and the shouting stopped abruptly.

It took my eyes a few seconds to adjust to the darkness of the interior after being out in the bright sunshine of the afternoon. When my eyes had adjusted and I took in the scene of the living room, I didn't know what to say.

Mom was standing, her eyes wild with anger and grief, her hands gripping her hair at both sides of her head, as if covering her ears to protect them from the volume of her own voice. My grandmother, Mom's mom, sat on the edge of my open sofa bed. My grandfather stood with his back to the kitchen doorway, his hands clasped behind him in a rigid military posture.

"Ma?" I said, my voice a question.

My grandparents were mostly strangers to me. I had met them only a few times in my life. They disowned Mom when they found out she was pregnant with me at the end of her senior year of high school. Mom didn't speak to them for a long time and I was six the first time I ever met them.

"Jason," my grandmother said with an attempt at a smile. "How are you?" she asked.

The question was so stupid, so inappropriate, that my shocked reaction was to laugh. My grandmother's eyes went wide, as if I had slapped her or screamed a curse at her.

"Don't even talk to him," Mom said, her voice a strangled cry.

"Ma," I said, holding up a hand to quiet her. "Calm down."

"Claire, you aren't doing Jason any favors by keeping us

away. We want to help," my grandmother said. Her eyes were traveling over the room, taking in the tangled sheets I had left that morning on my sofa bed, the pile of dishes on the table that filled the small dining area. I had been meaning to clean up the mess but I spent so little time in the apartment it was easier to just ignore it. A pair of my jeans was draped over the arm of the couch—not dirty enough to warrant a trip to the Laundromat but not clean either. Beside the couch was a laundry bag full of my underwear and shirts. I knew they were seeing all of this and judging the way we lived. In contrast with my grandmother's neatly pressed skirt and blouse and my grandfather's precision-trimmed hair and beard, I felt like I always did when someone from the outside saw our living conditions.

Mom gave an angry, garbled cry. No words, just an expression of grief and frustration. Then she turned and fled to her bedroom.

My grandmother stood with a small sigh and moved as if to follow Mom.

"Leave her alone," I said as I put myself between them and the hall door. "She doesn't want you here."

"She's upset," my grandmother said, her mouth in a grim line. "She's sick, Jason. She needs help."

"You think you're telling me something I don't know?" I asked with a mirthless laugh. "Where were you a month ago?"

"It's a long drive from Florida," my grandmother said after casting an uncertain look over her shoulder at my grandfather. "Gladys called us. She thought we might be able to help."

"Ma and I can take care of ourselves," I said. "You've never been there when we needed you before. I don't get why you think now's the time to start."

"Jason," my grandmother said, her eyes turning sad as she tried to decide what to say next.

"You should go," I said and turned my back on them to walk to Mom's room. Her door wasn't locked and I let myself into her dark bedroom, shutting the door behind me. There was a sour smell to the room, strong, like she hadn't done her laundry or washed her sheets in a long time. At first I held my breath against the smell. As much as I had been out of the house lately I hadn't really noticed how much further she had slid into despair.

Mom was curled up in a ball in the corner of her bed, her back pressed against the dingy-white wall. Her hands were over her face and her breathing was ragged and loud from the snot that filled her nose. Her crying was no longer the desperate sobs that had become so familiar. Now she only whimpered, like an injured animal that doesn't understand the source of the pain it's experiencing.

"Ma, Ma, Ma," I moaned as I climbed onto her bed and pulled her arms away from her face. She didn't fight me, just went limp as she continued her whimpering. "Hey. Hey, they're gone," I said in almost a whisper as I sat down with my back against the headboard and put my arms around her shoulders. I pulled her against my chest as she sniffled loudly.

"Don't let them come back, Jason. Don't let them come back."

"I won't," I said, wondering as I did how I would stop them if they tried to visit her again.

"They don't care about me," she said as fresh tears spilled onto my shirt and soaked the front of it. "They never cared about me. They kicked me out. Their own daughter. Kicked me out when I needed them the most."

I shushed her and held her tighter as her body shook with sobs. She was like a child in my arms and it made me uncomfortable. Like maybe she really was too sick for me, for anyone, to help her. I was still alive, still here with her, but it would never be enough.

"And now I'm just like them," she said. "I don't know how to be a good mother. I wanted there to be more. So much more. I can't ever seem to do anything right."

"Don't say that," I said, though just to make her feel better. It was killing me, listening to her cry and go on and on about what a failure she was, what a disappointment her life had been. I wanted to push her away and leave, be someplace—anyplace—else. But there was no way I could leave her. All I could do was sit there and hold her and silently promise myself that I would never end up like her.

"I killed her," Mom said, the confession rushing out on a gust of breath that warmed the wet patch on my shirtfront. "I killed her by not being there when she needed me."

"Don't say that," I said again, wanting to beg her to stop talking altogether as my own tears broke the dam of my lower eyelid. The wetness burned my cheeks and I put out my tongue to catch the line of tears before they reached my chin, the taste completely foreign because it had been so long since I had let myself cry. About anything.

I buried my face in her hair and held her tighter as she started to calm down, her breath slowing toward sleep.

"I'm sorry," she mumbled. "I wanted to be more."

I shushed her again and tipped my head back against the headboard, my eyes closed.

"It's just the two of us, Jason," she said, her voice muffled

against my chest. "It's just the two of us now. We don't have
anyone else."

"I know," I said dully.

Once she was asleep I carefully slid off the bed and pulled
a blanket from the end of the bed to cover her, deciding as I
did that I would wash her sheets and remake her bed for her
the next time she was out of the house.

Though I took care to shut the bedroom door silently
behind me, I probably could have slammed the door and it
wouldn't wake her, she was so out of it. It was like she was getting the first real sleep since Sylvia had died, and I hoped she
would stay asleep all night.

It was just now turning to evening though it seemed much
later, as if many hours had passed since I got home from school.
There was a light tapping at the door and I went to open it.
Mario and his mom stood on the stoop. He was holding a large
basket and a shopping bag and handed me the basket as they
came through the door.

His mom didn't make a point of looking too carefully but I
could sense her taking in the condition of the apartment—
the stale air, a rancid smell emanating from the kitchen.

"She's sleeping," I said.

"*Bueno,*" Mario's mom said with a nod of approval.

They were silent after that, Mario working under her direction as she spoke to him in quiet Spanish, telling him to
dust this and wash that, with him never managing to do anything to her satisfaction the first time. He was used to that. I
sat at the small table eating a plate of steak with rice and salad,
the contents of the basket they had brought, as they worked
around me.

The sun had long set by the time they left. I sat at the table once again and tried to finish my homework but my eyes kept sliding closed. Soon after Mario and his mom were gone I fell into bed and was asleep before my mind had time to drift anywhere it shouldn't go.

CHAPTER NINETEEN

I was standing in the lunch line contemplating the choice between a salad and overcooked broccoli. The salad was just a small cup of lettuce with a wilted slice of tomato on top—the slice so thin it was like they only had one tomato to go around for the whole school so they had to be tight with it.

Between the free breakfast at school and the occasional dinner with Mario's family I managed to get a decent meal here and there, but I was still hungry most of the time. I had to always be planning a meal ahead, thinking all the time about whether I had exhausted my welcome at Bad Habits for a burger or if Mario's parents would think it was weird that I was stopping by to eat, again.

Sometimes Aunt Gladys would come by the apartment with a casserole or cookies or something, but usually I was going most of the day on coffee and some kind of day-old pastry from the convenience store that I passed on the way to school.

Though she had been barely functional before, somehow

Mom was worse since my grandparents' visit. Seeing them had made her retreat further into her own misery, though she didn't mention anything about her latest breakdown and I didn't bring it up. Now I was doing everything to manage our small apartment, including Mom's laundry. She hadn't done any grocery shopping since Sylvia died.

Mom had been losing weight. Her face was thin, the lines around her eyes more obvious than they had been a month ago. I never saw her eat, assumed she was eating at work, which was where she spent most of her time lately unless she was in her room. She was working double shifts a few days each week. Sometimes I worried about her but since that was a futile exercise, I tried not to think about it. It just made my stomach hurt.

My dad did send Mom money every month for my expenses. I don't know how much. The way Mom told it, the money was never enough, just enough to keep us out of the poorhouse. I thought we were already living *in* the poorhouse, but I suppose it could have been worse. Besides, when Sylvia was alive there was always plenty of food in the house, and even though we qualified financially for the free breakfast at school and lunch vouchers, I hadn't used them much until after Sylvia died.

If I wanted the free breakfast at school, I had to get there at least twenty minutes before classes started, which meant that if I waited for the school bus, I got there too late to get anything to eat. If I did go to school for breakfast, I had to be up by six so I had time for the thirty-minute walk to school. Some rubbery eggs and a few withered pieces of sausage weren't enough of an incentive for me to get up before the sun.

Since I got a free lunch at school I couldn't just use the

voucher to buy whatever I wanted. If you accept a free lunch, you also have to accept the absence of choice. I had to take the protein dish, even when it was the disgusting goulash they were serving today, and at least two servings of fruit and vegetables. The fruit consisted of those cups of little oranges or peaches packed in sugary syrup, so at least it was kind of like getting dessert. Dessert is not included in a free lunch.

As I stood there contemplating my vegetable choice, someone stepped up beside me in line, too close to be socially acceptable, and it dragged my attention away from the vegetable servings.

"Hi," Raine said with a shy smile as she crowded my space.

"Hi," I said. Though we had Civics together every day we never spoke other than to exchange the occasional hello. Sometimes she would still give me the finger if she caught me looking her way, but now it was more of a playful thing, almost a flirtation.

"I hope that disgusting smell is your lunch and not you," she said.

I lifted one arm and sniffed at my armpit. "No, it's definitely the food," I said.

"Gross," she said as she hit my shoulder with the side of her fist. She reached across me to grab a yogurt and an apple from the cold food shelves, and her right breast pressed against my arm. Raine didn't show them off much but she had a perfect set of breasts. Not too big, and not too small. Perfect. I could feel the soft roundness of her breast pressing against my arm, just a fleeting thing, but I would be able to conjure the memory of that feeling, and would often, over the next few days.

She smelled good too. Not like perfume or shampoo, but like the earthy good smell of the part of a girl's neck that is warmed by her hair.

"You're like a gorilla," she said. "I wouldn't be surprised to find out that you also fling your own poo around."

"Do gorillas do that?" I asked, but she ignored the question.

"How's your eye?" she asked as she studied my face.

"Better," I said, wondering if she knew the abuse I had taken at the W & L game was because of her.

"It was horrible to watch when you got knocked out," she said. "I was really worried."

"Yeah?" I asked, raising my eyebrows with interest as we inched along the lunch line.

"I mean, not just me," she amended quickly. "We were *all* worried."

"It was worth having a headache for a week to beat those guys for once," I said.

"There was a party after the game, down by the cliffs." Raine was talking about a place in the woods that overlooked the Potomac River. A popular place for major parties because it was so remote—a place the cops never bothered to look. "It was mostly W and L people even though they lost the game."

"Yeah? Who'd you go with?" I asked, keeping my voice casual—didn't want to give her the impression I was all that interested.

"I went with Madison. Jordan and Cheryl went out to dinner or something so just the two of us went."

"You walked down to the cliffs just the two of you?" I asked in surprise. "That wasn't exactly smart. Pretty girls attract all kinds of unwanted attention."

"Did you . . . Did you just give me a compliment?" she asked in mock astonishment. "You did, didn't you? You just called me pretty."

"I suppose before now you thought guys were into you for your stunning intellect," I said.

"Don't worry," she said. "I won't tell anyone you said something nice to me. I know you have a rep to protect as the stoic tough guy."

"When have I ever not been nice to you?" I asked.

"You're joking, right?" she asked. "Look, now that Jordan and Cheryl are a thing, you and I should have a truce. Despite her personality flaws, Cheryl *is* my best friend, and you and Jordan are tight. So, you and I should get along. You could start by eating lunch with us." As she said this she gestured toward a table by the floor-to-ceiling windows that lined one end of the cafeteria where I could see Jordie sitting with Cheryl and a few other people.

Before I had a chance to answer, the line shuffled forward and Raine and I were suddenly at the cash register, where a bored-looking woman in a smock and a hairnet didn't even bother to acknowledge us. I handed her my lunch voucher, fighting down the feeling of shame that was rising because I was getting the free lunch, a fact that couldn't possibly escape Raine's notice.

"ID number," the cashier said. I rattled off the five-digit number that identified me as a freeloader, like an inmate number in a prison.

The woman spent a minute typing in my number and considering the information on the screen in front of her. "This voucher doesn't match your student number," she said, her tone accusing, like I had been trying to steal the disgusting school lunch. Who would try to steal a lunch if they could afford to buy something better?

"I don't know what to tell you," I said. "I brought that from home and that's my ID number."

"Jason Marshall?" she asked.

"Yes."

"Well, the voucher is supposed to match your account."

"Like I said," I said slowly, feeling Raine's eyes carefully studying my expression, "I brought that voucher from home."

The woman gave an impossibly long sigh, like it was the biggest inconvenience in the world, as she looked at the voucher number and typed it slowly into her keyboard, her index finger stabbing the keys one by one. After a long minute she said, looking at me over the rims of her glasses, "This voucher number belongs to a . . . Sylvia Donaldson. You don't look like a Sylvia to me."

"Just ring ours in together," Raine said as she opened her purse and started to dig out some money. "I'll pay for it."

"No," I said quickly.

"If you want to pay cash," the woman said, "it's two-fifty for the lunch."

"I don't have any cash with me," I said.

"Jason, just let me pay for it," Raine said. "You can pay me back tomorrow."

"I don't want you to pay," I said, my voice rising with anger.

"Stop being ridiculous," Raine said, her own anger matching mine. "What? You can't stand the thought of a girl paying for you?"

I couldn't stand the thought of anyone paying for me, much less a girl. Even less Raine.

Now there was a crowd of people behind us, watching our exchange intently as I refused to back down. The cashier still just looked bored, picking at a hangnail as Raine and I continued our standoff.

"Forget it," I said as I shoved the tray toward the cashier. "Keep your lunch."

"Jason!" Raine called after me, but I just walked away. A few heads turned at the sound of her voice calling after me but I didn't care. I headed for the exit and didn't look back.

I walked out of the main entrance toward the parking lot, like I was going to the gym, but at the last minute I veered off the paved walkway and picked up the trail that had been beaten by the tread of many feet along the shortcut that would take me out to the main road. Once I was out of sight of the school I started to jog and kept running even after I was breathing hard and had a stitch in my side.

Home was not my destination. It would never occur to me to run home. My feet carried me to Bad Habits, to the kitchen door, which was the only entrance I ever used.

The outer door, a security gate made of iron bars, was shut, but when I tugged on it the door swung outward. I tested the handle of the interior door and it turned freely. As I stepped into the kitchen I almost stumbled over the rubber mats that sat in a pile near the door. Chris was standing in the middle of the kitchen, surrounded by tall stacks of boxes, a clipboard in his hand as he checked in inventory.

He didn't ask me what I was doing there in the middle of the day, why I wasn't in school, or why I was out of breath and sweating. One look at my face seemed to be the only answer he needed.

"I want my job back," I said, still panting. "I want you to give me some shifts."

He looked back to the invoice on his clipboard and didn't say anything for a minute while I wiped at the sweat on my forehead with my sleeve. Finally, he said, "Bernard's going home to visit his family in Haiti for a few weeks. You can take his shifts while he's gone."

I nodded in agreement, not even asking what hours it would mean I was working. "And after that?"

"We'll figure it out," he said. "I've always got someone calling in sick or wanting to take time off. Each time you're late I take away a shift. If you get fired it will be because you fired yourself. Got it?"

I was itching to make a smart comeback but bit down hard and just nodded again. "I know how it works."

"Good. Finish checking this stuff in and get it loaded in the cold box," he said, meaning the walk-in cooler at the back of the kitchen. "I've got some errands to run. Anything's missing from the orders just write it down and I'll call them later. And don't forget to clock in."

After he left me alone in the kitchen I took a minute to get a drink and punch in at the time clock hanging on the wall near the alley doorway. I was glad for the solitude in the kitchen, knowing the bar wouldn't open for another five hours and no one in the world, other than Chris, knew where I was. It would give me some time to get my head straight, try to forget about the humiliation of the scene in the cafeteria.

I looked at the clock on the microwave and there was still

thirty minutes until Civics started, when Raine would get to class and sit behind my empty chair for all of sixth period. I spent the next thirty minutes checking in the weekly inventory, distracted every few minutes by looking at the time.

At one fifteen I knew Civics class had started. Raine would be looking at my empty seat, thinking about my lunch voucher. Thinking about how I had tried to use my dead sister's lunch voucher to get a free meal. I hadn't even realized they would know the difference when I took the booklet of vouchers from Sylvia's dresser at home.

"Shit!" I shouted in frustration, forcing my mind to let it go. I started lifting the boxes, two and three at a time, my neck and shoulder muscles aching from the strain of lifting the heavy boxes and loading them into the cold box. When I finished moving the inventory I sat down on one of the kegs in the cold box, savoring the cold air as it lifted the sweat from my skin.

When Chris returned I was still sitting on one of the kegs, my elbows rested on my knees. He stood with his shoulder leaned against the doorjamb, watching me but saying nothing.

He spoke first, asking, "You want to tell me what happened?"

"Nothing happened," I said.

"Uh-huh. Okay," he said in his gravelly drawl. "You don't want to tell me, it's fine."

"I don't want to talk about it."

"So, what else is new?" he asked. "You want something to eat?"

"Yeah," I said as I realized suddenly that I really was hungry, had gone all day without anything to eat. And thinking about the fact that I had missed lunch reminded me again of why I had walked out of school. Chris left me alone then, went to fix us both something to eat as I waited for the feeling of humiliation to pass after replaying the scene with the lunch lady in my head.

I thought about how nice it would be if I never had to leave the solitude of the kitchen at Bad Habits, never had to go back out into the world at all.

CHAPTER TWENTY

Mario wasn't at practice Monday or Tuesday and Arturo was just pissed off enough about it that he would probably keep Mario out of the Friday game. We had all just finished dressing for practice on Wednesday when Mario strolled into the locker room.

"Hey, Mario, where've you been?" Chick asked.

"I've been busy," Mario said.

"You gonna be at the game on Friday?" Jordie asked.

Mario hesitated before saying, "I don't think so."

"What do you mean, you don't think so?" Jordie asked hotly. "Either you're on the team or you're not. Which one is it?"

Mario's jaw was set in an angry clench as Chick and Jordie waited for his answer. I was tying my laces, ignoring them, because I already knew his answer.

"I'm off the team," Mario said. "I just came to tell Arturo that I'm done."

"Son of a bitch!" Jordie said as he slammed the side of his

fist into the metal lockers. "You're a real asshole, you know that," he fumed.

"I don't get what the big deal is," Mario said. "I just don't want to play anymore, that's all. And I'm tired of Arturo always riding us about grades and stuff. I just want to relax my senior year."

I noticed that Mario wouldn't even look at Chick, who seemed ready to cry, his face flushed red.

"Yeah, I forgot. You're too busy getting stoned with your loser friends to show up for class or practice," Jordie said.

"What do you care, Jordie?" Mario asked acidly. "Your new popular girlfriend doesn't approve of you hanging out with us anyway."

"You keep Cheryl out of it," Jordie said as he stabbed a finger at Mario. "This has nothing to do with her. It's about you being an unreliable asshole."

"Oh, yeah?" Mario asked. "How many times have you invited Jaz to go to the country club with you to hang out? Huh?" He didn't stop to wait for an answer. Instead he continued his rant, asking, "How many times have you invited Chick to go with you to your family's beach house for a weekend? Have you introduced him to all of your awesomely cool new friends?"

Jordie was silent, his eyes on the floor as Chick and I both waited to see what he would say.

"That's what I thought," Mario said when the silence had stretched on for a solid minute. "You know as well as I do that you would be too ashamed to take any of us to the country club with you. You'd never own us as your friends in front of those people. So, what I don't get is why you think I have some obligation to you. The only person you care about is yourself."

"Man, shut up!" Jordie shouted. "I'm so tired of your shit,

Mario. If you don't want to play for the team anymore then just get out of here."

"Gladly," Mario said as he shifted his backpack onto one shoulder and turned to leave. Chick was crying by this time. He was muttering to himself as he started to rock from one foot to the other.

"It's okay, Chick," I said quietly. "It's just a fight, man."

"Screw Mario," Jordie said as he shoved dirty clothes into his gym bag. "I'm sick of his shit." Then Jordie was gone too and Chick and I were alone in the locker room.

Chick was crying for real now, his body shaking as he sniffled and wiped at his eyes.

"Take it easy," I said to Chick as I stepped closer to him. "It's nothing worth getting upset about."

"You and Mario are barely speaking to each other," he said as he gulped air. "Now Jordie and Mario are fighting. Nobody's friends anymore."

"It's just a fact of life, man," I said as I put a hand on his shoulder and shook him gently. "Everybody leaves eventually."

"Are you going to leave me too?" Chick asked as he lifted his gaze to my face, his eyes desperate.

"Of course not," I said, but I couldn't muster the emotion Chick wanted me to feel. As I said it, I realized it was an empty promise.

CHAPTER TWENTY-ONE

I suppose if I hadn't been fighting my own demons at home and at school I might have noticed sooner that Chick wasn't doing so well. The thing was, he had always been sickly, missed a lot of school and soccer practice because of his health, usually some kind of bad chest cold. A few times I may have noticed that he was unusually scattered and unkempt—his hair unwashed and his clothes wrinkled and stained—but I didn't give it more than a passing thought.

At the time I also wasn't paying much notice to how much Mario was fucking up—skipping class to spend more time getting high with his friends and pissing off his mom and dad, who complained to me about it every time I saw them. Even the way he had blown off Arturo, who he had always treated with a certain amount of respect, would have been troubling if I had really been paying attention. And though Mario and I were drifting apart, I was still tight with his parents, still held honorary big brother status with his little sisters.

Now I was working at least three shifts a week at Bad

Habits. Other nights Chris would either take me on as an extra dishwasher when they were expecting a busy shift, like on the nights they had bands play in the small stage area, or I would fill in for someone who wanted a day off or was sick. On the nights I was covering for Bernard or I filled in for one of the other bar-backs, I got tipped out, a share of the tips from whoever was bartending. On the nights I washed dishes, I just got a straight hourly wage—so, of course, I preferred to fill in for a bar-back, but I took whatever shifts I was offered.

After a couple of weeks Chris stopped looking up at the clock every time I walked in. I never gave him any cause to be unhappy, came on time and worked hard. I always got a free shift meal, got served whatever Carmen, the weeknight line cook, offered me. Usually she gave me something healthy, like grilled chicken and vegetables, but sometimes I got lucky and she would give me a burger and fries.

Most of my time was spent over the steaming water at the dishwasher, my hands chapped and red at the end of each shift from scrubbing Carmen's pots and pans to her satisfaction. It was work that didn't really require any thought and my mind tended to wander from one worry to another—usually when I was exhausted by thinking about Sylvia or Mom, I would find myself thinking about Raine, wishing I had never made such a goddamn fool of myself in front of her in the cafeteria. At least since I was working again, I didn't have to worry about lunch vouchers, not that I would ever set foot in the school cafeteria for a meal again.

I wanted to work for more than just the money. I hated going home to the empty apartment or seeing Mom when she was home. At the bar I had friends of a sort—they were the people I had known for a while because most of the people who worked for Chris had worked for him for a long time. He was a good boss, took care of the people who worked for him, and he had a way of inspiring loyalty from them. Don't get me wrong, he could be a total hard-ass and was quick to correct someone's work if they weren't doing it the way he liked, but he had done all their jobs at some point, working his way up and learning the business. It's easier to work for a boss when he's done your job before.

By the time Friday night rolled around, I was so tired from school, soccer practice, and work that I really only wanted to go to sleep. It was a bye week for us, no game on Friday, so I could just have gone home to bed. As tired as I was, my mind and body were restless and the thought of being at home was too depressing. I decided to go to a party at the house of some girl I knew whose parents were out of town even though I knew I would probably run into Raine there. I had a feeling, on my walk there, that it wasn't really where I wanted to be, but I didn't have any place better to go.

I ran into Chick almost first thing, in the front yard of the house. It was only about ten, so the party wasn't out of control yet—the noise still confined to the house and only a few people arriving. Chick and I were standing in the front yard talking when Mario got there with Travis in Travis's hipstermobile. I had planned to ignore them but Chick called Mario's name and waved frantically. From the look on Travis's face, you knew he didn't want to talk to us but just shrugged when Mario gestured toward us with a jerk of his head.

"Hey, Chick, Jaz," Mario said with a nod.

"Hey, Mario," Chick said, "I talked to Arturo. He said he would still take you back on the team."

I caught the roll of Travis's eyes as he did his best to pretend he wasn't in a conversation with us.

"I'm not worried about it, Chick," Mario said, looking over his shoulder as if already bored by the conversation. "I'm not coming back."

"But the team needs you, Mario. We can't make it to regionals without you. Isn't that right, Jaz?"

Mario still hadn't looked at me. He studied the ground, his shoes, the back of Travis's head, but his gaze never landed on me.

Finally I said, "We'll be fine without him, Chick."

Now Mario did look at me, his eyes narrowed as he digested the meaning of my words.

"Yeah, well, see you around," Mario said as he fell in behind Travis to head into the party.

Chick followed them, as if we were all going to party together, but I hung back and let Mario and Travis disappear into the house before I followed.

It was easy enough to find the keg, the one room in the house full of people. Someone was working the tap, filling one red Solo cup after another, and I stepped in to take a beer, more than half of it foam. Not that it mattered. It was some shitty, domestic light beer like Natty Light or Busch. I just took it to have something to do with my hands. I'd spend most of the night nursing the same beer.

As I walked through the house, greeting a few people but not committing to a conversation with anyone, Alexis found me and right away started putting her hands on me. Her breath smelled strongly of some sickly-sweet malted beverage and she was a little unsteady on her feet. It took me a few minutes to untangle myself from her and I promised that I would come back to her once I had gone to the bathroom. This was a lie. I'd spend the rest of the night avoiding her. Either she would try to hook up with me again or she'd want to talk about Sylvia. Neither welcome.

I retreated to the basement, figuring it would take Alexis a while to find me there. It was a full, finished basement with a bar and a pool table and a jumbo-screen television the size of the one in Bad Habits where they showed the games. A few of the guys from the soccer team—Eli, Chick, and Mario among them—were hanging out around the fireplace, sitting on the floor and sectional couch. Chick was at Mario's side, eyeing Travis as he lay a strip of toilet paper on the coffee table, saying as he did, "Nah, man, you got to separate it and just use a single layer. Otherwise the ball of paper you get is too big." Talking like he was some kind of fucking expert about something. Goddamn rich kids and their two-ply toilet paper.

Travis pulled the two layers of toilet paper apart and then started to split it into the small squares along the lines of per-foration. Then he took a prescription bottle out of his pocket, probably had his grandmother's name on it, and shook out small piles of white powder on each of the squares of toilet paper.

I thought about yanking Chick up by his collar and pulling him behind me out of the room. But I didn't.

Jordie was at the pool table with a few people from his country club crowd, Raine and Cheryl sitting on tall stools along the wall watching the guys play pool.

"Hey, Jaz," Cheryl called out happily as I joined the group. It grated on my nerves to hear her use my nickname, but it's not like I could tell her to stop using it.

"Hey, Cheryl," I said. Raine looked at me but said nothing, crimped her mouth in a tight line like she was mad about some-thing. I figured after what had happened in the cafeteria she was done ever talking to me again. I decided not to care. I had spent too much time worrying about it as it was.

I shot a couple of games of pool, winning easily since everyone else was getting liquored up as we played. Raine kept up a quiet conversation with Cheryl. Sometimes I got the sense she was looking at me, but as soon as I turned my head to check she had already looked away. After a few times I kept my eyes on her, waiting to catch her in the act of looking at me. When she finally did look my way I realized my mistake. Now it looked like I couldn't take my eyes off her.

I felt stupid after that so I surrendered the pool cue even though I had been winning and running the table. As I was headed out of the basement I ran into Chick, literally ran into him, as his feet slid out from under him and he thudded down the top three steps, his arms wheeling crazily.

"Jesus," I said. "What's wrong with you?"

He groaned and put a hand on the wall to steady himself.

"What are you on?" I asked. "If you say you took any of that Molly shit I'm going to knock you the fuck out."

He shook his head, then seemed to think better of it. "Rum," he said. "Drunk."

"Man, you know you can't hold your liquor," I said with impatience. "What are you taking shots for?"

"Where you going?" he asked, speaking slowly and carefully the way drunk people do, trying to make like they aren't.

"Get a beer, I guess," I said.

"Mario's upstairs. He's totally out of it. C'mon." Chick turned so suddenly that he swayed on the stairs. I put a hand out to steady him and followed him to the living room on the first floor. "He was just here," Chick said with a frown as he put a hand on the back of the couch and bent over, as if he might find Mario under the coffee table.

We found Mario on the front porch, smoking a cigarette, his eyes open only slits. He was sitting propped up against a large ceramic urn that held a potted plant. Even with his back resting against something, he was having trouble holding his head still and it bobbed from side to side like the head of a puppet.

"¿Estás bien?" I asked him as I leaned back against the porch rail, arms crossed over my chest.

It took him a long minute to answer, like he was really thinking about how he was before he spoke. "I need a beer," he said as he picked up a plastic cup that lay on its side beside him, looking at it as if he couldn't remember what had happened to the contents, his words coming out a garbled mess. "So thirsty."

"I'll get you one," Chick said quickly and turned to go back inside, but I grabbed him by the back of the jacket and held him there. He looked at me questioningly and I just shook my head.

"You seem wasted enough," I said. "You trippin'?"

"Trippin' balls," Mario said as he took a sudden interest in his cigarette, his brow wrinkled as he stared at the glowing ember, like he was unsure how it had ended up in his hand. He tipped his head back against the ceramic planter and shut his eyes. "Man, Jaz, you just need to chill. You don't get it, but I'm getting in touch with something, some part of me that's deeper than all this bullshit around us. Maybe we'll never go anywhere, you and me, five years from now we'll still be living in the same hood, you working for Chris. At least when I'm trippin' I'm going somewhere."

Even if Mario's speech hadn't been so slurred from being wasted, he still would have sounded like a fucking idiot. My eyes rolled back into my head but I held my tongue.

"Is that bad?" Chick asked. "Is it bad if we're all still living in the same neighborhood five years from now? At least we'll still be able to hang out together."

"Things won't stay the same," Mario said to Chick.

"Yeah?" I asked. "You going to be all fucked up in the head then, living in your parents' basement?"

Mario ignored my insult and returned his gaze to the lit cigarette in his hand. "I get that the idea doesn't appeal to you so much, getting inside your own head, taking a deeper look," Mario continued. "You've had a lot of fucked-up shit happen to you. Thinking too much about it while you're tripping could make you crazy. You just have to learn to let all of that shit go," he said, as if it had any meaning.

He stopped talking as he went on the nod and the cigarette burned, forgotten. I slipped the cigarette easily from between his fingers and he didn't notice, his eyes still shut. I took a drag before tossing the cigarette into the front yard, thinking about a time when I would have put him in a fireman's hold and carried him home.

While I stood there contemplating Mario as he sat huddled against the potted plant, two cop cars pulled up at the curb, no lights or noise. Stealthy. "Cops," I said. "Let's go."

When Mario didn't react I kicked his shoe. No response. Nothing.

"Wake up, man," I said as I grabbed him by the sleeve of his jacket and shook him. Still nothing.

I didn't really decide anything, just turned and let myself

back into the house, left Mario to his fate. Once upon a time I would have stayed with him, wouldn't have let him go down with the bust by himself. I don't know what had changed or even when. But I knew we were both on our own now.

CHAPTER TWENTY-TWO

Chick followed me and we left Mario on the front porch and went back into the house. I wasn't going to raise the alarm, figuring we had about two minutes for a head start.

"We're leaving Mario?" Chick asked, his voice rising with worry. "Really leaving him?"

"Stay with him if you want," I said over my shoulder. "Or carry him yourself. I'm not getting busted."

Chick stumbled behind me to the kitchen, the brightest room in the house. The keg was dead now and was tilted on its side as it floated in a tub of melted ice. A few people were hanging out, talking and sipping from a bottle of liquor.

Raine, her distinctive head of hair immediately recognizable, was leaned over the sink, the back of her hand pressed against her mouth. As I drew close to her the stink hit me like a wall. Before I even saw the mess in the sink, I knew she had just finished emptying the contents of her stomach into it.

She turned at the sound of my approach, her eyes widening as she saw me, but she seemed too sick to care all that much that I had just caught her puking. Chick was so out of it he didn't even notice the puke and gave Raine a goofy smile and a wave, his eyes narrowed into a stoner slit against the glare of the kitchen light.

Without really thinking, I picked up Raine's hand, the one that gripped the edge of the counter and said, "C'mon. Cops are here." I pulled her along as I walked toward the door on the far side of the kitchen. Mutely she followed me as I pulled her behind me through the door and into the garage. I didn't bother to look for a light switch but headed for a door at the back of the garage, ambient light from outside dimly glowing through the four panes of glass in the top half of the door.

"What do you mean the cops are here?" Raine asked, looking to both Chick and me for an answer.

I only grunted in response as I fumbled with the door that opened into the backyard. "Shit," I said. "Dead bolt." A few seconds later I located the lock, feeling for it in the dark, and had the door open.

"Where are we going?" she asked.

"Cops are out front getting ready to bust the party so I'm taking the back way out," I said.

"What about everybody else?" she asked, her voice vibrating with worry.

"What about them?" I asked.

"Man, Jaz, I think we should go back for Mario," Chick said, bobbing on his toes like he was anxious or had to pee or something.

"You want the cops to find you here? Drunk?" Instead of waiting for an answer, I picked up Raine's hand again and jerked my head at Chick for him to follow, then started walking across the backyard toward the fence.

We reached the fence, an eight-foot wooden privacy fence, and I started to walk along the length of it, hoping to find a back gate. After a minute I stopped and said, "No gate. We'll have to go over."

"I can't," Raine said. "I'm wasted."

"I can't either," Chick said, "wasted or not."

"Sure you can," I said with confidence I didn't feel. They were both pretty trashed. "There's a ledge. About halfway up. Just pull yourself up onto that and you can get your leg over."

"The ledge is four feet off the ground," Raine said, ready to accept the fact that it was hopeless. "Maybe if I wasn't wasted. Maybe if I wasn't wearing this," she said, gesturing at the short skirt she was wearing over tights.

"I'll help you. C'mon, Chick," I said. "Up and over, man." Chick looked up at the fence like he was looking at a mountain. I gave him a leg up and he managed to get one leg over the fence. He lost his grip as he struggled to get his feet under him on the other side, then disappeared suddenly over the top and landed heavily with a yelp on the other side. Jesus, between the two of them weighing me down, I thought we were busted for sure.

Then I put a hand on the top of the fence and pulled myself to a standing position on the wooden cross-brace. As I steadied myself by holding on to the top of the fence with one hand, I offered my other hand to Raine. I pulled her up onto the ledge beside me, a narrow strip of wood barely two inches wide, then said, "Now throw your leg over and I'll lower you down the other side."

She did as I said though it took her three tries to get her leg high enough to reach the top and then she couldn't get her leg hooked over. Rather than give her empty encouragement, I just waited patiently while she struggled. Half my attention was on the background noise as I expected any minute for a flashlight beam to catch us in this awkward pose.

When she finally did get her leg up she gasped as the sharp edge at the top of the fence bit into her leg. But then we heard confused shouts and the slam of the back door as people started to run out of the house and scatter in every direction. "Cops! Cops!" someone shouted to announce the obvious. I thought we were dead for sure when she finally got her bottom half all the way over the fence.

"I'm going to fall," Raine said, her voice tight from pain and fear.

"I won't let you fall," I said simply.

"What now?" she asked.

"Dig in with your toes," I said and shifted my weight so I could lift her under the armpits and lean over the top of the fence to lower her toward the ground. "You're only a foot or two off the ground. I'm going to let you go," I said. "Ready?"

She took a small stumbling step as she landed but Chick stepped in to try to steady her and got knocked ass over elbows for his trouble. They both broke into nervous giggles as Raine bent over and tried to help him to his feet.

I hurried to follow them over the fence and landed with a twinge of pain in my ankle. Raine was bent over, rubbing her hands over her tights, as if to make sure she was still in one piece. Chick stood swaying, studying his hands as if he had never seen them before.

"You okay?" I asked them, dropping my voice to a whisper.

"I ripped my tights," Raine said. "And I left my purse in Jordan's car."

"It'll be all right," I said.

As we started walking down the street, Chick fell into step between us. The two of them were slowing me down. Alone I would have been walking much faster, and I had to keep slowing up to stay beside them. The temperature had been dropping steadily during the party. I hadn't really noticed how cold it was, because of the exertion from climbing over the fence, but as a breeze lifted the sweat from my face I heard Raine shiver, her teeth chattering.

"You cold?" I asked.

"A little," she said.

"Just a little, huh?" I asked, teasing her because she was hugging her chest and rubbing her upper arms with her hands. I unzipped my hoodie and tugged at the sleeves then handed it to her, though Chick probably needed my jacket more than she did.

"Now you'll be cold," she said as she took the jacket from me. And she was right, I was cold in just my T-shirt, but I wouldn't let her know that.

"I'm fine," I said.

"Well . . . thanks," she said.

Chick was quiet, thoughtful, kept bouncing off both of us, like a pinball, back and forth between us. Raine was tall enough and Chick short enough that we could speak to each other over his head. Like he wasn't there, yet at the same time, kept us apart.

She dug her hands into the front pockets of my sweatshirt and tucked the bottom of her face into the neck of it, as if to warm her nose. After a minute she let the hoodie settle back onto her shoulders and said, "Your sweatshirt smells like you."

"Oh, yeah?" I asked. "It smells offensive, you mean?"

"No, it just smells like . . . you. I can't really describe it."

The thought of her being close enough to know what I smelled like was kind of a turn-on. When I was around Raine I had to be a little bit of a dick, keep her at a safe distance. If I let my guard down, let myself say the kinds of things I wanted to say to her, there was no safe outcome. I was distracted, thinking about her, and realized she had still been talking and I hadn't been paying attention. "You know, most guys smell like an overapplication of Axe body spray or Old Spice deodorant. I hate to say it, but Jordan is the worst offender when it comes to spray cologne."

Her comment reminded me suddenly to think of Jordie and Mario. I had just left both of them at the party to take their chances getting busted. Mario had gone down for sure, passed out as he was on the front porch. Two months ago that never would have happened. He would have been with me instead of with Travis, and I never would have left him, even if it meant getting busted myself.

"I'm texting Cheryl," she said as she pulled her phone out of her pocket. "Maybe she and Jordan got away and are wondering where I am. They could pick us up."

"You think Cheryl's worrying about where you are?" I asked out of curiosity.

"Sure, why wouldn't she be?" Raine asked, her eyes on her phone as she finished typing her text to Cheryl.

"Should we go back?" Chick asked me, his forehead wrinkled with a concerned frown. "I hate that Mario and Jordie will get busted."

I snorted at that. "If Jordie gets busted out drinking and the cops call his parents it will be the last time the Colonel lets him drive that car."

"The Colonel?" Raine asked. "You mean Jordan's dad?"

"Yeah," I said absently, my mind already skipping ahead to figure how I was going to get us all home. I was used to walking everywhere, wouldn't think twice about walking the thirty minutes it would take me to get home. But Raine's house was too far from where we were and I wouldn't let her walk home alone, which meant I'd be just getting home when the sun came up if I walked her home first.

"The Colonel is a hard-ass," Chick said. "Not that we ever see him. He doesn't like for Jordie to have company over. But Jordie's always complaining about him, about what a ballbreaker he is." Chick's head jerked up suddenly, his eyes wide. "Uh, sorry," he said to Raine.

"About what?" she asked, her nose wrinkling with the question.

"I didn't mean to cuss in front of you. In front of a girl, I mean."

Raine laughed, loud on the quiet street. "Believe me," she said, "I hear much worse from my brother. I've been *called* worse by my brother."

"Oh, well, I don't like to cuss in front of girls," Chick said.

"That's nice," Raine said as she put her arm through Chick's and moved in close to him. "That's really nice. I like the idea of a boy showing respect like that."

"Yeah?" Chick asked, his voice catching. "You do?"

"Yeah," Raine said. "I do." And she sounded like she really meant it, her voice becoming warm and soft as she looked on Chick with something resembling affection.

"It's too late to catch the bus," I said, breaking into their little romantic moment, "not that I would know where to catch the bus in this neighborhood anyway."

"So, how the hell am I supposed to get home?" Raine asked, keeping her arm linked with Chick's.

I wasn't really sure. There was only one option I could think of, and not a very good one, but I would still try to make it happen. "We can walk to Bad Habits from here," I said. "It's only about a mile. Chris will let me borrow his car so I can drop you at home."

"Who's Chris?" Raine asked.

"He's—" Chick started to answer her, but I cut him off.

"He's the owner of Bad Habits," I said. "He'll be there. He's always there on Friday and Saturday nights until close."

"Oh," she said. "God, I really need a ginger ale or something." She covered her mouth with her free hand as she burped and grimaced. She laughed then checked the time on her phone and said, "I only have thirty minutes until my curfew."

"We'll make it," I said. "As long as Chris lets me use his car."

"What time do you have to be home?" she asked.

"I'm all grown," I said. "I can stay out as late as I want."

"Really? Your mom doesn't care how late you stay out?"

"I don't think my mom gives a shit about me one way or the other," I said, unsure why I was relating this information.

"What about your parents?" Raine asked, turning her attention to Chick.

"It's just my dad," Chick said. "My mom's dead."

"I'm sorry," Raine said quietly.

"No biggie," Chick said in his usual affable way. Dead mother. No biggie. Poverty. No sweat. "But my dad doesn't really worry about where I am."

An awkward silence followed as Raine digested what we had said and I felt her judgment settle on us. Somehow I always managed to disclose things in conversation with Raine that I would never say to anyone else. Every conversation we had ended up being an accumulation of regrets for me.

"Well, I've always been a huge disappointment to my parents," Raine said. "I'm used to it. Maybe they give me a curfew, but they only really care about our family image. My brother and I are supposed to be the best students, best athletes, best everything, just so they can brag about us. If my mom had her way I'd be wearing clothes that were color-coordinated to match our curtains."

I laughed at that. "I guess that explains the pink hair. You wear it like that just to piss off your parents?"

"Maybe," Raine said with a halfhearted shrug, and I could tell she didn't really like the suggestion that her pink hair was just an act of rebellion. "Maybe I figure if my hair is pink, they'll find at least one thing about me exceptional."

When we got close to Bad Habits, I led them through the dark alley, instead of walking out onto the Pike. Chris would lose his shit if I brought a drunk underage girl through the front door of his bar. In the alley there was a sweet, rotten odor as we passed a line of Dumpsters, and the metallic smell of stale beer from the large cans holding the bottles for recycling.

"Stay out here," I said to Chick. "You're too drunk. Chris will know as soon as he sees you. He won't let me use the car if he thinks we're all hammered."

Chick waited obediently as I took Raine with me into Bad Habits. I didn't want to leave her in the alley with Chick since he would be pretty much useless if someone came along looking for trouble. And maybe I just wanted her with me.

The door to the kitchen stood open and Víctor, a Dominican guy who worked in the kitchen, stood against the brick wall, smoking a cigarette and looking at his phone.

"*¿Qué lo que?*" I asked with a chin thrust.

"*Ella es muy bonita para ti,*" he said with a sly smile.

"*No te pregunté,*" I said, and he laughed.

Then we were inside the kitchen of Bad Habits, loud with the dishwasher running, people shouting to each other to be heard above the clatter of dishes, and a radio blaring salsa music.

"What did he say?" Raine asked.

I shook my head. "Nothing."

"Was it about me?"

"He just said you were pretty. You don't speak any Spanish?"

"I speak French."

"I bet that comes in handy. Wait here one minute," I said, nodding toward the coatrack just inside the door. "I'll be right back. Hopefully he's in a good mood."

The bar was packed with people and Chris was so busy I had to wait a few minutes before he noticed me standing there.

"What's the matter?" he asked when he came to the end of the bar to pull some bottles from the cooler.

"I need to borrow your car."

"Is this a joke?" Chris asked. "Tell me it's a joke."

"No joke," I said. "My ride left without me. I've got a girl with me. I need to give her a ride home. There and back. That's it."

"Wait a minute," he said, then went to give the bottles to a customer.

Chris called out to the other bartender—they always had

two behind the main bar on weekend nights—then followed me into the kitchen. Raine was leaning against the wall in the short hallway that led to the alley door, arms crossed over her chest and her nose tucked into the neck of my sweatshirt. She stood up straighter as we approached, as if she was trying to appear as sober as possible.

"Raine," I said, "this is Chris. Chris, Raine."

"Hi," she said quietly with a shy smile.

"Nice to meet you, Raine," Chris said with a nod. Then he turned to me and said, "You been drinking?" He held up his keys, as if he was ready to snatch them back if I admitted to having had anything to drink.

"I had one beer," I said, "three hours ago. I'm fine."

"Where do you live?" Chris asked, turning back to Raine.

"Um, over near Ridge Road," she said and I could tell Chris was sizing up her condition with the practiced eye of someone who got people drunk for a living.

"About fifteen minutes from here," Chris said, directing his comment to me. He pointed at me with a meaty finger. "You've got one hour. One minute after that and I call the cops and report the car stolen."

I took the keys from Chris's hand and gestured for Raine to follow me.

"God, he's really scary," she said quietly once we were well away from the entrance and walking through the alley toward Chris's car.

"Chris is all right," I said. "He likes to talk tough but he's not so bad."

CHAPTER TWENTY-THREE

When Raine and I returned to the spot where we had left Chick, he was gone.

"Should we look for him?" Raine asked.

"Nah," I said, though even as I said it my eyes were searching the shadows along the alley for Chick's familiar form. "He probably forgot why he was here and just walked home. His apartment isn't far from here."

"Are you sure?" she asked, her tone uncertain.

I thought about it for half a minute then said, "Yeah. Yeah, I'll take you home, then swing back by his place to make sure he got home okay." The night, and the hours of sleep I would get, suddenly disappeared in a puff of smoke. "C'mon. I'd better get you home."

"I hope you don't have any ideas about me getting in that car with you," she said.

"Ideas like what?" I asked with a frown.

"I mean . . . ," she said, speaking slowly as she tried not to slur her words, "do you think I'm going to sleep with you or something? Because I'm drunk? Because you're taking me home?"

"Wow, you really do have a high opinion of yourself, don't you?" I asked. "You think I can't get laid anytime I want? That I have to take advantage of some drunk girl who doesn't have sense enough to wear pants when it's this cold outside?"

"I'm wearing tights," she said haughtily. "And I wasn't expecting to be out in the cold. I thought I would be riding in a nice warm car."

"That's the problem with you rich kids," I said, hearing myself turn snide. "You're never prepared for life when it happens."

"You are so annoying," she said with a sigh.

"Oh, come on," I said, then started walking away backward toward Chris's car while she stood there in the middle of the alley. "I take it back, okay?" I said, and waited for her to relent.

She looked pissed, like she might slap me again. "You know, just because my family has money doesn't mean I don't have any feelings," she said. "And it doesn't mean my life is all unicorns and rainbows. I have problems too." She had one hand on her hip but was still unsteady on her feet so she looked more ridiculous than menacing.

"I said I took it back. Friends?"

"Maybe instead of taking it back, you should try not to say stupid, insulting shit in the first place," she said, not wanting to give in.

"I think you like it," I said. "I think I'm the only honest person you know."

She sighed as she followed me to the car. "So, is that a fact?" she asked. "You get laid anytime you want?"

I cut my eyes in her direction but didn't turn my head to look at her. "Unless I'm sleeping with you, it's none of your business."

"Gross," she said. "Jason, you will not be sleeping with me. Ever."

"You know, I'm never sure whether I think you're entertaining or irritating," I said as I looked up to survey the night sky. "I guess it depends on my mood."

"That's so funny," she said. "I feel the same way about you."

We both laughed and our truce was restored, at least until our next argument.

On the drive, we killed the time talking about music. Raine and I liked a lot of the same bands, especially Arcade Fire and Foals. Once we weren't bickering about something, our conversation fell into a natural rhythm—so comfortable I was almost able to forget I had ever been embarrassed in front of her that day in the cafeteria.

While we sat at a red light, I dug through the CDs in Chris's car. Not much to choose from, since he listened to a lot of classic rock. I was hoping for at least Nirvana or something. I stopped looking when I found an Allman Brothers CD. I hit the advance button until the song "Melissa" flooded the car.

"I love this song," Raine said as she tipped her head back against the seat.

"Everybody loves this song," I said. "If someone doesn't like this song then there's something wrong with them."

Raine kept her gaze fixed on the window as we drove. She was pretty drunk, so it wouldn't have surprised me if she passed out. I hoped she wouldn't.

"We'll stop to get a drink or something," I said, figuring it would help to sober her up, "so you don't smell like such a booze hound when you get home."

She turned her head to give me a wilting stare but then her face spread into a lazy smile. I pulled the car into a 7-Eleven and parked right up against the front wall of the store. There were a few guys hanging around the entrance to the convenience store, smoking and talking. As I got out, I locked the driver's-side door with the key. Raine still had her head tipped back against the seat and she looked small and vulnerable wrapped in my sweatshirt. I leaned over and tapped on the glass of the driver window, then gestured at her to lock her door too. After a few seconds she got my meaning and pushed the lock down on her door.

I had just enough money to buy us each a drink and a hot dog. Raine was the kind of girl who was probably used to guys buying her a nicer meal than a 7-Eleven hot dog, but when I got back to the car, she was really excited that I had brought her something to eat.

"I'm starving," she said as she opened the wrapper and dug in to her Big Bite. Then, almost like an accusation, said, "You got me a ginger ale."

"Isn't that what you said you wanted?" I asked.

"Like an hour ago, yeah. I can't believe you remembered."

I took my eyes off the road long enough to look at her as I said, "Doesn't your boy, Brian, buy you nice things like ginger ales and hot dogs?" As soon as I said it, I wished I could take it back. It came off sounding jealous and insecure, which, maybe, I was.

"What do you care if he's my boyfriend?" she asked in that way girls do when they're trying to trip you up, make you say something stupid.

So I said nothing. Just rode in silence while she ate her hot dog and drank her ginger ale.

"Brian doesn't really know me," she said, her gaze on the scenery out her window. "Nobody does. Every time I'm around my friends it's like I'm always pretending to be someone else."

"What about Madison and Cheryl? They're your friends, right? I see you hanging out with them all the time."

She snorted at that and blew out a weary sigh. "Cheryl and I have known each other for a long time. I'm not sure that just knowing someone for a long time qualifies them as a friend. Madison is a mean girl. I could never tell her anything personal because she can't be trusted. She betrayed me once already. I'll never forgive her."

"How's that?"

"Do you remember Robbie Slade?" she asked as she studied her thumb, then licked a dab of ketchup from it. "He went to school here until tenth grade when his family moved away."

I shook my head. "No."

"Well, anyway, I had a huge crush on him all through middle school. I was completely in love with him. Madison and Cheryl both knew I had a major crush on him. So, one night we were all hanging around at the skate park. Remember that skate park over near the library? Everyone used to hang out down there in middle school. People would make out behind the half-pipe and sneak in beers and stuff. Anyway, we were all hanging out there one night and Robbie and I were talking, he was totally flirting with me. There were a few of Robbie's friends hanging out with us but Madison was interested in Robbie Slade too. He was the hottest boy in our middle school.

"Madison is such a bitch. In front of everyone she told this

really embarrassing story about me just to make me look
stupid."

"What story?" I asked, and was surprised to find I genuinely wanted to know.

"It was so embarrassing. I had just started my period the
year before and the first time I tried to use a tampon I accidentally tried to get it in the wrong hole. You know, it's not like I
had ever had any reason to put something in my vagina before
then. How was I supposed to know? I told Cheryl and Madison
about it because you're supposed to be able to tell your girlfriends everything. But she blabbed it to everyone, right there
at the skate park, and Robbie and all of his friends were laughing at me. I was so humiliated, I could never even look him in
the eye again."

"Oh my God," I said with a groan. "Why did you have to
tell me that story?"

"What?" she asked, turning to look at me. "What's wrong?"

"That's the worst thing I've ever heard. In case you didn't
know, guys don't want to know anything about tampons."

"Oh, give me a break," she said, her voice dropping with
disdain. "Guys are such babies. All you think about is sex and
vaginas, but when a girl talks about it, you can't handle it. It's
a double standard, you know? You look at your own dicks all
the time, touch them—Christ, you probably even measure
them. But if a girl talks about a vagina you get all squeamish
about it."

"I don't have a problem talking about . . . a vagina," I said,
the word feeling foreign and awkward on my tongue. Sure, my
friends and I talked about pussy all the time. Obsessed about
it, in fact. But I had never had a conversation with a girl about
it. "Guys just don't like to think about . . . it . . . in that way."

"In what way? You mean because we have our periods? If you can't even talk about a period or a woman's vagina then what are you doing having sex with one?"

"If you don't stop talking right now," I said, "I am going to drop you and your vagina off at the next corner."

She huffed out a laugh through her nose, almost spitting ginger ale all over Chris's car, then swallowed audibly. "You are too much," she said.

When I pulled onto her street, I stopped a few doors down from her house and cut the lights, figuring she wouldn't want her parents to see her coming home with me. "I'll watch to make sure you get in," I said as I put the car into park and cut the engine, loud on the quiet street. "Ain't Wastin' Time No More" was playing and I adjusted the volume down as the music was loud now without the road noise to accompany us. "I just don't feel like getting shot by your old man."

"My dad's a lawyer," she said. "He doesn't shoot people. Just sues them."

"Sounds like a great guy," I said as I leaned into the armrest on the door. I didn't want to seem in a hurry to leave but, all the same, wasn't going to encourage her to stay.

"I should have thanked you earlier," she said. "You know, for saving me from getting busted and . . . everything."

"Anytime," I said with a nod.

"And thanks for the ride," she said.

"You're welcome, Raine."

After that there didn't seem to be much else to say so she reached for the door handle to let herself out, then stopped with one foot on the curb, the other still in the car. "Jason?"

"Yeah?"

"I was just thinking. . . ."

Pause. I waited patiently but she didn't say anything else.

"Thinking what?" I asked.

"There's this gallery opening this Friday and I was planning to go," she said quickly, like she was nervous. "Would you want to come?"

"With you?" I asked. "Just the two of us?"

"If the idea isn't too repulsive to you, yeah," she said with a small laugh.

"I didn't mean it like that," I said. "I'm just . . . surprised."

"I'm not asking you out on a date," she said as she turned to look back at me over her shoulder. "Okay? It's not like a dating thing. You don't have to get a big head about it. I'm just asking if you want to hang out is all."

"Sure, I'm down with that," I said. "You gonna pick me up?"

"How about six o'clock? Friday night," she said.

"I have a home game on Friday," I said, and for a second I could have sworn I saw disappointment in her eyes. "You can come watch the game and then we can go from there. That cool?"

"I'll come to the game if you promise you aren't going to get in any fights," she said.

"I guess you'll have to show up to find out," I said.

She just shook her head as she shut the car door but she was smiling. I didn't start the engine until after she was inside the house with the door shut behind her.

I stopped by Chick's place on my way back to Bad Habits, pushing the curfew Chris had given me to return his car. I found the apartment door unlocked, Chick asleep on the couch when

I got there. I left as quietly as I had arrived and set the lock on the door as I let myself out into the stairwell.

When I returned Chris's car to Bad Habits it was late, almost closing time. I hung out in the kitchen shooting the shit with the guys and waited for Chris to finish his shift so he could give me a ride home. It was cold outside and I had forgotten to get my hoodie back from Raine so I didn't feel like walking.

"That your girlfriend?" Chris asked me as we climbed into the car later.

"Definitely not my girlfriend. Just a girl."

"She's pretty," he said. He studied my expression while we were stopped at a traffic light.

"Mmph."

"Oh, what? You telling me you didn't notice?" he asked with a laugh as he twisted his shoulders to settle more comfortably into his seat.

"I noticed," I said.

"Yeah, I'll bet you did," Chris said as he adjusted the volume up on the Allman Brothers CD, still playing through the car speakers.

"But she's so crazy, I never know whether I'm coming or going with her," I said, and Chris laughed at that.

By the time I got home, I was completely wiped out but was at least relieved to find that Mom was asleep. She usually slept only a few hours each night, and the sound of the television was almost constant. I had learned to hate the noise of the late-night shows she watched, the canned laughter and applause grating on every nerve in my body.

I stood over her bed, watching her sleep for a minute. She

was still in her clothes, her hair tangled in a mess around her face. In sleep the lines in her face were smoothed and she looked much younger than thirty-six. I turned off the television and dropped a blanket over the bottom half of her body, then went to settle onto the couch.

CHAPTER TWENTY-FOUR

The next morning I slept in. Mom was gone when I woke so I spent some time cleaning the apartment and decided I would go to the grocery store with some of my carefully hoarded earnings from the bar. I kept the money hidden in the kitchen, since Mom never spent any time in there other than to make coffee.

Until I went to the store, there would be nothing to eat in the house. The refrigerator offered up some molded leftovers that I tossed in the trash, the plastic containers so gross that I tossed those too without trying to clean them. I decided to shower and get dressed and go out for a meal before taking the long bus ride to the grocery store.

When I left the apartment, instead of turning to walk down the hill toward the diner, my feet carried me to Mario's house, along a path so familiar I couldn't have strayed from it if I tried. His building was part of the same apartment complex as mine though his family lived in a small brick duplex instead of an apartment. It was an unseasonably warm day, the temperature near seventy degrees, so the inner door to their house stood open and just the screen door was shut. A small grill sat out on the concrete patio, the smell of cooking meat sharpening my hunger. My stomach ached and I could taste acid at the back of my mouth.

I let myself in without knocking and walked into the kitchen where Mario's mom stood over the stove talking on the phone in such rapid Spanish I understood only scraps of the conversation. She waved when she saw me and a minute later ended her conversation.

"*Hola,* Jason," she said, making it sound as if my name had three syllables instead of two.

"Hey, Mama," I said as I bent down to accept her kiss and hug. She smelled like the marinade of her meat and an earthy scent. "Is he here?"

She waved a dismissive hand in disgust. "He here. In his room. I no like that boy Travis he hanging around with. He bad boy. You want something to eat?" she asked as she lifted the lid from a steaming pot of rice and started spooning it onto a plate without waiting for my answer.

Primo, Mario's dad, was seated at the dining room table over a plate heaped with sliced steak and beans, his glasses hanging toward the end of his nose. His wife called him Primo, as a joke, a way to poke fun at the fact that even if he called himself the head of the family, she was the one who ran the household. The kids called him Primo since it was the only thing they had ever heard their dad called in the house, though sometimes Mario's sisters called him Papi. I had known him since I was a little kid and had always just called him Primo too. Mario's mom could call him Primo in that ironic way she had, making a joke every time she used the word, and it kept him humble.

"Hey, *mi hijo*. She's making me loco." He said this last part in a voice loud enough that his wife could hear him from the kitchen. "Mario was brought home by the police last night. Drunk out of his mind is what I tell her, but I know he was on something else. *Colocado*." Stoned. Primo wasn't so easy to fool as most parents. It figured he would know what Mario was up to.

Primo worked in a restaurant and spoke much better English than his wife. I had sat at this table many times listening to Mario's parents yell back and forth to each other between the dining room and kitchen in rapid-fire Spanish. I used to always think they were arguing and wondered why Mario didn't ever seem concerned about it. After a few years I began to realize they just put on a good show but probably had a more functional relationship than any other married couple I had ever met.

I experienced a momentary twinge of guilt about Mario getting busted. Not because I felt bad about leaving Mario to his fate the night before at the party. He deserved whatever trouble he got for being a dumb-ass. But I hadn't really thought about Mario's parents when I left him behind. If nothing else, I could have tried to keep him out of trouble for their sake. Especially since they always worried about their resident alien status. Mario and his sisters were all citizens, since they were born in the United States, but his parents still only had green cards.

"She's worried," Primo continued. "Doesn't like that *hijo de puta* Travis. I tell her not to worry so much. Just boys. It's what boys do."

"I hate that guy," I said as I began shoveling food in my mouth. "Travis. He's a dick." Primo and I both used language we wouldn't use if Mario's mom were in the room. If she heard

me using bad language, she would pinch me, hard, on the soft
fleshy part under my arm. It hurt like hell. "I don't even hang
out with Mario when he's with that guy." Which was never
now that Mario hung out with Travis virtually 24-7, though I
left that unsaid. I held my tongue about the drugs and Mario
blowing off the team and school lately, since I wasn't a rat,
wasn't going to tell his parents the truth. If he kept going the
way he was going, he would get busted for real eventually. He'd
get his own ass in trouble without me meddling.

When I finished eating I stood and took our plates to the
kitchen and started to wash them. "Such a good boy," Mario's
mom said as she nudged my hip. "Now you go. You talk to him.
Give him some sense," she said as she nodded toward the basement door.

"He doesn't listen to me any more than he listens to you," I
said, but she just shook her head and turned back to polishing
the worn linoleum counter to a dull shine.

Mario's bedroom was the cramped basement room that
also housed the boiler, water heater, and washer and dryer. The
upstairs had only two small bedrooms where his parents and
two younger sisters slept.

As I opened the basement door the smell of stale pot smoke
mixed with incense hit me right away. The basement was
dark, the sound of music the only evidence someone was below.

"What's up?" I called out before I reached the bottom of
the stairs.

Mario was reclined on his bed, the television on but muted,
the music coming from an old CD player that rested on a stack
of milk crates.

"Hey, Jaz." Mario's voice, but different. He didn't get up
when I came in, just kept his gaze fixed on the television. The

Ronaldinho poster that once held a place of honor above his bed had been covered by stickers of some bands I recognized, some I didn't.

"What's going on, man?" I asked as I shifted a pile of dirty laundry off the one chair so I could sit. "Primo says the cops brought you home last night. Your mom's flipping out."

"Man, she's always flipping out about something," Mario said as he folded one arm under his head like a pillow. "I barely even remember getting home last night, but she tried to drag my ass out of bed this morning to go to confession and Mass."

Even though our conversation was totally natural, no different from a million other conversations we'd had over the past ten years, there was an uneasiness between us now that I couldn't shake. Or maybe I was the only one who felt it. Mario didn't seem to remember seeing me at the party the night before and I didn't bring it up.

"She wants me to talk to you," I said as I leaned back in the chair and crossed my arms over my chest.

"Give me a break," he said as he picked up a dirty sock from the floor and tossed it at me. "Is that why you came down here? To take sides with them and give me a bunch of shit?"

I plucked the sock off my lap and tossed it in the general direction of the washer and dryer. "She's worried about you. And you're acting like a selfish little prick. You think I wouldn't give anything to have a mom and dad who actually gave a crap about me?"

"Is that what this is about?" he asked, incredulous. "I'm supposed to be grateful because my immigrant parents work so hard to give me a better life? Man, if you want to buy into their little piece of the American dream, be my guest. They've always liked you better than me anyway. Mama's boy." His little speech was practiced, like he had already thought it through, or performed it for others.

A few months earlier the things that Mario was saying wouldn't have made me angry. I would have laughed them off or given him shit right back. The fact that he was so determined to hurt everyone around him made me want to walk out and never look back.

I leaned forward, my elbows resting on my knees as I tried to cool my anger before I spoke again. "Man, I'm not giving you shit because you went to a party or because you had a good time," I said, keeping my eyes on his face though he refused eye contact. "You and I both know that someone who doses on the kind of shit you've been taking can't be trusted."

"Why the fuck are you even here then?" he asked.

My hands were clasped in front of me and I was squeezing them together so tightly, the skin at the point where they met had started to turn white. I dropped my head and shut my eyes as I took a deep breath and fought to keep from pounding his scrawny ass against the wood paneling.

"You know what, man? I have no fucking idea why I'm here," I said. As I stood I realized I wasn't really angry with Mario. I was sick of his shit, sure. Sad to lose my closest friend, maybe. But too tired to give a fuck. I had my own problems.

CHAPTER TWENTY-FIVE

The void on the team left by Mario was now a daily reminder of how strained and awkward things were among my friends. Jordie and Mario never spoke to each other as far as I knew, and I barely saw Mario at all. Occasionally I would still drop in to see his mom and would share a meal with his parents, but usually Mario wasn't there. He had stopped going to church, and every time he was home was fighting with his parents. Mario's mom grew more and more depressed about it, to the point where I could barely stand it. Once she even got up from the table and left the room because she couldn't keep from crying in front of Primo and me.

"Mi hijo . . . ," Primo said, then paused for a while as he chewed his food and stared at the print of the Virgin Mary that hung at the top of the wall full of family portraits, a pyramid of pictures with the Virgin Mary at the top and, just below her, Mario's paternal grandparents, who had died in El Salvador without ever seeing Mario in person.

"It's good you still come," Primo said finally. "You must

always come. Understand?" he asked, and I knew what he was saying. Mario was lost to them, the same way he was lost to me. I was the son who still ate dinner with them.

In the middle of the wall, under portraits of Mario's parents, aunts and uncles, and older cousins, was a picture of Mario, a school portrait from when he was about twelve. His black hair was cropped close to his head, his front teeth enormous because his face hadn't grown into them yet. In the photograph, Mario was wearing his Ronaldinho jersey from when Ronaldinho played for Barcelona. Mario still owned the shirt as far as I knew. Once upon a time he had worn it several days a week.

I stayed to work at Bad Habits until close one Wednesday night. Chris and I didn't discuss it, but since the place was slammed when the end of my shift came I just stayed on and kept working, helped the late-night bar-backs clean the floors and bathrooms after the last customer left.

At the end of the night when I was getting ready to leave, I stopped by Chris's office where he sat drinking a beer and counting out his cash drawer.

"I'm out of here," I said, "unless you need something else."

"No," he said, and took a swig of his beer. "Hey, thanks for staying, Jaz. We'd still be cleaning up if you hadn't stuck around. Here," he said, and held out a couple of folded twenties to me, a share of his tips.

I took them with quiet thanks and pushed them into my jeans pocket. Chris put the cash from his drawer in the safe and I waited as he locked the office door and put the key back in its usual hiding place.

The guys who had all just finished their shifts were sitting at the bar, having their shift drinks and chewing the fat. Chris's friend Ahmed, who he had known since high school, sat at the bar with the rest of them. Ahmed's tight black T-shirt strained against the muscles in his arms and chest. His stomach had started to round a bit with middle age but he and Chris lifted weights together on the regular. It was hard to tell if Ahmed had started to lose his hair or if he just chose to keep his head shaved clean, but he wore a slick black goatee. Ahmed's dark skin had not started to wrinkle at all while Chris, the exact same age, had laugh lines around his eyes and deep creases flanking his mouth.

"Hey, it's the kid," Ahmed said as I slid onto the barstool next to him. He held out a hand to shake mine and clapped me on the back with his other hand. I tried not to wince from the slap to my back. He balled his hands into fists and pretended to punch me first in the kidney and then in the shoulder, his fists landing gently. To Chris he called out, "Hey, man, I'm the oldest friend you got and this is what you give me when I order a beer?" He held up the bottle of cheap domestic beer, his nose wrinkled with distaste.

"You can order whatever you want," Chris said as he held his hand out in an expansive gesture to indicate all the bottles behind him. "But if you're expecting to drink for free, then yeah, that's what you're drinking."

"All these years of friendship," Ahmed said, then leaned an elbow on the bar and took a swig from his beer, "don't mean shit."

"All these years of friendship is how I know what a cheap bastard you are," Chris said. "You order like Jay-Z, but you tip like DMX during his crack phase."

I laughed at that and Ahmed cut me a warning look.

"Man, a brother can't get any love in this place. I'll remember this next time you show up at the club, begging to get in to see one of those cracker bands you love so much." Ahmed gave me a wink as he waited to see if his comment would elicit a rise out of Chris.

Chris set a beer on the bar in front of me. A beer I really didn't want because I was so tired from school all day, hitting the weight room in the afternoon, and then a solid seven hours of manual labor. I was so tired I was just trying to work up the energy to walk home.

Hoping Chris or Ahmed would offer me a ride if I stuck it out, I sat on one of the barstools along the wall, watching while they shot a game of pool.

Ahmed pulled a small bag of weed out of his pocket and some rolling papers and started to roll a joint.

"Hey," Chris said with a gesture toward me, "what're you doing? Not in front of the kid."

"My bad," said Ahmed, and slipped the half-rolled joint into the plastic bag before shoving it all in his pocket.

"What?" I asked Chris. "You worried about being a bad influence or something?" To Ahmed I said, "Believe me, people do ten times worse shit at parties all the time. I'm not into it."

"You're all grown," Ahmed said with admiration, but he left the weed in his pocket.

"I saw Stacie the other day," I said to Chris. "At the diner. Chick and I stopped in and she was there."

"Yeah?" Chris asked, not acting like he was too interested. His eyes were on the Internet jukebox as he fed money into the machine. A few seconds later the honey melody of "Wish You Were Here" by Pink Floyd started to play. "How's she doing?"

"Good," I said. "She looked good."

"Stacie always looked good," Ahmed said. "Never anything wrong with the way she *looked*. That's for sure, right?"

"What did you tell her about me?" Chris asked, his tone still casual but he was definitely interested.

I shrugged. "Nothing. Your name didn't come up."

Ahmed laughed in appreciation at that but Chris kept his face expressionless. He was a good poker player.

"How long have you and Chris been friends?" I asked Ahmed, suddenly curious since their friendship was so much like mine with Mario. I wondered what had kept their friendship from falling apart while my friendship with Mario seemed to be mostly over.

"Shit," Ahmed said as he wiped his mouth with the back of his hand. "We go back like a recliner. Almost twenty-five years. Back then this neighborhood was almost all black folks. Chris got his ass kicked on a daily until I started sticking up for him. Used to have to walk his skinny ass to school every day, just so he'd get there in one piece."

"Hmph," Chris grunted as he bent over to line up the cue ball.

"You've been hanging out with each other the whole time?" I asked. "Ever since then?"

"Sad, ain't it?" Ahmed said. "I guess there was that one time we got into it over a girl we knew. She was stepping out with both of us and it came to blows. You remember that?" Ahmed asked Chris. "We didn't speak for almost six months."

"I remember," Chris said, taking a step back from the pool table to chalk his cue. "Can't remember that girl's name, though."

"Natonya," Ahmed said with a wistful smile. "She was half black, half Cambodian. So hot, she could melt glass. If she hadn't blown us both off for some college boy, I still wouldn't be speaking to him," Ahmed said as he gestured at Chris with his beer bottle.

"The truth is I can't stand him," Chris said, directing his comment to me, "but he keeps coming around. Never been able to get rid of him."

"So, what's going on with you, Jaz?" Ahmed asked me as if Chris hadn't spoken.

"Not much," I said.

"He's got a girlfriend," Chris offered as he leaned over to line up his next shot.

"Oh yeah?" Ahmed asked. "She hot?"

"She sure is," Chris said before I could answer.

"I don't have a girlfriend," I said firmly.

"Does she know that?" Ahmed asked, and laughed at his own joke.

"We don't sleep together," I said, disclosing to him something I would never admit to my friends.

"That's good," Chris said. "That means she's got some self-respect. That's a good thing," Chris said with a meaningful look at Ahmed.

"I'm not interested in sleeping with her," I said as I unconsciously rubbed the hair at the nape of my neck. This wasn't exactly the truth. The truth was I would have slept with Raine in a heartbeat if I didn't consider the prospect completely off the table.

"Yeah, okay," Ahmed said in a tone of mock belief.

"No, I'm serious," I said, unsure why I was saying any of this. "I don't sleep with anyone. I wouldn't sleep with a girl unless I was willing to have a kid with her. My dad was the one who said that to me," I said, shifting my gaze to make eye contact with Chris. "He said, accidents happen. Don't sleep with a girl unless you want to have a kid with her."

"Did he?" Ahmed asked idly as he kept his eyes focused on the pool table.

"Yeah. He did," I said flatly. "And so I don't sleep with any-one, because I know what it feels like to be an accident. Some-one else's mistake."

"Kid, that's messed up," Ahmed said, his voice earnest and quiet now. "Don't say shit like that."

I drained the last of my beer and stood, the room filled with tense silence after my confession, but I didn't care. "I'm tired," I said. "I'm heading out."

"Ahmed," Chris said, his back to us as he straightened the pool cues in the corner and took care to hang the rack on the wall. "You want to give him a ride home? He shouldn't be walk-ing home by himself this late."

"Sure. Yeah, sure. Come on," Ahmed said to me and gestured for me to walk in front of him. "I'll catch you later, loser," Ahmed said to Chris. I didn't say good night to Chris, was too tired to muster the energy, and he didn't say anything as we left.

CHAPTER TWENTY-SIX

Raine showed up for the soccer game on Friday about twenty minutes after the game started. I was half expecting her not to show, had been watching for her so was distracted by her arrival. She looked fierce, with a pleated gray wool skirt and black boots, her outfit meant to mimic the classic schoolgirl's uniform, but she wore it with a white tank top and a cropped plaid jacket so you could see the slim line of her waist. The hemline of her skirt rippled at the curve of her thigh.

We won the game, which put me in a good mood even if the win was meaningless. We had no chance at making regionals based on our season record, but it was good to go out of the season on a win.

When I headed off the field, Raine was leaning on the low fence that surrounded the field, talking to Eli. They seemed friendly, like they knew each other pretty well. Eli had one hand resting on the fence and was standing close enough to her that I felt the familiar flash of white-hot jealousy knife through my chest.

For half a minute I thought about just walking off to the locker room, ignoring Raine as long as she was talking to Eli. They were joking about something now, Raine laughing at something he said. What the hell?

I had to swallow my jealousy, like a dose of nasty-tasting medicine, because it wasn't like I could say anything. For one thing, Raine wasn't even my girlfriend. We were just friends. Only a psycho would act possessive about a girl he'd never even kissed. For another thing, even if she was my girlfriend there was no way she would tolerate a guy who acted like an insecure, jealous prick.

When I was about ten feet from Raine and Eli, she turned to look at me, and maybe it was just my imagination, but her eyes seemed to brighten a little. Her face was already fixed in a smile but it reached her eyes as she watched my approach.

"Hey, Jason," she said.

Eli turned to look at me and I expected to see something like guilt in his eyes but he was smiling too, his expression completely unguarded. "Nice game, Jaz," he said. "Sorry it wasn't enough to keep us in the regionals."

"No worries," I said.

"I'm glad you won," Raine said to me in that playful, flirtatious way she had when she was having fun at someone else's expense. "I would have been pissed if I drove all the way over here just to watch you guys lose."

Eli laughed at her joke and slapped my shoulder as he turned to go and waved good-bye to Raine.

"I didn't think you would show," I said once Eli was out of earshot.

"I thought you would get in a fight," she said. "I guess we're both full of surprises."

"How do you know Eli?" I asked, almost blurting out the question.

She shrugged. "I have a few classes with him."

"Yeah?" I asked. "You into him or something?" *No! Stop talking. Immediately.*

She tilted her head to one side as she considered my question and I felt like she could read every thought in my head. "Am I into Eli?" Her brow wrinkled. "Like, do I have a crush on him or something? Is that what you're asking?"

"Is there another way to interpret that question?"

"Are you—?" Her frown deepened and her eyebrows twisted in question. "Are you jealous or something?"

"Jealous of what?" I asked, feeling heat creep up my neck. I hoped that my face was already red enough from exertion to cover the blush of embarrassment.

"Forget it," she said. "Please tell me you are planning to shower—with soap—before we go anywhere."

"It'll only take me a minute."

"Take all the time you need to wash the stink off."

She turned as if to walk along the length of the fence toward the gate, but I tossed my bag on the other side and hopped the fence. As I bent down to retrieve my bag Chick came over to the fence to talk to us.

"Hey, Raine," he said, his voice quiet and uncertain. He never had learned how to talk to a girl. Never had any practice.

"Hello, Chick," she said warmly and my chest swelled with gratitude that she treated him like a human being.

"Are you guys going somewhere?" he asked.

Raine looked to me first and when I didn't answer said,

"Jason and I are going to a gallery downtown. There's an exhibition opening tonight."

"Cool," Chick said. "Do you guys mind if I ride along?"

I could see that she didn't really want Chick to come along but didn't know how to say it without hurting his feelings. The truth was I had been looking forward to being alone with Raine all week. Ever since we had gone to have coffee, I had been thinking about her, thinking how easy it was to talk to her.

"We were just planning on the two of us going, Chick," I said. I didn't want there to be any misunderstanding, because there was no way I was going to let Chick tag along. It's not as if I had planned on some great romantic evening. Raine had made it clear this was not a date. But I wanted her to myself, didn't feel like sharing Raine's attention.

"Oh," Chick said, and his cheeks went pink as he looked at me, then Raine, then back to me. For a second I thought Raine might jump in and say that it was okay if Chick went with us. The pity in her eyes was obvious and it made me like her more, to know that she felt sorry for Chick.

Raine started to open her mouth, as if to relent and invite Chick along with us. But I didn't know when the next time I would get to see her or spend time with her would be, so I wasn't about to let Chick spoil everything.

"Sorry, man," I said as I swung my backpack onto my shoulder. "Next time."

Raine and I fell into step together as we walked back toward school. She waited out in the hallway while I took a quick shower. By the time I finished getting dressed, we were the last ones in the school besides Arturo. Chick was gone, but when I saw Raine waiting for me I forgot to wonder about him.

•   •   •

Raine drove to the north side of town, where the subway line stretched out from the city, and the streets were choked with parking meters and bus shelters and ethnic restaurants. She had her iPhone docked on the stereo, the music turned up kind of loud—so there was no mistaking it when suddenly Miley Cyrus's "The Climb" blared into the car.

Raine's hand shot out to hit advance on her playlist, but I got my hand there first and stopped her. "Own it, girl," I said.

"I don't listen to Miley Cyrus," she said as she tried to push my hand away so she could change the song.

"Yeah, I know," I said as I slapped her hand away and then kept my hand over the iPhone so she couldn't touch it. "This isn't Miley Cyrus. This is Hannah Montana. I can't believe I'm hanging out with a closet Hannah Montana lover," I said, raising my voice as if in alarm. She grabbed my wrist and tried to pull me away from the iPhone. I held her off with one hand and reached over with the other to turn the volume up as high as it would go. Then I opened the sunroof to let the music spill out of the car. She started laughing. "Sing along," I said as I nodded my head in time with the music, as if I were really into it. "You know you want to."

"I do not like Hannah Montana!" Now she was laughing too hard to say anything—almost crying, she was laughing so hard.

"Sing it!" I shouted as I rolled down my window, the music really loud now that it had reached a crescendo. People on the street and in the cars near us were staring as we passed.

Then she started to sing, just let go and belted the song out at the top of her lungs. I was singing along with her and people were really staring now. I held back on the a cappella parts, leaving her to solo, then joined her again for the final chorus.

It was a full minute after the song ended before she was able to stop laughing long enough to catch her breath. "I can't believe you know the words to that song," she said. "Be honest. You're a closet Hannah Montana lover too."

I just smiled out the window, my arm rested along the top of the door. "No," I said with a chuckle. "I just have a little sister."

We both went quiet in the same second, our faces falling out of mirth, all humor sucked out of the car like air sucked into the vacuum of space. My cheeks still ached as a reminder that we had just been laughing hysterically a moment before, though nothing was funny now.

"Had," I said. "I *had* a little sister."

She bit her lower lip—I was so jealous that she could bite her lower lip anytime she wanted, while I could only imagine it—as her forehead wrinkled and her eyes were desperate and sad. Her chin quivered, as if she might actually start to cry. Her hand was on the gearshift between us and I started to put my hand over hers, then stopped myself and instead punched her gently on the shoulder. Weird, but maybe less weird than putting my hand on hers.

"Stop thinking about it," I said.

"I'm sorry, Jason," she said, and she said it with such feeling that it warmed a small part of the cold hollow in my gut.

She parked on a residential street and we walked back toward the busy road. Even in her boots her chin only reached my shoulder and I thought about putting my arm around her—not because I wanted to put the moves on her or anything, but because somehow I craved the warmth of her body next to mine, like hugging a pillow when you go to sleep at night.

But I kept my hands to myself.

The smells coming from all the restaurants reminded me that I was starving, and I nodded in the direction of Pho 75. "Mind if we stop? I'm starving."

"Not at all," she said. "I love pho."

"Me too. Though Jordie's mom makes the best."

"She does?"

"Yeah, she's Vietnamese," I said. "She makes it all the time."

"Right," Raine said with a nod, "I forgot."

"I think he prefers it that way," I said, not really thinking about it as I said it.

"What do you mean?" Raine asked with a puzzled frown.

"I just think he doesn't like feeling like he's different. Most of the people who live in your neighborhood are white. It's important to him to fit in with your crowd."

"My crowd?" she asked, her tone shifting to disdain. "I don't have a crowd."

"I just mean the folks who live in your neighborhood. Kids whose families have plenty of money. Stop getting pissed. I'm not making a thing out of it. I'm just saying is all."

"I'm not pissed," she said, not entirely the truth.

"Anyway," I said with a shrug, "I always figured Jordie started hanging out with Mario and me because he felt like he fit in better with us than he did with the kids in his neighborhood. That's all."

"We have time to stop," she said. "The gallery will be open until nine."

We ran across three lanes of traffic to get to the pho place.

I put my hand at the small of her back as we approached the curb. It just felt natural to do it, but as soon as I realized what I had done I pulled my hand away and put it in my pocket.

We sat side by side at the counter in the window overlooking the street and ate spicy Vietnamese soup with thick noodles. I ate the noodles and meat with chopsticks and drank the broth from the bowl, the way Jordie and his mom ate it, while Raine daintily ate hers with a spoon. Or at least she tried to eat it without making a mess, which is almost impossible with the thick noodles in the bottom of the bowl.

After we ate we walked to the Metro station and caught the train headed downtown. Most of the seats were full since it was still close to rush hour, so we stood in the space just inside the sliding doors. I leaned back against the Plexiglas window that separated the seating area of the train car from the space where we were standing just inside the door. Raine was standing in the middle of the aisle, her arm hooked around the metal bar as the train car swayed and rocked through the tunnel. I looked through the window into the blackness of the tunnel. Most of the time there was nothing to see other than a reflection of the train car interior. I could see Raine's legs, clad in boots, and her short skirt, reflected in the glass. I didn't let my gaze linger there. I couldn't look at any part of her directly for too long without feeling like I might explode if I didn't touch her.

As the train slowed to a stop at the Rosslyn station platform I could see a group of guys waiting to get on our car. When the doors opened, the guys spilled inside, loud and smelling like Bad Habits on a busy night, their laughs booze soaked.

I didn't want to end up in a fight, didn't want to start any kind of trouble with Raine there, but I knew if one of the guys bumped her or even looked at her with interest I would lose it. Raine didn't like that I got into fights, would frown disapprovingly if the subject ever came up. She definitely would be pissed if I went looking for a fight now.

In the interest of keeping the peace, I took a handful of Raine's jacket and pulled her closer to me while I kept half an eye on the rowdy group of guys who were crowding the entire aisle of the train car. They were talking loudly, laughing hysterically at everything, had obviously been out drinking for happy hour and were now oblivious to the ruckus they were causing. I pulled her in close to make it clear to these guys that she and I were together.

As the train started up again, Raine took a stumbling step back and reached for my arm to stop her fall. I was holding the edge of the wall I was leaned against but put my free hand around her waist to steady her. She didn't lean into me, but as the train car slowed or sped up she relaxed into the movement and her body would bump mine. We had never been this physically close to each other before and I was constantly distracted by the smell of her hair, the weight of her hand on my forearm. And when the train did lurch and sway and her body bumped against mine, I wanted to tighten my arm around her waist and press her against the length of my body.

But I didn't.

There was an invisible line that Raine and I didn't cross with each other. She had made it clear from the beginning that she thought all guys were out for one thing. If I wanted to be around her, it was as a friend. That much I knew. And I liked hanging out with her. Once you got to know her she was a lot like Mario and she could give me shit as well as she could take it.

It was a few blocks to walk to the museum from the Farragut West station, the streets alive with people traveling home from work or heading to happy hour or dinner in the business district. A few guys noticed Raine as we walked, took the time to look at her, their eyes passing over her legs and chest. I tried to ignore it but would stare hard at anyone who looked at her with too much interest.

At the main entrance of the museum, Raine showed an invitation to get us into the gallery, the event not open to the general public.

"How did you get invited to this shindig?" I asked her as we walked through the lobby on our way toward a marble staircase.

"My parents are donors," she said with a flutter of her hand, as if it were no big deal her parents having so much money. "They have some special membership that gets them into gallery openings like this."

"Donors?" I asked. "Like they have so much money they just give it away?"

"Screw you, okay?" she answered hotly. "Don't make me sorry I invited you."

"Why do you always act like it's an insult if someone points out that you're rich?" I asked.

"Because that's how you mean it, isn't it?" she said quickly. "How would you like it if I brought up the fact that you were poor all the time?"

"I *am* poor," I said. "It doesn't bother me."

"If it doesn't bother you, then why are we even having

this conversation?" she asked angrily. "You know, I haven't forgotten how mean you were to me in the cafeteria that day. You can't just take out your bad moods on people and expect them to always forgive you."

My face burned as she brought up the embarrassing episode when I lost my temper with the lunch lady. "Okay, yeah," I said, relenting a little. "Sometimes maybe it bothers me. But it's not as if kids from my neighborhood grow up thinking they're going to be astronauts."

"Why can't you be an astronaut?" she asked as she stopped in the middle of the stairs and turned around to face me. People behind us eyed her curiously or with some annoyance as they had to step around her. Her feet were planted defiantly as she stood on the step above me, waiting for my answer. "You're a good athlete and you're in Calculus—"

"Jesus, Raine, I don't really *want* to be an astronaut," I said as I glanced nervously at the people walking up behind us, most of them trying to eavesdrop on our conversation as they moved around us. "I'm just using it as an example."

"Why do you always try so hard to make me not like you?" she asked, her expression softening as she studied my face.

"What are you talking about?" I asked. With her on the step above me we were the exact same height, her face close to mine, and I thought again about what it would be like to take her lower lip into my mouth for a kiss. I tried to keep my eyes on hers instead of on her lips, figuring it would just piss her off if she could tell I was distracted.

"It's like you don't want me to like you," she said. "You always say insulting things, try to hurt my feelings on purpose. Why do you do that?"

"I . . . I guess because I'm a dick," I said with a smile but she didn't smile back—was giving me the silent treatment while she kept her gaze fixed exactly two inches to the side of my face, refusing to make direct eye contact.

She waited, not seeming to care that now we were causing a major traffic jam.

"Maybe I figure you'll hate me soon enough," I said finally, with a shrug. "I might as well give you the reasons ahead of time."

No answer, just an approving nod from her, as if to say, that's what I thought. Then she turned and resumed walking up the stairs and I followed, realizing, as I did, that if I wasn't careful, I'd end up following her all kinds of places just so I could get that look of approval again.

We spent an hour wandering through the galleries together, looking at the paintings and sculptures, each taking our own time to stop and study the works of art that interested us. Sometimes we would stop to look at the same work of art, but mostly we wandered on our own. Raine liked to look at the brightly colored landscapes and portraits of decorated women. She spent a lot of time in front of one painting that was a view of a crowd of people, but painted from the back so you couldn't see their faces.

There was a series of paintings that showed boxing matches between two guys wearing really tiny shorts, the strain of their muscles and expressions of pain on their faces told only in abstract. Raine said the artist was probably most famous for these boxer paintings. There were a couple of other paintings I was drawn to, though looking at them made me a little uncomfortable. They were paintings of scrawny young boys, one with his shirt pulled halfway off so it looked posed, like someone wanted to show off how pale and scrawny and sickly the kid was. That painting reminded me of Chick, and I experienced a momentary twinge of guilt about blowing him off after the soccer game. I would make it up to him by taking him to the movies one of my nights off work during the week.

After we left the museum we walked slowly toward the Metro station, like neither one of us really wanted to go home but weren't sure where else to go. It was full dark now and the white marble of the buildings in that part of town near the White House all glowed under the powerful security lights. I loved being in the city at night—knew that as soon as I finished school and found a job I would move into town to find an apartment instead of staying in the suburbs.

"Come on," I said to Raine. "Let's walk down to the Lincoln Memorial before we head back."

"Can we do that?" she asked uncertainly.

"Why not?"

"I mean, will we get in trouble? Walking through the park at night?"

"Like they say, it's a free country," I said. "I do it all the time. Come on."

From a distance the Mall seemed empty and quiet but once we crossed Constitution Avenue and entered the park area that housed the various war memorials, we saw several people, alone and in pairs, as they walked or jogged along the pebbled sidewalks. We ended up on the path that ran along the Vietnam Veterans Memorial, a black granite wall etched with the names of the people who were killed or MIA during the war. The wall stretched for the length of a city block and Raine trailed her fingers along the polished face of the stone as we walked along.

"People leave stuff here," I said. "Letters, photographs, flowers, teddy bears, trophies. All kinds of crazy shit. And someone comes out every night to collect the things people leave behind."

"Where does it all go?" Raine asked, her voice hushed as if we were in a church.

"No clue," I said. "They must have warehouses full of stuff. Or it gets put in the trash."

"No way," she said. "They wouldn't throw it away."

She was lost in thought after that and didn't say anything for a while. Most girls felt the need to fill every silence with senseless babble, but Raine would go quiet sometimes, like she had retreated somewhere inside her own head and had plenty in there to keep her busy.

"Have you gone to visit Sylvia's grave?" she asked. "I mean, since the funeral."

"I can't," I said.

"Why can't you?"

"Because," I said, taking a minute to find the words to explain. "At the funeral, I was supposed to be one of the pallbearers, you know, help to carry the casket." Raine just nodded to encourage me to keep talking. "I couldn't do it. I couldn't pick up her casket. Mario had to do it for me. I couldn't stand the thought of Sylvia's body inside that casket. It creeped me out," I finished lamely. I cast a sideways glance at Raine, wondering if she thought I was a complete tool for admitting something like that. She was looking at the ground, listening thoughtfully as we walked along.

Talking about Sylvia like that, it occurred to me that she had started to fade from my memory. I couldn't recall the sound of her voice, and even when I saw her face, in my nightmares and daydreams, it was just the suggestion of a face—dark hollows for eyes and the vague outlines of her features.

"Chick and I went to see this movie after Syl died," I said. "It was a horror movie with all these zombies, you know, the bodies of these people half decomposed, falling apart. All I could think about, while I was sitting in the theater, was Syl, rotting in some grave. Do you think that's weird?" I asked, figuring she would say no, whether she found it weird or not, just to be polite.

But when she turned to look at me her expression was intense. "No," she said. "I don't think that's weird at all."

"I don't think I'll ever be able to watch a horror movie again," I said. "And I can't go to her grave. Maybe never."

We reached the Lincoln Memorial and walked halfway up the steps before sitting down to look out over the reflecting pool and at the Washington Monument, up-lighted by a dozen massive spotlights. The stairs we sat on were solid rock, but had been worn in places by the tread of millions of feet. Raine sat one step above me while I leaned back on my elbows on the step so that my arm was close to her leg. When I looked up at her, the side of her face was in shadow, only her chin and bottom lip illuminated by the streetlights around us. Her hair, parted on the side, obscured most of her face and I wanted to push her hair back so I could see her eyes, what her mood was.

The National Mall was beautiful at night. The marble buildings, grimy during daylight hours from the exhaust fumes of a million tour buses, were luminous at night under the strategically placed spotlights. The long, shallow pool between the Lincoln Memorial and the Washington Monument reflected

shimmering points of light and echoed the distant noises of the
busy D.C. streets.

Raine pulled out her phone and scrolled through her Spo-
tify until she found a playlist that she wanted. "Volcano" by
Damien Rice filled the space between us, as if filling our own
private room with noise. I wasn't a big fan of his music, but it
was the exact right song for the moment.

"I was at Sylvia's funeral," Raine said suddenly, like a confession of guilt.

My face burned with embarrassment and I was glad for
the darkness. If Raine had been at Sylvia's funeral, then that
meant I didn't need to have told her. She saw me lose it, step
back and let Mario carry the casket for me because I was too
much of a pussy to do it myself.

"I didn't really know Sylvia," Raine went on, "but there
were a lot of people at the church who weren't really her friends,
just people from school."

She paused as if waiting for me to say something but I didn't
speak. The ache in my gut was starting up again, not as bad as
it had been in the past, but it was there.

"I'm sure you didn't even notice I was there," Raine said.

"I didn't notice anyone," I said dully.

"I watched you that day—at the cemetery," she said, sounding apologetic. "You looked so . . . lost. So alone. I felt terrible
for you. I mean, I know you have your mom and Mario and
Jordan. . . . Anyway, I guess I felt sorry for you."

I was too tired to work up any anger at her for giving me
pity I didn't want.

"Sylvia was all my mom really cared about," I said, more
forcefully than I had meant. "She hates the shit out of my dad

and I remind her of him. And now my mom wishes I had been the one to die, instead of Sylvia." Since Sylvia's death, I had thought this many times, but it was the first time I had said it out loud to anyone.

"Don't say that," Raine said quietly.

"Why not?" I asked. "It's the truth."

"She's your mom. I'm sure she loves you," she said lamely.

"I'm not saying she doesn't. I'm saying that if she had to choose, she would have picked Sylvia over me. Let's say your mom had to choose between you or your brother dying, which one of you do you think she would pick?" I asked.

"Definitely me," she said without hesitation. Then she laughed. "God. So twisted."

"My mom was young when she had me. Not much older than I am now," I said though I hadn't really thought of it that way before now. "I was a mistake. An accident."

"What about your dad? Was he at Sylvia's funeral?"

"No," I said. "My mom would have flipped if he had shown up. Like I said, she hates him."

"Is he awful?" Raine asked.

"He's not a bad guy. Just wasn't much of a dad. When I was a little kid it was harder. He never paid child support on time and was always blowing off his visitation times with me. Now he does all right. He sends my mom a check every month and he tries to be like a dad in his way."

"Parents suck," Raine said.

"Most do," I said, nodding in agreement.

"You're a good person, Jason. You look out for Chick. He wouldn't have any real friends without you."

Her comment sent another stab of guilt through my gut as

I conjured the mental image of Chick's crestfallen face when Raine and I didn't include him in our plans.

"What about you and Mario?" Raine asked. "I never see you guys together anymore."

"Yeah, he's so burned out, I don't have much interest in talking to him lately."

"You're not into that? Drugs, I mean."

"Nah. My life's fucked up enough," I said as I sat up and brushed the dust from my hands. "I don't need to be smoked to the filter to make it worse."

"That's too bad. About you and Mario, I mean," she said, and she sounded like she really was sorry about it. "I had him as my lab partner last year in Chemistry. I like him."

"Yeah," I said because I didn't know what else to say. Mario felt lost to me, like the person I had known since first grade was a complete stranger to me now. I realized then that my whole life had been a succession of people leaving me. Eventually Raine would leave me too. I had to be careful or that would hurt me as much as anyone else leaving, if not more.

Raine was talking and I realized I hadn't heard anything she had said for the last couple minutes. When I caught up with what she was saying, she was still following the same trajectory of our conversation.

"Not that I'm so into getting drunk or anything," she was saying, "but I figure my brain is already fucked up enough so I don't mess with drugs either."

"You seem to me like you have your act together pretty well," I said. "Why do you think your brain is so fucked up?"

The look she gave me was impossible to read and she didn't answer me right away. I waited patiently, and when she finally did speak she was looking off into the middle distance instead of looking at me. "My family are all crazy overachievers. My dad is a successful lawyer, a founding partner in his firm. My parents both went to Ivy League schools. For someone looking at us from the outside, we're perfect. Except for me. But even with their perfect educations, perfect careers, perfect genes, my parents still managed to have a daughter who is stupid."

"What are you talking about?" I asked scornfully. "I know plenty of stupid people. You aren't one of them."

"I'm dyslexic. That's why I have so much trouble with school," she said as she lowered her chin and took up a sudden interest in picking at a hangnail. She dropped her hands back into her lap and sighed, a long, weary exhale, and said, "I've been a disappointment to my parents from the beginning."

"I doubt that's true," I said. "I mean, it's not like you can help having . . ." Awkward pause as I realized what I had been about to say.

She smiled in understanding at my hesitation. "It's okay. You can say it. A learning disability. That's what it is. It was almost impossible for me to learn to read. I still struggle some-times, like I'm always two minutes behind everyone else. I don't know. I can't explain it."

"Well, you play it off well. I never would have guessed you were anything other than perfect." *Shit.* As soon as the words were out of my mouth I realized I had said something stupid again. "Not that, you know, being dyslexic makes you bad or anything. You know what? I should just stop talking."

"Yeah, that was offensive," she said, but without any real feeling, and I could tell she wasn't really bothered by what I had said.

"When I was a kid I was always getting in trouble at school,"

I said, maybe to make her feel better, maybe because I just like telling her things. "I couldn't sit still, couldn't concentrate. I was bored, I guess. Never could stay interested in one thing for very long. It drove the teachers crazy. My mom too. She took me to some special doctor and he said I was smart but that I had ADHD, was too impulsive, and offered to put me on some kind of meds. But my dad had been a big drug user and the idea of it bothered my mom. She didn't want them putting me on anything."

"So, what did they do?" Raine asked as she sat listening patiently to my story, her hands tucked between her thighs for warmth.

"My mom sent me to some stupid camp for kids with ADHD," I said, dimly remembering now an experience I hadn't thought about for a long time. "I think I was only there two weeks but it felt like fucking forever. The counselors would do activities with us, like hikes and shit, I suppose to give us something to do with all of our energy." I laughed to myself. "They would take us on these hikes and each kid would get assigned a llama."

"Wait, a what?" Raine asked with a small frown. "A llama?"

"Yeah," I said with a nod. "An honest-to-God llama. We had to lead them on the hike, keep them under control. Mine was the smallest but he would bite and kick and never wanted to go in the direction I was trying to lead him."

"A llama camp?" Raine said with quiet wonder. "What the hell?"

"I know," I said, and after a beat of silence, "My llama's name was Bud."

She laughed out loud at that. "Did it help? Were you cured?"

"I guess not," I said with a shrug. "My mom still always

told me I made her crazy. I guess I was supposed to learn something from it. Like my mom and my teachers felt the same way I did trying to manage me as I did trying to manage that fucking llama."

"Well, it seems like you turned out okay. Maybe Bud made a big difference and you just never realized it."

"They put labels on us to help them manage their own stress and disappointment," I said. "I'm ADHD, you're dyslexic. We just think differently from the way most people do. It scares them." I didn't know exactly who "they" or "them" was, but Raine knew what I meant—our parents, teachers, other old people who couldn't remember what it was like to think for themselves. "At least that doctor said I was smart, I guess. I have that going for me."

"You are smart. Unlike me. I guess I could never be an astronaut like you," she said with the flash of a smile in my direction. "It's true. I accept it."

"I don't want to be a fucking astronaut," I said as I pushed her shoulder to tell her to shut up, and she elbowed me in the ribs. "Ow," I said, though it didn't really hurt.

"Big baby," she said, and when she tried to dig her elbow into my ribs again I grabbed her arm and held it so she couldn't. She tried to pull away but she was laughing.

I thought about kissing her right then. Pulling her onto my lap and kissing her under the moon and stars and the stern gaze of Abraham Lincoln.

After a minute I realized I was still holding her arm, my gaze fixed on her full lower lip. I could feel her holding her breath as she waited to see what I was going to do.

I released my grip on her arm but allowed myself to give her hand a brief squeeze. "We should go," I said.

"Really?" she asked, sounding surprised, confused, and maybe a little hurt.

"Yeah," I said, then took in a deep breath and blew out my disappointment. "Yeah, we should go."

On the drive home to my house I was preoccupied, thinking about what I was supposed to do when we finally said good-bye at the end of the night. Though Raine had made it clear when she asked me that this wasn't a date, I knew she had expected me to kiss her when we were at the Lincoln Memorial. She had stayed quiet for most of the ride back on the train, talking only as much as was necessary. I couldn't tell if she was mad or sad or what, and there didn't seem to be any way to ask her.

When she pulled the car up in front of my apartment building she turned off the car headlights but didn't shut off the engine.

"I had a good time tonight," I said as I rubbed my palms against my jeans in a nervous way, like I was trying to rub warmth into my legs.

"Me too," she said. "Thanks for coming with me."

The seconds ticked by as the engine fan shifted into high gear. If it had been any other girl, I don't think I would have hesitated. Either I would have gone in for the kiss I wanted or I would have opened the door and left without another thought. With Raine I was always second-guessing myself, afraid to put too much out there and get shot down, or not say enough and let her walk away without telling her that I liked being with her.

Raine laughed softly and startled me out of my private thoughts.

"What?" I asked.

She just shook her head. "Nothing. Just . . . this," she said as she gestured at the space between us with a wave of her hand. "Awkward silence."

"Oh," I said, and then I took the plunge. "I was just trying to decide if I should kiss you good night. Thought maybe I'd get hit again."

"If you kiss me, I promise I won't hit you," she said.

"Wow. That was almost . . . romantic," I said. She was laughing again when I leaned over the console and put a hand on the side of her face. The kiss I gave her was quick, almost missing her mouth entirely as my lips caught just the corner of hers. But I pulled away and didn't linger on her side of the front seat.

She leaned her elbow on the door handle, her body angled toward me as she slid her left hand under her hair and raked her fingers through it in a nervous way. "The fall cotillion at the club is this weekend," Raine said, her gaze on the windshield. "My mom organizes it so I have to go."

"Cotillion? What's that?" I asked. She said it as if I should know, but I had never heard the word before.

"It's a dance. A really lame dance," she said, dropping her voice conspiratorially. "Ballroom dancing."

"Oh. I guess that does suck."

"I was thinking—" Raine said, and shifted in her seat so that her body was angled toward the front of the car now. "I was just going to go to the dance by myself, just see my friends there, but most of them are going with a date."

"You saying nobody asked you to the dance?" I asked skeptically.

She didn't answer, just kept raking her fingers through

her hair as she seemed to be thinking. Finally she said, "I was thinking I would ask you to go with me."

"Does that mean you're still thinking about it?" I asked, my eyebrows raised in question. "Or are you actually asking me?"

The corner of her mouth lifted in a smile. "I guess I'm asking you. Will you go to the cotillion with me?"

"You sure about that?" I asked. "I mean, I know it wouldn't be like a date or anything," I added quickly.

"Exactly," she said. "But you have to wear a suit and tie. Deal breaker?"

"Not at all," I said, already wondering how I was going to pull that one off.

CHAPTER TWENTY-SEVEN

When Raine got to my apartment building that Saturday night, I was standing in the living room waiting for her. I hadn't been able to sit still all afternoon, watching the clock and thinking this was all a huge mistake.

She was already out of her car and walking up the cracked and uneven sidewalk to my door when I stepped out onto the stoop. "Holy shit," I muttered under my breath at the sight of her. She was wearing a formfitting black dress that flared out at the knees and settled into a silky pool at her feet. Her hair was pulled back from her face but hung in loose curls down to her shoulders. The dress wasn't particularly low cut and didn't show a lot of skin. What it did show was every curve, and I couldn't keep my eyes from traveling over each of them, imagining what it would feel like to run my hands over her body, to hug her against me. I was going to have to spend the better part of the night thinking about soccer or my mom just to keep from touching Raine.

I was wearing a shirt and tie but I was warm in it and so

had my jacket hanging over my arm. The funeral suit. I hated it, but there was no other option. The only person I knew who wore almost the same size I did was Chris, and I couldn't imagine him owning a suit.

"You look really nice," Raine said as she gave me the once-over.

"I—uh . . . You look fucking amazing," I said.

She smiled at that but I instantly wished I could take it back. Jesus, the first words out of my mouth and I'm cussing at her like a sailor.

"I'm sorry," I said. "I mean . . . I meant that you look nice too."

" 'Fucking amazing' is better than 'nice' any day," she said.

"You changed your hair," I said, noticing it for the first time. Her hair, which fell in long waves to the middle of her back, had been all one length before and now was cut with bangs to frame her face. And she had changed the color to a dirty blond. "Is that your natural color?"

"Close enough," she said.

"Why did you change it?"

"My mom wanted me to," she said, wrinkling her nose with distaste. "Because of the dance. Do you hate it?"

"It makes your eyes look more blue," I said.

"Yeah?"

"Yeah."

"You ready to get out of here?" she asked.

We fell into step with each other walking to the car. I headed for the driver's side so I could open Raine's door for her.

"I was wondering if I was going to meet your mom. Is she home?" Raine asked.

"She is," I said, "but she's not much for company these days."

"I'm sorry," Raine said.

"Don't worry about it."

"Did you want to drive?" Raine asked as I stepped off the curb and reached for the car door handle to open the door for her.

"Why?" I asked.

"I don't know," she said with an uncertain shrug.

"You think it bothers me to have a girl drive me around?"

"Does it?" she asked.

"Not if that girl is you," I said as we stood with the open car door between us, her hand resting on top of the door.

Raine frowned and said, "I'm not . . . sure I'm in the right place. I was here to pick up Jason Marshall. You know, about six-two, dark hair, nice smile, kind of a dick."

I laughed at that. "If it will make you feel better, I'll be a dick on the drive there," I said.

"I don't know," she said. "I guess I could get used to this Jason."

As we drove along the parkway that followed the river to the country club, I stared out the passenger window at the last rays of sun shining through the trees, most of them now in full fall colors.

In a few minutes we reached the entrance to the club. A large wooden sign announced it as the WESTWOOD COUNTRY CLUB, but there was nothing but rolling green fields and a patch of woods in sight. Raine turned onto a road that was lined with a perfectly straight row of trees along both sides.

The temperature of the air dropped suddenly as we drove under the canopy of trees and Raine shut the sunroof. We drove for what seemed like a mile before we saw a building, a large white stucco building with a portico covering part of the circular driveway. When we pulled up in front of the building, a guy in a white uniform with a burgundy bow tie ran over to open Raine's door.

"How you doing?" I asked one of the other uniformed valets with a nod as he came to shut my own door behind me.

"Good evening, sir," he said, calling me sir like I wasn't just some punk kid, but somebody whose dad had money and influence. I thought about the look Mario would have shot me if he had been there to hear the valet call me sir, and it made me feel suddenly lonely. I wished for a friend with me who I could turn to and with just a look ask, "Sir? Did you hear that?"

I took a minute to study the building up close while Raine handed over the keys to her car and gathered her purse from the backseat. Fountains flanked either side of the entrance, water splashing playfully against stone statues. There were potted plants and benches all along the veranda that ran from one end of the building to the other and a red carpet marked the path that would lead us inside the building.

"You ready?" Raine asked.

"Sure. Yeah," I said as I pulled my jacket on and buttoned the top button. Raine put her arm through mine and held my forearm. Her whole body was touching mine, her breast pressing against my arm. Walking with Raine on my arm, in that moment, I felt like I was the man. The feeling was fleeting since once we walked into the lavish club I was reminded that I was a stranger here and the loneliness settled in again.

The foyer of the building was bigger than my entire apartment, and black marble columns separated the main part of the foyer from a row of fireplaces, all burning with fires to ward off the autumn chill. People sat alone and in small groups at couches and wingback chairs near the fires, talking and drinking. Some of the men were dressed in tuxedos, but most wore suits. I was struck by how at home Raine looked in this place, almost like she owned it. I felt completely out of place and wished that I had at least had a more recent haircut.

"Nice place," I said as we mounted a large central staircase, climbing to the second floor. "I feel like I've hit the big time."

Her lips tightened in a little purse and I could tell my comment had her miffed. "Don't start," she said.

"I just said it was a nice place."

"Uh-huh," she murmured, but let it go without a fight.

At the top of the stairs, the doors were propped open to a large room that included a stage draped with red velvet curtains. A band was seated on the stage with music stands in front of each musician. They were playing an upbeat, jazzy song when we entered and there were a few couples out on the dance floor, most of them older people. Otherwise, people were just kind of milling around, talking or getting drinks from the bar. I recognized a few people from school, including Jordie, who was standing with Cheryl and other people our age.

"I have to introduce you to my mom," Raine said with a sigh. "We might as well get it over with. So embarrassing."

I didn't ask if she was embarrassed by me, or her mom. Maybe both. Even though I knew Raine's parents were members of the club and her mom was an organizer of the event, it still hadn't occurred to me before that moment that I would have to meet her parents. My hands started to sweat as I thought about the prospect of meeting her mom and just hoped she was too preoccupied to take much notice of me.

Raine's mom was pretty in a made-up kind of way—blond like Raine but clearly an expensive dye job—and gave you the impression right away that she was running the show. People were hanging around her, asking questions and for direction about things.

"My mom's in charge of the cotillion," Raine muttered to me out of the corner of her mouth. "She's like a Nazi with her organizational skills." Then she turned back and stepped up to her mom, dropping an airy kiss on her cheek. "Hi, Mom. This is my friend Jason."

Mrs. Blair's cool blue eyes landed on me and gave me the once-over, but I didn't feel any judgment, more like she was just mentally cataloging everything about me for later reference.

"Hello, Jason," she said, her tone friendly enough. "It's nice to meet you."

"Nice to meet you too, Mrs. Blair."

"It's Ms. Anderson," she said. "Mrs. Blair is my mother-in-law. I thought I'd wait to change my last name once I'm sure my first marriage is going to work out."

She was funny, even if she delivered the joke without a smile. I got the sense from the way Raine rolled her eyes that she had heard this one many times before.

"Fair enough," I said. "A good-looking woman like yourself, it's smart to keep your options open."

Now Raine's mom did crack a smile and cut her eyes to Raine as she tilted her head with a meaningful lift of her eyebrow. "I'd be careful, if I were you," she said to Raine. "I'm glad to have met you, Jason. You two have a good time."

"Yes, Mother," Raine said as she took me by the elbow and steered me away from her mom. "Gross," she whispered to me. "Stop flirting with my mom."

"I wasn't flirting," I said. "I see where you get your smart mouth."

"You *were* flirting. And it's gross. Come on," she said. "Let's dance."

"This isn't really my kind of dancing," I said as the band started up a new song, a slow one.

"Well, if you don't mind me driving, maybe you won't mind if I lead," she said. "Come on." She picked up my hand and we walked onto the dance floor together. In the center of the dance floor, Raine stopped and put her hand on my shoulder. The other she rested lightly in my hand. There were just a few seconds of awkwardness as we settled into each other. This was the first time for us touching each other in such a familiar way, so there was a moment of uncertain fumbling. But I had thought about holding her often enough that I already knew how I wanted her to fit in my arms.

I put my hand at the curve of her waist and she stepped in close to me, her head tipped back slightly to look up into my face. "When I was in middle school, I had to take cotillion every week," she said. "I was always taller than the boys so their faces would end up somewhere near my boobs. It's nice to dance with someone taller than I am."

I smiled at her comment but didn't trust myself to say anything, afraid my voice would break like I was twelve again. My heart was pounding insistently and I knew Raine had to feel it as close as we were.

I slid my hand to the other side of her waist so I was holding her closer and tried to breathe normally, though my breath kept catching in my chest. Raine turned her head to look at some of the other people dancing and she let out a quiet sigh, almost like she was content, or happy. I put my face closer to her hair and breathed in her scent. We weren't moving much, just barely, but each time we did move our bodies rubbed together in a way that was setting off alarms in my head. I had thought about holding her for weeks, and now that I was holding her, it was in front of a roomful of strangers and it made me distinctly uncomfortable.

Other couples were talking as they danced but Raine and I were quiet. She slid her hand up my shoulder, closer to my neck, and I felt the collar of my jacket press against my skin. She shifted her hips, just a little, but she was suddenly closer to me and my mind was racing at a hundred miles an hour.

Her eyebrow came just to my chin and I thought, totally crazy, about brushing my lips against her forehead. The people around us were a blur now, the room a kaleidoscope of shimmering light and the chatter of conversation, all of it meaningless.

When the song ended, it took us an extra few seconds to let go. Our eyes met as we stepped away from each other and I savored the look she was giving me. If we had been alone that moment, nothing short of death could have stopped me from kissing her, regardless of how much restraint I had shown up to this point in life.

"Let's get a drink," Raine said, her comment casual, but a tremble thrummed under her voice.

A group of people our age was clustered near the refreshment table as Raine and I approached, and some of them stopped to greet Raine. A few of the people I knew, like Madison and Cheryl, with Jordie at her side, but the rest were strangers to me. I hadn't told Jordie ahead of time that I was coming and I noticed his eyes widen in surprise when he saw me with Raine.

As we stood talking to Raine's friends, Brian approached with a group of guys, all of them in tailored suits, their hair perfectly gelled. My hand was balled in a fist in my pocket as I fought the urge to chew nervously on my thumbnail. Subconsciously I had known I would see people like Brian when I agreed to come with Raine, but thought with a little luck we'd be able to avoid them for most of the night.

"Hey, Raine," Brian said, ignoring everyone else.

"Brian," she said with a small nod as her eyes wandered over the crowd of dancers to avoid his gaze.

"Hey, Jason," Brian said, the friendliness in his voice so fake, it made me want to wince.

"How you doing?" I asked as I thought about stepping closer to Raine.

"Hey," Brian said, his voice too eager, "we were just going outside to hit the bottle for a bit. This shindig is lame. I can't deal with being sober. You should come with us, Jason."

Raine's eyes narrowed as she studied Brian's expression but she said nothing.

"I probably shouldn't," I said. "We just got here."

"Oh, come on," Brian said, chiding me. The way he was able to turn on the fake charm was pretty impressive—his parents probably thought he hung the moon. "You worried Raine is going to be mad. You don't care, right, Raine?"

"Jason can do whatever he wants," Raine said with a small shrug in that way girls do when they won't admit to being mad about something yet can't hide it anyway.

"I'll be back in just a few minutes," I said to Raine.

"Don't worry," Brian said to Raine, giving her that "aw shucks" tilt of his head that made up half his practiced charm. "We won't let him talk to any other girls."

"Very funny," Raine said, and she turned away with Cheryl to talk to her girlfriends.

"You coming?" Brian said to Jordie, his tone almost a challenge.

Jordie shook his head, his jaw tight with some unspoken criticism. "Nah, man. Cheryl will lose her shit if I go."

"Pussy," Brian said to Jordie. "She's got you whipped." In this, Brian and I, possibly for the only time ever, were in agreement about something.

I walked with Brian and his friends through a side staircase, not the big main staircase I had walked up with Raine. At the bottom of the stairs, there was a single door with a crash bar that opened to the outside. Brian led the way out of the building and across the gardens as we headed toward a small outbuilding.

A silver flask winked in the moonlight as Brian pulled it from his inside jacket pocket. Probably monogrammed with his initials, was the thought that flitted through my mind. He took a long swig from the flask, then handed it to me. Figuring I would need it, I took a long draw from the flask before passing it back. The liquor spread like a fire through my gut and loosened my muscles. It was exactly what I needed in that moment.

Brian's buddies were talking and laughing, their behavior almost frenetic as they ambled along behind us. We were headed for an outbuilding near the tree line that separated the golf course from the landscaped gardens. A lone security light mounted on the building cast a broad path of light across the manicured lawn, painting long shadows. The twisted shadows of the old trees seemed sinister because of my mood and anticipation of what was to come.

Brian handed me the flask again as we stepped behind the

outbuilding. It was dark here, the only light coming from the moon and stars. The other guys were drinking from their own flasks but had fallen quiet as they waited for Brian to take the lead. I held the flask out to Brian and he waved his hand toward me, a gesture for me to keep it.

"Have some more," he said. "There's plenty more where that came from. You're our guest."

"I get that you have to pretend in front of Raine," I said, then hit the flask again. "But you don't have to keep up the act on my account."

"What do you mean?" Brian asked, all innocence.

"I know why we're out here," I said, "so why don't we just get to it."

The silence closed in as they all held a collective breath.

"If Raine really cared about you, she wouldn't have brought you here," Brian said. "If she wanted to make me jealous, she should have set her sights a little higher."

"I get that," I said with a nod. "But there's nothing going on with me and Raine." If Brian thought of himself as her boyfriend, technically she hadn't been cheating on him with me. "I've never even kissed her. We're just friends."

"I'm sure that's all you want. To be her friend. You gay or something?" A few snickers from the guys, nervous laughter.

"I don't need to tell you what I am," I said.

"Oh, I already know what you are," Brian said. "You're nothing."

"Yeah?" I asked. "So, why are we out here then?"

"I'm not going to do anything," Brian said. "This is just a friendly warning."

"And what?" I asked. "I stay away from Raine or you come after me with five guys backing you up?"

"Something like that," Brian said.

"You worried about going one-on-one with me?" I asked.

"What I'm worried about," Brian said as he stepped in closer to me, his posture threatening, "is that you think that a guy like you is good enough to be going out with Raine. You must have some white trash girls from your own neighborhood you can hang around."

"I'm done talking," I said. "If you want to fight let's get to it. I'm not listening to any more of this shit."

"I'm telling you that if you leave right now," Brian said as he retreated a couple of steps and slung one hand casually in his pocket, "there won't be any trouble."

"And if I don't?" I asked.

Brian chuckled. "Then we'll make what happened to you at the last soccer game seem like a cakewalk. You won't be walking out of here."

"You think I'm just going to walk out on Raine?" I asked. "You must not know me all that well."

"We'll tell her you got bored or that you left with another girl," Brian said. "Whatever you want."

"What I want," I said, knowing I should hold my tongue but too pissed off to care, "is to wipe that fucking smile off your face."

His face went slack with surprise and if I hadn't been so tense with anticipation it would have made me laugh.

When Brian came at me I was ready for him, my hands already balled into fists. I figured he had brought his boys for mop-up, didn't expect that they would go straight for the group attack. It wasn't even a fight since I had to spend all my energy trying to keep out of the grip of his buddies as Brian swung at my face and gut.

I fought them off for as long as I could, but there were five of them. That's not to say that I didn't get in a few punches. Each time one of them tried to grab me I kicked out, and swung my fists when I could. My fist connected with flesh a few times and there was the occasional howl or yelp when I landed a solid punch.

But then they had me up against the wall of the outbuilding and two of them pinned my arms while Brian worked me over. I kept my head down as I struggled against the guys holding me. As long as the top of my head was pointing forward Brian had to swing at me from the side or use an uppercut so it diminished the power of his punches.

Finally he stepped back to catch his breath. I still had some fight in me though my chest was tight from exhaustion and pain.

"Let him go," Brian said, confident now that I was worn down, swaying slightly on my feet.

They both released me and I stumbled forward and circled Brian so my back wasn't against the wall anymore.

"You can leave now," Brian said. "We won't chase you if you leave now."

"Not yet," I said, stupid with anger. I didn't really have a hope of doing any damage to them, but pride wouldn't let me back down.

I bent double to nurse the ache in my gut and took a few deep breaths, testing the feel as my lungs expanded with air. At first I thought some of my ribs were cracked, but after a few breaths was fairly sure I was just bruised. As I collected my thoughts, I wondered why I was still in this fight. It wasn't like I had any expectation for things to work out with a fairy-tale ending.

They were silent again as they all watched and waited to see what I would do. My mind was already made up. After a minute I stood quickly and rushed in to grab Brian by the collar. There were confused shouts at this unexpected turn of events as I got hold of him and landed a punch on his cheekbone. Then they were kicking at me, each of them jumping in to take hits at me and then retreating quickly before I could face off with any one of them.

I went down on one knee when someone got me in the side of the head with a hard elbow, my eyes squeezed shut to force the stars from my vision. While I was down, Brian stood over me and grabbed me by the back of my jacket. He held me steady while he drove a knee into my chest. Then another.

Brian dropped me after the second knee to my chest and they all took turns kicking me some more. I curled into a ball to protect my sensitive underbelly but one of them kicked me from the back, drove his foot hard up into my balls, and I thought I might piss myself.

"Okay, enough," Brian said finally. "He needs to be able to walk out of here."

The pain from getting kicked in the balls was so intense it drummed all the other pain out of my head. With the wind knocked out of me all I could do was fight to breathe, my chest heaving but not enough oxygen reaching my starved lungs.

"If you try to come back inside I'll tell everyone what happened," Brian said, panting heavily. "That you jumped me and my friends had to step in to protect me. Got it?"

I didn't answer. Couldn't, in fact. But he didn't wait to see what I would say.

As soon as I knew I was alone I let out the groan I had

been holding back, it ending on a whimper as I started to shake with cold. The shaking hurt almost every inch of my body and I knew the sooner I could get off the ground, the sooner I would feel better.

Jordie was the one who came to find me.

"Jaz?" His voice vibrated with worry and maybe a little bit of fear. He hadn't been willing to come outside with me and face an ass-kicking the way Mario would have. Actually, the way things were now, Mario probably wouldn't have taken the ass-kicking either, but once upon a time, Mario would have come with me and taken the ass-kicking without question. Maybe Jordie never would have. It was hard to tell anymore.

I had seen the look in Jordie's eyes when Brian asked him to join us outside. He knew what was about to go down and had chosen to stay out of it. It hung there between us, the knowledge that Jordie had chosen not to back me up. Not that I faulted him for it. Jordie had to live in this world. I was just a visitor.

"You okay, man?" Jordie asked as he crouched beside me. "Can you stand up?"

"Yes," I said with more conviction than I felt. It was still another minute before I rose from the ground with Jordie supporting me under one arm.

As soon as I was on my feet I pulled back from him—and left with nothing to do with his hands, he hung them by the thumbs from his belt in an awkward gesture. "Brian said you left," Jordie said quietly.

"Yeah?" I asked as I brushed at some of the dirt and grass clippings that clung to my pants.

"Yeah. You want a lift home or something?"

"Nah, I'll be all right," I said, maybe not entirely the truth.

"You're sure?" he asked uncertainly but with some relief, grateful he didn't have to explain to anyone why he was leaving the dance.

"Yeah, man. I'll be fine." The truth was, I knew I either had a very long walk ahead of me, or I'd have to find a pay phone where I could call Chris and see if he would come and pick me up. Small chance of that happening on a Saturday night when the bar was busy.

Left with only two choices—to walk out on my own or go back inside and face whatever Brian had cooked up for me, face Raine's probing and pitying stare—I took the only option I saw for myself, and chose the walk alone.

CHAPTER TWENTY-EIGHT

Sunday I had to be at work by ten to get the bar set up for the crowd that would come in to watch the football games. I was actually glad to go to work, to have something I could focus on besides thinking about Raine.

It's not as if I hadn't known from the beginning that everything between Raine and me was only temporary. We both knew that even if she wasn't into Brian, eventually she would end up with someone like him. Someone who had money and who would go to college. I never for a minute believed that she would stick around. I just hadn't been ready to let her go this soon.

My shift ended at seven, just as the night shift people were coming in to work, including Chris, who would work until close. When Chris stopped to talk to me in the kitchen I could see him eyeing the marks on my face from my fight with Brian and his boys, but he didn't ask about them or mention them at all. It wasn't a big secret that I got in a lot of fights. Even Chris knew that.

When I left work I lifted a bottle of booze from the office to take with me while Chris was busy at the bar. I was walking through the alley, toward the hole cut in the fence that opened onto the back side of the park. It saved me ten minutes on the walk home, though I had no plans to head for home right then. I was headed for the park to drink myself into oblivion.

"Jason! Hey, Jason," Chick called after me as I walked along the alleyway behind the bar. I stopped to wait for him to catch up, and when he fell into step with me he was breathing hard. I was too angry to walk slowly and wait for Chick to keep up with me, so he just had to scamper along beside me.

"I've been looking for you, man. Thought we could hang out or something," Chick said to me, his voice drowned out by the crunch of gravel and broken glass under my feet. "You okay, Jaz?"

"Yeah, Chick. I'm fine," I said dully.

"You sure?" he asked. "Your face is messed up. Were you in a fight? Is that what you're upset about?"

I wanted to scream at him to shut up, stop talking. I had been an idiot, a complete and total tool. Every time I thought about the things I had said to Raine, how I had shared details about my life with her, it made me cringe.

I had wanted the way things ended with Raine to be on my own terms. At the end of the school year she would be headed off to college while I would probably end up working for Chris and living in some shitty apartment. But, damn, I couldn't even imagine what she was thinking about me at the moment.

"I don't want to talk about it, Chick," I said.

"Is it about Raine? Because if it is . . . I don't know. Maybe it would make you feel better to talk to someone about it."

I stopped so suddenly that Chick ran into me and bounced off my back. "Talk with who? With you?" I asked hotly. "How the fuck is it going to help me to talk to you? You've never even been with a girl before."

"Yeah, I know," he said and I could hear the tears in his voice.

"Go home, Chick," I said. The hurt was so plain on his face as I turned my back on him that I felt pain knife through my stomach. I walked away quickly, hoping to avoid another word with him. I was too mad at the world to apologize to him, too caught up in feeling sorry for myself to be able to spare any pity for anyone else.

At first I just walked aimlessly, but after a while my feet carried me to the pavilion where we went with Cheryl and Jordie on my doomed first date with Raine.

With the sun down it didn't take long to get cold deep in the woods under the trees, but I didn't get up to head home, just kept drinking until I felt warmer. Every once in a while I thought about walking to the Pike to catch a bus to Raine's neighborhood but would then quickly dismiss the idea. The sooner I forgot about her, the better.

I don't know how long I sat there, drinking and trying to forget everything, when a pair of headlights cut through the trees. A car was coming down the road into the park, its only possible destination the parking lot next to the pavilion where I sat. My first thought was that it might be Raine, coming to look for me, wanting to talk things through. And, honestly, that was what I was hoping. I went back and forth between wishing she would magically turn up down at the park to find me, and wishing I would never see her again.

By the time I realized the car was not Raine's, that it was, in fact, a cop car with two uniformed officers in it, it was too late for me to get very far. Sure, I could have cut into the woods and easily outrun them, but I was just so tired. Tired of fighting. Tired of running.

So, I sat there, doing nothing but hitting the bottle a couple more times before tossing it in the metal wire trash can a few feet from where I sat.

They got out of the car slowly once they realized I had no intention of running. An older cop had been driving, with a younger cop, probably only a few years older than me, riding shotgun. They sauntered over with that kind of walk unique to cops, forced rigid posture from their bulletproof vests, the movement of their hips stiff from all the gear they wore on their belts.

I saw the older one sizing me up, but he looked almost bored, like he couldn't believe he got the shit assignment of busting kids drinking down in the park.

"Evening," the older cop said, his friendliness too forced to be real.

I just nodded at him and stayed where I was, didn't want to come across as a threat. I kept my hands on the picnic table where they could see them. The older cop was still eyeing me closely, taking in my hoodie and the marks on my face from last night's fight. It didn't take him long to make his assumptions about me, fit me into a neat little box of limited potential.

"If I look in that trash can, am I going to find some booze?" he asked. The younger cop still hadn't said anything but he kept a hand on the nightstick at his waist as if in silent warning.

"Yes," I said. "A bottle of rum."

"That right?"

It wasn't a real question that demanded an answer. I had

already told him everything he needed to know, so I kept my mouth shut.

"You got ID on you, kid?" the older cop asked as he shifted the weight of his gun belt on his hips.

"No," I said.

"What's your name?"

"Jason."

"Last name?" he said impatiently.

"Marshall."

"Uh-huh," he said absently as he wrote something down on his pad of paper.

"Your folks know where you are?" he asked, watching my face for the lie he thought was coming.

I shrugged. "I guess not."

"Oh, you guess not?" he said, his tone chiding. "How old are you?"

"Seventeen," I said.

"Well, since you're a minor, we're going to have to take you home to your parents. Release you into their custody. Where'd you get the booze?" he asked, not really expecting a straight answer.

"I got some homeless guy to buy it for me at the liquor store up the road," I lied easily. The wrath of the cops didn't scare me, but Chris would rearrange my face if the stolen booze got traced back to him.

"That still works, huh?" the older cop asked as he and the younger cop exchanged a laugh. To me he said, "What's your address? And just so you know, if you give me a fake address I'm taking you straight to the police station to let you spend some time in the drunk tank and your folks will be picking you up there."

"It's just my dad," I said. "He's at work." This was the lesser of two evils. I didn't want the cops coming to the apartment. There was a good chance Mom would be too out of it to handle me getting brought home by the cops. I didn't want her to have one of her freak-outs in front of strangers, especially not ones who were armed and carried handcuffs. They might be tempted to take her away to a loony bin.

"Where does your dad work?"

"Bad Habits, the place on the Pike. He owns the place."

"Chris Marshall is your dad, huh?" the older cop asked. "I know him. Went to school with him, as a matter of fact. He know you're out? Or does he think you're at home watching television?"

"I'm not sure he spends much time thinking about it either way," I said.

The cop looked a little uncomfortable, maybe sorry for me, and for a second I thought he was just going to turn me loose, let me off the hook. He sighed and said, "Well, we can't leave you out here on your own. I know you kids think it's cool to party down here, but it's dangerous. Lots of bad types hanging around. Come on." His partner moved to stand behind me as the older cop came alongside me and put a hand on my elbow. As I stood he directed me to one side and started patting my pockets, the sides of my hoodie, and put a hand at the small of my back to make sure there was no weapon tucked into my waistband.

"You got anything on you that you shouldn't have?" he asked as he patted down the sides of my legs and then had me turn to look at him.

"No, sir. Just the booze."

"You on anything else? Been doing any narcotics?"

"No."

"Okay," he said once he was sure that I wasn't concealing a weapon. "Hop on in the back." He gestured for me to get in the backseat of the squad car as he went to open the door.

It was a short ride to Bad Habits, only about three minutes from where the cops found me in the park. They pulled around to the back door, and I sat in the car with the younger cop while the other one went in through the kitchen to find Chris. The older cop and Chris emerged a few minutes later, talking and laughing about something.

"Here he is," the cop said as he opened the car door and gestured for me to climb out.

Chris didn't say anything, just pursed his lips as he shook his head.

"When he told me you were his dad I thought he was pulling my leg for a minute. Didn't know you had a kid," the older cop said. "But once he said it, I could see the resemblance. Looks a lot like you did when you were that age."

"Yeah, unfortunately he got my shitty attitude too," Chris said wryly.

The cop laughed. "Seems like an okay kid. Didn't get an attitude with us like most of them do."

"Hey, thanks for bringing him to me, Hugo," Chris said as he stuck out his hand to shake. "I appreciate you bringing the boy to me instead of making me come and get him out of the holding tank. Say thank you," Chris said with a threatening tap on my shoulder.

"Thanks for being cool about it," I said to the older cop, Hugo, and directed a nod at the younger one, who had barely looked up from his phone while the rest of us stood talking.

The cops saddled up and drove away, and before their taillights had cleared the building, Chris directed me inside with a gesture. "You wait in the office while I get someone to cover the bar." He walked me to the office to make sure I didn't split as soon as he turned around. He stood in the doorway and waited while I took a seat on the couch. As he turned to walk out of the office he stopped in the doorway to say, "Hey, and just so you know, I'm not a total idiot. When I take liquor from the office to restock the bar I take it from the *front* of the row, not the back, so you aren't fooling anyone. And don't think I didn't notice when you helped yourself to a bottle of vodka either. I'll be taking both of those out of your paycheck."

"Can I get it at the wholesale price?" I asked. His eyes went hard and the muscles along his jaw bunched as he clenched his teeth. He left without another word and banged the door shut hard enough that he almost split the wood on the doorjamb.

My feet were up on Chris's desk when he came to get me a few minutes later and he shoved my legs so that my feet fell to the floor. We exchanged glares while Chris waited to see if I would give him any lip. I just shrugged and averted my gaze, let him win that round.

Chris drove me home and we rode in silence until he said, "I'm not going to get all preachy, partly because I know you won't really listen, and partly because I don't have a right to say much, but you got lucky tonight. Lucky those cops were cool about bringing you to me instead of dragging your ass down to the station. You're going to be eighteen soon. Which means real trouble for you if you keep making bad choices."

"Who the hell are you to talk to me about bad choices?" I asked.

"I'm your goddamn father. That still counts for something, doesn't it?" he asked, not taking his eyes off the road.

"It doesn't count for much," I said. "Man, you were never around. You think because you sent a check every month you get to have some say in my life?" I posed it as a question but didn't give him a chance to answer. "Oh, that's right. I forgot. You were too busy partying to give a shit."

The leather steering wheel cover groaned as he twisted his grip around it. "I'm sorry, Jaz. I really am. I was a kid when you were born. But I've been trying. These past few years I've been trying to be there for you. I haven't even been a day late on a support payment in years."

"It's not about the money!" I said, my voice raised to almost a shout. "It's about every time I needed you and you weren't there. Every time you said you were going to show up for a game and then blew me off. Every time you showed up late for weekend visitation because you were too hungover to get there on time. I don't give a fuck about the money."

"I know that," he said, his voice sounding thick, like he might cry. "I know I fucked up by not being around more when you were little."

"You know what, why are you even trying to act like you care all of a sudden?" I asked. "Just forget it." My gut was starting to ache and I wanted the conversation to be done. I thought about telling him to pull over and let me out on the side of the street, but I knew he wouldn't.

"Is that what you think?" he asked. "That I don't care?"

I rested my head against the cool of the glass window, my anger spent. "I don't think about it much," I mumbled. "Not anymore."

"Don't give me that shit," he snapped. "You take hits at me

all the time. You want me to feel bad about it. Want me to feel like shit for the rest of my life because I wasn't the father you wanted me to be. Well, you know what? I feel bad about it every time I look at you—hell, every time I think about you. But I can't change it now. I can't go back in time and make it right with you." He was out of breath, his chest rising and falling quickly as he slammed the side of his fist against the steering wheel.

The silence stretched on for so long I thought that would be the end of the conversation. When he spoke again his voice sounded hollow, like all the emotion had left him. "Your aunt called me when your sister died. She thought I should know. As soon as I answered the phone, I could tell from her voice that something was wrong. At first I thought she was calling to tell me something had happened to you. When she said that Sylvia had died it was such a relief." He paused, but I knew he wasn't finished. "I felt bad about that later, bad that I was glad it had been her instead of you. But there it is.

"Maybe I'm not any good at showing it, but you're my son, Jaz. I do care about what happens to you. I love you. You're the only good thing I ever accomplished with my life. I hope you know that."

"Yeah, sure," I said, though without much conviction. "Just don't expect me to start calling you Dad." He laughed, like I knew he would, and let me have the last word for once.

CHAPTER TWENTY-NINE

Monday morning, Mom was at the table drinking coffee when I woke up. I went into the kitchen to pour a mug for myself before getting in the shower. I walked right by her on the way to the kitchen without saying anything, and she kept her gaze on the table so we didn't have to make eye contact. As much silence as there had been between us over the past few months it was impossible to break it, like if you did it too suddenly it would shatter whatever comfort was left in the apartment for both of us.

That's why it startled me so much when Mom said, "You got home late last night."

"Working," I said. Chris would never in a million years call her to tell her I had been busted by the cops so I knew she wasn't digging for any dirt.

"Oh. You've been working a lot lately," she said quietly as I moved into the kitchen doorway, one shoulder leaned against the doorjamb. "Thanks for doing the shopping."

"You're welcome," I said with a nod.

"And I know you've been staying on top of keeping the house clean. I appreciate it."

She looked so small, and young, like a little girl with her hair pulled back in a ponytail, her face scrubbed clean of makeup. She sat holding her coffee mug with both hands, as if it were all that was holding her up, or holding her together.

"Were you in a fight?" she asked as her eyes searched my face, as if seeing me for the first time.

"It's nothing," I said, though my face ached more now after a day of healing than it had on Saturday night.

"A girl called for you yesterday," Mom said. "Her name was Raine. She called a couple of times, actually."

"Yeah?" I asked, keeping my voice casual though my heart had started to race at the mention of Raine's name, the heat creeping up my neck as I thought about how I had walked out on her like a coward Saturday night.

"She seemed eager to talk to you," Mom said.

"She was probably just selling something," I said with a shrug.

It wasn't much, her mouth just turning up at the corners so that it was barely perceptible, but it was the first time I had seen Mom crack a smile since Sylvia died. It was like a rainbow or a unicorn in the apartment after so many months of misery.

"I'd better get ready for school," I said, figuring I should end the conversation while we were still on a positive note.

At school I kept to myself, left campus during lunch, mostly to avoid Raine but also not being in the mood to talk to anyone. I made a point of getting to Civics class before Raine and keeping my head down and eyes on my desk so we wouldn't catch each other's eye when she walked into class.

Even with my eyes locked on my desk, I actually felt it when Raine walked into the classroom. The tension between us was like a physical presence as soon as she stepped through the door. She stopped beside my desk, like she was waiting for me to look up at her, but I didn't. Ms. Conroy saved me, asking Raine to take her seat so we could get class started. I felt Raine's eyes on the back of my head throughout class. She never raised her hand or spoke up during class. A first.

As the bell rang to dismiss class I was already out of my seat and heading for the door. I didn't look back to see if Raine tried to catch up with me. In fact, I went straight to the bathroom and stayed in there until I knew the halls were empty, then showed up late for seventh period.

It was late in the fall now and it got dark early. The days were mild, but it got chilly as soon as the sun went down. That night I was back at work and taking a break, sitting on an overturned milk crate out in the alley, my back resting against the brick wall and my eyes closed, when Chris stuck his head out the back door and called my name.

"I'm just taking a quick break," I said.

"Don't get defensive," Chris said. "That girl's here. Looking for you."

"Raine?" I asked as I stood.

"Come on," he said. "Bring her out back to talk to her. She looks like she has people who would get my liquor license yanked if they found her here."

I followed Chris back through the kitchen and into the bar. Raine was waiting, her hands clasped in front of her as she tried to ignore the leers from the guys at the bar.

"What are you doing here?" I asked as I put a hand on her shoulder and steered her toward the kitchen, glancing back at Chris, who was watching us with interest. "This isn't a place for someone like you, Raine. You shouldn't be here," I said in a low voice as I led her through the kitchen and out into the alley.

"I'm sorry," she said. "I tried calling you at home but you're never there. Jordan said I could probably find you here."

As we stepped out into the alley I was conscious of the rancid smell of the Dumpsters—spoiled food and stale beer—and I knew those smells were on me too. My clothes, my hair, the filthy apron I wore over my T-shirt and jeans—everything about me smelled like trash and dirty dishes. I tried to keep my distance from her so she wouldn't notice that the odor of the alley was my smell too.

"What are you doing here?" I asked again.

"Will you get in trouble? Because I'm here?" she asked, and her voice trembled slightly, like she was really afraid.

I laughed a little at that, though she wouldn't understand what was funny. "No," I said with a shake of my head. "I won't get in trouble. You might, though, if your parents find out you're hanging around here."

"Are you mad at me?" she asked.

"No, of course not."

"Are you okay?" she asked. It sounded like she was getting ready to cry, and she quickly bit her lip to keep it from quivering.

"Why are you crying?" I asked.

"It's nothing," she said. She wiped at her nose and sniffled as a fat tear spilled over her lower lid and rolled down her face.

"Seems like something," I said.

"I'm just"—She paused as she thought about what she would say next.—"sorry about what happened Saturday night. It's my fault. I should have known Brian would do something stupid like that."

"It wasn't your fault. I knew what I was getting into when I went outside."

"What do you mean? Are you saying you knew that Brian was planning to kick your ass when you agreed to go outside? You *intentionally* went out and got your ass kicked?" Her voice was rising at the same rate as her frustration.

"I wouldn't say I got my ass kicked exactly. . . ."

She jerked her head in surprise and narrowed her eyes as she waited for me to take it back. I had gotten used to taking things back without being told.

"Okay, I know. I take it back."

She ignored my comment and said, "So, you just left on Saturday? Without talking to me?"

"They didn't really leave me much of a choice," I said, trying to keep my voice neutral.

"What? You think I actually believed Brian?" she asked. "His bullshit about you deciding you were bored and wanted to leave?" She stepped in closer to me and I took a step away, but did it casually, as if I were just shifting my stance. "I went looking for you. Did you walk home?"

As she waited for me to say something, she took another step toward me and I was starting to run out of places to go to avoid her, unless I stepped around her, back toward the kitchen, like we were boxers circling each other before a fight.

"Why are you running away from me?" she asked.

"I'm not running anywhere," I said.

"Yes, you are. You're always running away from me." She was so close to me now that I was afraid to look her right in the eye, and I put my hands on my hips as I tried to regain my cool.

"I should get back to work," I said. "I only get a few minutes for my break."

"Okay," she said. "I just want to ask you one question, and tell you one thing, and then I'll go. Okay?"

"Okay."

"So, I wanted to tell you that I'm not interested in Brian." She waited after she delivered this little bit of news. There was no appropriate response to that, so I just waited for the question that was coming.

After she had let the silence drag on until it got awkward she said, "And my question is, do you like my hair like this?"

"That's your question?" I asked. "You want to know if I like your hair?"

"Uh-huh," she said as she mimicked my stance and put her hands on her hips. "Yes. I want to know. Do you like my hair like this? Or did you like it better when it was pink?"

This was obviously some kind of test. She was asking in that way that girls do when they want to catch you in a lie, make you start fumbling your words and tripping all over yourself. Even though I was a virgin, I had spent my life living with two women. I knew that I would lose either way I played it, so I might as well tell the truth.

"I liked it better pink."

"That's what I thought," she said as the corner of her mouth turned up in a smile. She seemed to be waiting for me to offer something else, but I was still processing what she had said about Brian, the reason why she felt it was so urgent she had to come to find me at work to tell me about it.

"You'd better go," I said. "I'll walk you out."

I walked her back inside and through the bar on the way to her car, ignoring Chris's gaze as it followed us across the room. Out front, when I opened her car door for her, she moved closer to give me a hug.

"Don't," I said as I pulled away. "I'm gross from working."

"I don't care," she said, looking up into my face.

"Well, I do."

"So, are you going to call me or something?" she asked.

"Yeah, I'll call you," I said, looking back over my shoulder so I'd have something to focus on other than her face. She was looking at me in that way she had that made me feel too exposed, like she could read my thoughts.

"You know, because I'm always the one who has to call you, ask you to go places," she said. "You never act like you want to see me."

"What are you talking about?" I asked, and her comment really did surprise me.

"I mean every time we get together, I always have to be the one to ask you out," she said, her voice tightening with frustration. "In fact, every time we've done something together, I was the one to ask you."

Maybe that was true, but it had never occurred to me to ask her to go out and do something. I figured if I asked I'd get laughed at, or hit, or turned down for my trouble.

"Because I'm not going to ask you again," she said as she slid into her car and put the key in the ignition. "You have to ask me. And if you don't, I'll just figure you aren't interested in seeing me. Okay?"

"Sure. Okay," I said with a nod. I said good night quickly and headed back inside, my mind already tripping over the problem of having to figure out how I was going to set up a date with her.

CHAPTER THIRTY

Wednesday night I was lying in bed, still dressed, mostly asleep. It was early, barely eight, and I had just returned from the bus stop, where I met Mom to walk her home. Lately she would call me when she was leaving work and I would walk up to the bus stop, wait for her so she didn't have to walk home through the labyrinth of apartment buildings in the dark by herself. We never spoke much but the silence between us was more comfortable than awkward now.

The phone rang as I lay there in the twilight between awake and asleep, and I rolled out of bed to walk to the kitchen and answer the phone.

"Jason." Mario's mom, her distinctive accent extending my name to three syllables in response to my mumbled hello.

"Yeah," I said, rubbing the sleep from my face. "What's up?"

"You come," was all she said, and cut the connection.

I debated as I pulled on my shoes and jacket whether to knock on Mom's door and tell her where I was going. If she was asleep I didn't want to wake her since she didn't get enough rest lately. Finally I decided it was better to tell her, not make her worry in case she came out and found my bed empty.

I knocked gently on her door, figuring if she didn't answer right away she was asleep and I would leave her be, but she answered my knock with a question.

I opened the door and stood in the light from the hallway. She was sitting up in bed reading, the television off. Without the blue light from the television and her face scrubbed clean of makeup, she looked healthier than she had in a while.

"What's up?" she asked as she put her thumb in the crease of the book and shut it.

"Mario's mom called. Something's wrong. I'm going to walk over."

"I'll come with you," Mom said, already climbing out of bed.

"No. It's okay. I'll call you if it's something."

"I'm coming with you," Mom said as she reached under her bed for her shoes and took a big sweater from the chair to pull on over her yoga pants and T-shirt.

Mom walked behind me, hands buried in the pockets of her sweater, as I followed the familiar path to Mario's house. Even in the dark I knew instinctively where to avoid obstructions in the broken sidewalk, eruptions of concrete created by the roots of trees that struggled against the pavement.

The door was open when we got there, every light on the first floor turned on. I didn't knock, just let myself in as I had a million times before, but as soon as I walked into the house, I could sense the terror, shock, and anger that filled the space I usually regarded as a safe haven. The muffled sounds of water running and tense conversation drew me up the stairs, where there were two small bedrooms and the only bathroom. The scene that greeted us was Mario's mom, holding the crucifix that she always wore around her neck, tapping her teeth against the gold as she hugged herself and rocked from one foot to the other. The door to the girls' room was shut.

"*¿Lo que pasa?*" I asked as I put an arm around Mario's mom's shoulders and hugged her to me.

She just gestured to the bathroom. Mom stepped in to take my place and put her arm around Mario's mom, then guided her into the bedroom to sit on the edge of the bed with her. I could hear Mom's soft voice, soothing, as she tried to comfort Mario's mom, asking what was wrong. I went to find out on my own.

Primo was in the bathroom, sitting on the edge of the tub as he cradled Mario's head in one hand. Mario was lying in the tub, naked but for his boxers, a ropy string of drool trailing from his lower lip. Primo looked up at me as I stepped into the bathroom, and I could see the anguish in his eyes. I said nothing, just sat down on the edge of the tub beside him and put my hand under Mario's head to relieve Primo.

"I don't know what to do," Primo said. "He won't wake up. I found him like this on the doorstep."

I wanted to offer something other than my silence, but there was nothing to say.

"Should we call the ambulance?" he asked.

"I don't know," I said. I lifted the back of Mario's neck in my hand and gave him a shake. "Mario? Wake up, dude."

He didn't respond but I noticed that his eyes had rolled back in his head. His eyelids were open only slits and I could see nothing but the whites of his eyes.

I shook him again. "Wake up, asshole."

He moaned and turned his head to one side, then started to jerk involuntarily, like he was going to throw up.

"Turn the water off," I said to Primo. He complied and I sank into a crouch so that I could support Mario's weight as I encouraged him onto his side. Mario's body started to lurch and I held him by the shoulders, hoping that he would puke and then miraculously return to normal.

My arms were straining to hold up his dead weight, keep his face above the six inches of water in the bottom of the tub. As the water drained I was able to relax him onto the floor of the tub and relieve the aching in my shoulders and biceps. Then Mario started to vomit, the strangling, choking noises frightening me into thinking he might actually suffocate.

Primo handed me a washcloth and I tried to wipe Mario's face clean, but it was no use. His vomit, a seemingly endless supply, came out orange at first, probably a mixer for the booze I smelled on him, the sour odor reminding me of the stink in Bad Habits after a busy night. After a while his vomit turned to a mottled brown, the color of shit. Finally he was just lurching and gagging but there was nothing else to come out.

I heard a sharp intake of breath over my shoulder and looked up to see Mom standing in the doorway. She had one hand over her mouth as if to hold in a sob.

"Maybe get him some milk or something," I said to Mom. "His throat must be burning." I said it as much to get rid of her as I did because I thought a glass of milk might actually help the situation. Mom would be thinking about Sylvia, thinking about Mario's family losing him the way we had lost my sister. Mom was better now, had started to get back into life a little bit. I didn't want this to ruin her small recovery.

Mario's breathing was a ragged wheeze, wetness still gurgling in his throat as he recovered from the vomiting. I had been like that only once before—the first time I ever touched liquor, when I was fourteen. Puked until my insides hurt and my chest and stomach muscles ached, my throat burning. I hadn't been stupid enough to drink myself to that point again.

When Mom had gone I turned on the shower, let the water run cold to pound down on Mario, rinse away the filth of the vomit that was in his hair and covered half his face. He started to shiver and shake with the cold, his lips turning purple. I left the cold water running for a little while longer, hoping he would sit up and start cussing at me.

When he was clean I turned the water to lukewarm and reached into the tub to shake him again. "Mario. Wake up, man. You don't wake up, we're taking you to the hospital. You want to go to the hospital? Get your ass thrown in rehab? Wake the fuck up." Primo said nothing, and I wanted to apologize for the way I spoke to his son. But he seemed to understand, knew that my words came from a place of love rather than anger. He held his breath and waited silently to see if my efforts had any effect.

Mario's forehead wrinkled with a frown, the only response I could get out of him, but at least it was something, showed there was still some kind of emotion functioning within his brain.

Mom came back then with a glass of milk and set it on the side of the tub.

"I think he'll be okay. Go on and stay with his mom," I said to her.

Mom didn't listen to me, just stood there staring at Mario, tears in her eyes.

"Go on," I said, gently but firmly.

Somehow, between the two of us, Primo and I managed to get Mario out of the tub, dry him off, and get him into a clean

pair of boxers and sweats. By then Mario seemed to be somewhat more with it. Could hold his own head up and even drank
some of the milk I offered him.

Primo was still worried that we should take Mario to the
hospital, but I just brushed the idea off when he asked about it.
"Let's put him to bed. If he shows up like this, they'll call the
cops."

Primo murmured in agreement and I could see how con-
flicted he was, wanted to do right by Mario but was worried all
the same what people would think of him if he rolled into the
hospital with his underage son who was clearly drunk and
cashed out. I wasn't even sure what Mario's drug of choice was
these days.

The night had obviously taken its toll on Primo, his face was
haggard looking. "Go to bed," I said. "I'll sit up with him, make
sure he doesn't start puking again."

Together we got Mario into bed and put him to rest on his
side.

Primo insisted on walking Mom home and I was glad for
that. I didn't want to let her go by herself.

The rest of the night I sat up in the chair and watched a
movie on the small television in Mario's room. I stayed awake
long enough to watch two movies, but fell asleep somewhere
near the end of the second one. I woke slumped in the chair,
my arms crossed over my chest and my head hanging forward.
My neck was stiff and sore, but I jerked instantly awake and
looked to the bed, where Mario lay in the exact same position
I had left him. He was breathing deeply, his face slack, making
him look like a little kid.

It was just starting to get light, the birds calling to each
other, as I let myself out of the house and walked home, my

shoulders hunched against the cold morning air. At home I fell into bed to try to catch some more sleep before I had to be up for school.

Mom woke me with an offered cup of coffee about fifteen minutes before the time I would have to leave.

"How's Mario?" she asked.

"Okay," I said as I rubbed the sleep out of my face. "He'll live."

"I've never seen anyone that drunk before," she said as she tugged nervously at her hair. "Or was it something else?"

I shrugged. "Probably a combination. He's been screwing up a lot lately. I don't know what he's using."

"But you—?" she started to say, but I cut her off.

"No. I don't use anything. I barely drink. I hated the way Chris was as much as you did," I said, looking at my coffee instead of her.

She seemed relieved by what I'd said. "That's good. It's good that you think that way. I never could get Chris to . . . Well, anyway, I'm glad you feel that way. Because I worry, you know."

I nodded, though I didn't really know, not like I should know. That she thought about me. Worried about me.

"I love you, Jason," she said. "You have to take care of yourself. I couldn't stand to lose you too." She started to cry. But this time it was okay. Like maybe she was crying for both of us, for me, not just for Syl.

"I know, Ma," I said, and pulled her into a hug. I was going to be late for school. Again. "But you have to take care of yourself too. It's not like I have anyone else either."

"I know," she whispered as she wiped her face with the back of her hand. "I know."

I didn't really want to leave her then, but she had to get to work and I was beyond late now. Seeing Mario that way had freaked her out, but maybe it was a good thing. Like waking from a bad dream and, with some relief, finding the world still as you'd left it.

CHAPTER THIRTY-ONE

Friday after the last bell of the school day I hurried out to the parking lot so I was waiting when Raine got to her car. As she walked across the gravel lot hugging two books to her chest, her backpack full and hanging from both shoulders, I was leaning against her car. I had considered that she might come out walking with one of her friends but was grateful to see she was alone.

Though we had seen each other that week during school, neither one of us had brought up the past Saturday night or our conversation at Bad Habits. I could see from the way she looked at me that she was waiting for me to say something, her unspoken impatience with me hanging between us every time I saw her.

"You bumming a ride?" she asked when she was close enough to speak without raising her voice.

"Maybe," I said as I shut the paperback book I had been trying to read for class while I waited and tucked it into the back pocket of my jeans. "What are you doing tonight?"

She shrugged. "There's a party going on at some guy's house who graduated last year. I told Cheryl I might meet her there. Why?"

"You want to go to 9:30 Club? See a show?"

"What show?" she asked.

"It's a secret," I said. "But I don't want you to get your hopes up. It's not Miley Cyrus."

"It's not One Direction, is it?" she asked as she threw her backpack in the backseat. "I know you love your boy bands."

"I guess you'll just have to come if you want to find out," I said as I leaned my arms on the roof of the car and spoke to her over the top.

"I have the power of the interwebs right in my hand," she said as she held up her phone. "I can just look up who's playing at 9:30 tonight."

"You have no sense of adventure," I said with mock disdain.

"And you are super irritating," she said. "But I suppose I'll go."

We caught the Yellow Line train at Pentagon City so we wouldn't have to change trains to get to U Street. The train was crowded with late commuters and people, like us, headed into town for the evening. Raine and I stood in the middle of the train car, between the sliding doors that opened on both sides of the train.

"What are you thinking about?" Raine asked me.

"I don't know," I said, caught off guard by her question since I had been thinking about her in that way. I could think of a hundred lies to tell her that would make her roll her eyes at me, another hundred that would make her blush, but I let them all go. I gave her the only answer I could that I knew would stop her from asking anything else. "Sylvia," I said. I pushed off from the wall as the train slowed in approach to our stop. "I was thinking about Sylvia."

At the U Street station we walked toward the Vermont Avenue exit and headed north. It was only a few blocks to the 9:30 Club and there were crowds of people heading in the same direction we were walking.

We fell into line behind a large crowd of people at the club entrance and waited to get to the security checkpoint. Ahmed was there, checking the IDs and tickets of the people waiting in line, beside him Darian, the other security guy who worked weekends. They both worked construction jobs during the week so their already intimidating size, over six feet tall, was compounded by their muscular builds and strong, thick hands.

Raine saw the name of the band over the ticket booth and drew in a sharp breath. "I love Thievery Corporation," she said in a whisper.

"It's not Hannah Montana," I said casually, not letting on how pleased I was that she loved the surprise I was able to give her, "but they're a pretty good band."

"I think I might pee myself," she said.

And then we were standing in front of Darian and Ahmed.

"Oh shit," Darian said when he saw me. "Did you know about this?" he asked Ahmed.

"I did," Ahmed said. "He asked me if it was all right."

"How you doing, Jaz?" Darian asked as his face split into an easy smile. "Man, you got big. I do think I'd have trouble kicking your ass now."

"Hey, Darian. Ahmed," I said by way of greeting. "This is my friend Raine."

"Mm-hm," Ahmed said as he waved us to the side so he could check the IDs of the next people in line. "She's too pretty for you."

"He said 'friend,'" Darian said. "He just told you, he already knows she's too pretty for him."

I knew I was going to have to withstand a certain amount of teasing when I showed up. It was the cost of admission. Maybe I'll admit that I liked showing up with a girl as pretty as Raine on my arm. Even if she wasn't really my girlfriend, Darian and Ahmed didn't know that, and I didn't correct their assumption about it.

Ahmed got in the last word, though his concentration had already turned to checking the ID of the next person in line. "You stay out of trouble, Jaz, or I'll turn you over my knee. You hear?"

"You hear that, boy?" Darian asked as his grin widened, his voice so deep, you could feel the vibration of it through the air between us. "You gonna get spanked." He slapped the back of his hand against his palm as he said this but was laughing, which I took for a good sign.

"Hey, thanks, guys," I said as I put my hands on Raine's shoulders and steered her toward the door. "Next time I go out with a girl I'll just bring you guys along to seal the deal, yeah?"

Darian and Ahmed broke up at my comment, their laughs high pitched and almost girlish. They were so preoccupied with their joke at my expense they didn't pay any attention as we walked past them and into the club.

There were two opening bands that played short sets. Neither of the bands were ones I had heard of, local acts who were riding the coattails of Thievery Corporation's fame. Thievery was a D.C. band, started out of Eighteenth Street Lounge, a club near Dupont Circle. They had a huge following but would still play a venue like 9:30 because it was a D.C. institution—like the Smithsonian museums or Ben's Chili Bowl.

I was still feeling a little nervous around Raine but once the headliners came on, we melted into the crush of people near the stage and I forgot to worry about it.

It was impossible to keep from bumping into people or getting your feet stepped on with everyone crowding the dance floor, but I loved it. I loved the energy of the people around us and it felt good to dance. We were caught up in the movement of the crowd, and even though other dancers would bounce off us and sometimes a drunk person would stagger and force the crowd to shift, it was like we were all together in the same happy place.

I stayed right next to Raine and used my size to carve out a space for us, but we danced with the same energy and enthusiasm as everyone else. She was totally into it and I could hear her singing along to the songs.

I was breathless and tired at the end of their first set and we retreated with everyone else, to get a drink and use the bathroom during the break. Raine and I separated while she waited in the long line to use the women's bathroom.

When I got back upstairs with our drinks Raine was standing against the wall outside the bathrooms. For that brief moment before she noticed me, when I could watch her face without her knowing I was watching, I could see her uncertainty, her feeling of self-consciousness about standing there alone. As guys walked by, they took notice of her, the way guys can't help but take notice when a beautiful girl is in their midst. With her hands clasped in front of her, her shoulders slightly hunched, she tried to make herself smaller than her tall frame would allow.

As I got close to her she finally noticed me, and her face beamed with such genuine gladness to see me that my heart did a stutter step in my chest.

The second set was even better than the first and I was glad Raine was the kind of person who would stay on the dance floor the whole time, not hang around the back putting down drinks and holding up the wall.

During the encore I started out dancing but after a minute was more interested in watching Raine dance. I was standing just behind her, and the way she was moving, rocking that body, with curves in places that a guy my age could only dream about because only women in their twenties and thirties had bodies like that. There was no conscious thought involved, but I was instantly hard and experienced a twinge of guilt about it. It wasn't as if I wanted to think about her in that way, but sometimes it was impossible for me not to.

The song ended and she turned around, caught me watching her. "What's the matter?" she asked, her face flushed, a glow of sweat across her face and chest. She wiped at the sweat above her upper lip.

"Nothing's the matter," I said, my voice raised so she could hear me over the announcer, now talking into the mic.

"You weren't dancing," she said, leaning in slightly so I didn't have to shout.

I was so hard by then that my groin ached, and I put my hand on the back of her neck, pulling her in so I could smell the sweat in her hair, and kissed her. Not on the lips or anything, but just let my lips graze her forehead. I put a hand on her arm to keep her from stepping into a hug. I was afraid she would press herself into me and feel that I was such a complete pervert that just watching her dance had given me an erection. Like middle school all over again.

She leaned in, her breath hot on my neck, and kissed the side of my throat. Which definitely didn't help. I almost passed out from all the blood rushing to my crotch.

The overhead lights came on then with an audible pop and people started to file past us on their way to the exit or toward the side of the stage, hoping the band would come out to sign autographs or something. If the lights hadn't come on then, if people hadn't started moving around us as we stood motionless on the dance floor, if I hadn't been so overwhelmed by the confusing flood of emotions I had every time I was around Raine, I probably would have kissed her.

I thought about it for the entire walk back to the Metro station, kept thinking I would grab her hand and pull her into one of the darkened doorways of the shops and houses we passed along the way. I would pull her into my arms and kiss her and . . . what? Tell her . . . something. Tell her I thought about her all the time, and not just because she was beautiful and sexy but also because she got my jokes and didn't put up with any of my shit and had a ton of sass. She would probably think I was crazy. And next summer, she would be gearing up to leave for college at some Ivy League school and I would be working full-time washing dishes and hauling trash for Chris. She would be planning a career as a doctor or a lawyer and I'd be making seventy-five cents above minimum wage.

I hadn't even kissed her yet but I already knew how this love story ended. It ended the way my life had begun—an accident, somebody else's mistake.

CHAPTER THIRTY-TWO

We stood on the Metro platform waiting for a train without speaking much. Raine kept staring off into space, obviously lost in thought. She held my hand as we stepped onto the train and stood closer to me than she usually did.

When the train reached our home station we still hadn't said more than a few words to each other. The air between us was charged with an electric current I could feel in the core of my body. It was like we were both thinking the same thing, that we wanted to touch each other or kiss, but neither one of us knew how to just suddenly start touching each other in a familiar way. I kept my distance, was worried maybe I had read the whole thing wrong and she would just push me away.

Once we were in her car she finally spoke. "You want to go back to my place? Hang out for a bit?" she asked.

"Your parents won't freak out?" I asked.

"They aren't home. They went away for the weekend."

"Oh," I said, now feeling more uncomfortable than ever. I didn't really trust myself to be alone with Raine, but I didn't want to let her just drop me off, didn't want to be away from her. "Sure, that's cool," I finally managed to say.

At her house she got drinks for us and led me to her room. I wasn't sure if her brother was home, or if he would care that I was there. If Syl had ever brought a guy back to our apartment when my mom was out I would have told him to keep his hands to himself and for her to leave her bedroom door open. Maybe Raine's brother wasn't protective of his sister in that way, but I didn't want to find out.

She shut her bedroom door behind us and docked her iPhone before kicking off her shoes and flopping onto the bed. Her room was a mess, which was totally unexpected. There were piles of clothes everywhere and books and papers scattered around. The bed wasn't made and there were more clothes and a notebook tangled in the sheets.

"I know," she said as she noticed me noticing the state of her room. "It's a mess. Sorry."

"How old is that piece of pizza?" I asked with a nod toward a plate that was half-hidden by a book on her desk.

She glanced over her shoulder at the desk but looked back at me before saying, "Why? You hungry?"

"No," I said with a meaningful glance around her room. "This was . . . unexpected. I thought you'd have a perfectly neat room. Pink, frilly bed. Maybe a Hannah Montana poster or two . . ."

She cracked a smile at that. "You just going to stand in the middle of the room talking about what a mess it is?" She patted the space on the mattress beside her, inviting me to sit down.

Fighting the urge to clear my throat, I set my glass down

on a pile of papers on the bedside table and sat down on the bed, leaving two feet of space between us. She raised one eyebrow slightly but didn't comment.

Then we started talking again, falling into conversation that was natural and easy, the way it had been when we still hated each other. It had always been easier for me to talk to her when I knew she hated me, didn't wonder whether she was judging every word that came out of my mouth. We talked about the show, the shows we wished we could see, as she lay back and stared at the ceiling. I was tired, so after a while I did the same, my arms folded behind my head as a pillow.

Almost as soon as I lay back she rolled onto her side and scooted closer to me. It startled me when she rested her head on my chest, just below my shoulder, and my heart started to pound against my breastbone. I put my arm down so that it lay against her back but didn't curl my arm around her, so she could pull away easily if she wanted to. I wondered if she was a virgin or if I wasn't the first guy to see the inside of her room when her parents were out of town. My mind was so busy I forgot to say anything for a while and she lifted onto her elbow to look into my face.

"Thanks for taking me to the show tonight, Jason."

"You're welcome," I said.

"I'm going to kiss you," she said, her eyes searching my face as she said it. "Okay?"

"Okay," I said, my voice coming out as a hoarse whisper.

She struggled a little to pull her face level with mine, and we made a few awkward false starts as she tried to find a place to put her arm so that it wasn't in the way and she could reach her lips to mine. We both laughed a little nervously but then she was kissing me and I was forgetting to breathe and my chest started to feel tight from lack of oxygen and the stress of knowing that I was crazy about this girl. It was a feeling I had been fighting for a while and suddenly here she was, in my arms, feeling soft and warm and smelling like the night air and some kind of earthy lotion. Within a couple of minutes I rolled onto my side and let her fall back against my arm so I could press my body against hers. She let out a soft little moan and I almost lost control of my bladder, realizing that I had to pee, but not wanting to pull away from her for anything.

We kissed for a while and she was rubbing her hand through my hair, then trailed her fingers down my arm, making me shiver involuntarily. Then I really did have to pee and I pulled back from her and sat up.

"Where's your bathroom?" I asked.

When I returned she was sitting up in bed, looking at the notebook that had been tangled in the sheets.

"What are you reading?" I asked, this time going straight back to sit on the bed beside her.

"My journal. I try to practice writing. You know, in a place that no one else will see, so I don't have to feel self-conscious about it."

"Oh," I said as I leaned back on the pillows and covered my eyes with my forearm.

"You tired?" she asked.

"Sort of. Just . . . thinking."

"You think too much," she said as she tossed her notebook onto the end of the bed and leaned over to rest against my chest. I put my arm around her and rubbed her arm, but didn't try to kiss her again.

"You can stay over if you want," she said. "But I'm not going to sleep with you."

"You want me to sleep in the guest room or something?" I asked.

"I don't mean that. I mean I'm not going to *sleep* with you."

I opened one eye to look at her, her head resting against my shoulder as she looked up into my face.

"What makes you think I would sleep with you?" I asked.

"You're a guy."

"So? Doesn't mean I'm easy."

She huffed out a laugh and shifted her head against my shoulder. "If you must know, I haven't slept with anyone. An honest-to-God virgin. I know that makes me like a unicorn, but I'm just not ready to go there."

"I'm a virgin too," I said.

"Really?" she asked, pushing herself up onto her elbow, her voice rising with disbelief.

"Really."

"Madison said . . . well . . ." She stopped and her hand drifted up to stroke the lock of hair she always favored, just behind her left ear, tugging on it nervously.

"Madison doesn't know shit."

"Yeah," she said, and sank back to rest her head on my shoulder again. "Yeah, I know. But Alexis . . . well, she made it sound like you guys were sleeping together."

"You worry too much about what other people say," I said as I turned to drop a kiss on her forehead. "If I was going to sleep with a girl it would be you, Raine. But I'm not going to go there. You've got everything going for you. You don't need to fuck it all up."

She didn't respond to that—or if she did, I didn't notice, because I must have dozed off shortly after that. I woke in the middle of the night, and Raine was still close to me, her arm folded against my chest, her head tucked up against my shoulder and our bodies tangled together for warmth like puppies sleeping in a litter. As I rolled onto my side so I was facing her, she murmured softly, half awake. I kissed her on the forehead and she snuggled in closer to me without waking up completely.

CHAPTER THIRTY-THREE

That was the beginning for us, for Raine and me. After that we became something like boyfriend and girlfriend—spent every free moment we had together even if at school we mostly still acted like strangers. We spent the golden hours between school and her parents getting home from work lying in bed talking, listening to music, or making out. We never brought up what would happen at the end of senior year, where we would be or go. We just lived in the moments we spent together. Every thought or experience I had didn't become real until I told Raine about it. Every new song or band I heard that I liked was irrelevant until I could share it with Raine.

Love, some people would call it. But we didn't call it anything. I never said I loved her. I didn't say it because those words were someone else's, not mine. I didn't say it, because anyone can say it and not mean it. I didn't say it, because saying it would make it harder when I had to let her go.

And Raine seemed to get all that. She seemed to get me. And with Mario and Sylvia gone, that made her unique.

•   •   •

The following week I got to work one night at the bar and found
Jordie there waiting for me. He was perched awkwardly on a
barstool, unconsciously twisting from side to side as he watched
the television suspended over the shelves of liquor bottles. Chris
was in his usual position, reading the paper with one elbow
rested on the rail of the bar.

"What's up?" I asked Jordie, giving him a chin thrust. Chris
didn't even look up to say hello.

"Hey," Jordie said, his voice quiet and apologetic. We hadn't
spoken since the cotillion, had gone out of our way to avoid
each other at school. With soccer season over, we had no reason
to see each other unless we made a point of it.

"Come on back," I said with a nod toward the kitchen. Chris
dragged his eyes from the paper for a lazy glance in my direction but didn't say anything.

"What's up?" I asked again as we walked through the
kitchen and I hung my jacket on the peg near the back door. I
didn't clock in. Would wait until I actually started doing any
work so I didn't have to hear anything from Chris about me
being a slacker.

Jordie shrugged and kept his gaze fixed on the floor. "I figured you and I needed to have words. Clear the air," he said.

"Yeah?" I asked. "About what?"

He scowled, his lips pursed, then said, "Goddamnit, Jaz.
Don't make it fucking difficult. You know about what."

I bit off an angry retort, didn't want to give him the
opener. I wasn't going to make it easy for him. While it was
true I didn't fault him for what had happened with Brian, for
him not having my back, I still didn't feel like just letting him
off the hook.

"You seen Chick lately?" I asked, diverting the conversation so abruptly that it startled him.

"No," Jordie said, and the weight of our discomfort with each other was lifted for a moment as we turned to safer topics.

"I'm worried about him," I said as I spun the knob that would drain the dishwasher and fill it with fresh hot water and detergent. "He came by the other day when I wasn't home. Mom said he didn't look so good. He's been missing school a lot lately. I thought maybe it was just because it was getting cold out, you know, as sick as he gets." I didn't finish the thought. Jordie would know what I meant. Once the weather turned cold Chick would miss more school than most other people. I hated to admit to myself or anyone else that I had been so preoccupied lately with spending time with Raine and working that I had forgotten to worry about Chick or Mario or Jordie much. If I was being completely honest, I hadn't really thought about them at all. I hadn't even been by to see Primo and Mario's mom, which I had promised I would do, even if Mario and I weren't speaking.

"I haven't seen him," Jordie said, and I took a moment to check my gut for anger with Jordie about that. But there wasn't any anger. I understood it. He was completely absorbed with Cheryl now, his social life and what he had going on with her. I was the same with Raine.

It bothered me sometimes, that I forgot to think about Chick and Mario in my preoccupation with Raine and trying to spend every free moment I had with her, but unlike Jordie, I would never forgive myself for it completely.

"I don't think he's doing so hot," I said. "We should go by and see him."

Jordie didn't say anything and kept his gaze fixed on his

shoes. He didn't want to go looking after Chick, but didn't feel comfortable saying it. "I came by because I wanted to talk to you about what happened at the cotillion," Jordie said, deciding it was easier to talk about the rift that already existed between us than open a new one by saying he didn't really have an interest in going to look after Chick.

"Go on then. Talk," I said as I turned my back to him and started rinsing plates before setting them in the hard rubber rack. "I have nothing to say about it."

There was a long pause while he decided what to say, the way sometimes even if you've already rehearsed in your mind what you plan to say, you can't really figure out a good way to start. "I didn't know Brian and his buddies were going to take you down like that," Jordie said, his words coming out in a rush. "I mean, I knew Brian had it out for you, knew he was going to talk to you about staying away from Raine, but I didn't think they would jump you like that."

"Really?" I asked. "You'd think if Brian just wanted to talk to me, he would have pulled me aside, one-on-one. Wouldn't need to bring five of his buddies just to talk to me."

Jordie grimaced slightly as his eyes searched the water-stained ceiling tiles. "Yeah, okay," he said. "But you have a reputation. It just made sense that he would want some backup. Just in case."

"So, why are you here?" I asked.

"To apologize, I guess," Jordie said. "To say I'm sorry I didn't have your back."

"You guess? Or you're actually apologizing?" I asked.

"Stop being a dick," he said, narrowing his eyes and cutting a glance in my direction. "I'm apologizing. I'm sorry. I should have stepped in or warned you or something."

"I knew what I was getting into when I showed up at that damn place," I said. "I willingly went outside and got my ass kicked. I didn't expect you, expect anyone, to have my back."

"Yeah," Jordie said with a sigh. "Yeah. Maybe that's the problem."

There was nothing I could say to that, so I kept my mouth shut. When Jordie left, it was on good terms, but somehow I felt more uncertain than ever about what, if anything, still bound us together as friends. As I made my way through the never-ending pile of dishes, I tried to find the part inside me that had ever felt anything about my closest friends.

CHAPTER THIRTY-FOUR

It was a Wednesday when I was pulled out of class during first period by a bored-looking student aide who came with a yellow hall pass from the office. Later I would remember thinking that Wednesday was a strange day for everything to go down. A Friday, or even a Monday, would have seemed more appropriate, but there it was, right in the middle of the week. It wasn't an exceptional week in any way—the weather was bad, but not bad enough to get us out of school for a day and so not really noteworthy.

Jordie and Mario were already in the office along with Jordie's dad and Mario's mom. It was never made clear if they didn't bother to call my mom or if she couldn't come. I never asked.

Jordie looked uncomfortable, Mario indifferent. Most likely Mario was stoned but I didn't bother studying his condition. Mr. Clemons, the guidance counselor, offered me a chair, but I just leaned against the wall and retreated into the background.

Mr. Clemons kept clearing his throat and stumbling over his speech, obviously out of his depth when it came to providing any actual guidance or counseling. "I . . . uh . . . hate to . . . well, that is . . . you see . . ." He went on like this for an almost incomprehensible amount of time. I shifted my stance against the wall, ready to shout at him or give him a good slap across the face to knock it out of him. My movement seemed to shock him out of his stammer and he delivered the news bluntly, without censoring for the impact.

"Walter Gunderson is dead," he said, followed by a loud gulp as he swallowed his own saliva.

"Who's Walter Gunderson?" the Colonel asked, his brow wrinkled in a frown.

"It's Chick, Dad," Jordie said quietly, his head down, eyes on his lap.

Probably texting his girlfriend about it, was the thought that ran through my head as I studied Jordie's reaction.

"*Madre de Dios,*" Mario's mother said as she crossed herself and covered her mouth with her hand.

"What happened?" the Colonel asked.

"He . . . uh . . . ," Mr. Clemons was back to fumbling. "It was suicide apparently."

"Well, the kid was a little off, right?" the Colonel asked as he glanced around at the rest of us for agreement. "I mean, it's tragic, but it's not like he came from a stable family. And they were poor, right?"

Jesus wept. Here was the Colonel, looking to all of us to agree that no one had been expecting Chick's life to amount to anything anyway. Suicide, prison, drug overdose, whatever— the kid had it coming.

"Where?" I asked.

"What?" Mr. Clemons asked stupidly, still processing the Colonel's reaction.

"Where did he do it?" I asked. "How did he kill himself?"

"I don't really think it's best for you boys to know all the details," Mr. Clemons said, his eyes on his desk blotter.

"I didn't ask you what you think," I said quietly. "I asked you what you know."

Mr. Clemons sighed and fidgeted with the folded glasses on his desk. "I guess I won't be telling you anything you can't hear on the news or learn on the Internet," Mr. Clemons said. "He hung himself from a tree in the park. A jogger found him early this morning."

I left then. Just walked out and didn't wait to see if anyone cared.

Poor Chick. Poor dumb, stupid Chick.

I stayed down at the park for almost an hour, sitting along the bank just upstream from the rocks where we had spent many nights drinking cheap beer or making out with the girls we brought to the park with us. Of course, Chick never got lucky. Before that moment it had never occurred to me to wonder what he did with himself when the three of us paired off with girls at the park.

A jogger. Always goddamn joggers discovering dead bodies.

It was bitterly cold and I thought about Chick down here alone in the dark, freezing in his inadequate winter coat as he climbed a tree to hang himself. As I sat there I knew why Chick had come to this place for his last moments. He came here to be at a place where he could remember what it felt like to be loved, to be part of something.

After a while I was near frozen, would end up being the second dead boy they found in two days' time if I didn't get up and move. My cheeks and ears ached from the cold as I walked to Bad Habits—stumbled there is more like it. Chris was at the bar, grinning and talking shit to a few guys there for an early happy hour when I blew in through the front door on a frigid blast of air.

When he saw my face his smile faded, and he came around from behind the bar to meet me. "What is it?" he asked, his voice sounding almost angry, but I knew he wasn't angry with me.

"I killed him," I said through chattering teeth as Chris put his arms around me to hold me up.

"Jesus, kid, you're freezing," he said, his own voice trembling now.

"I killed him," I said again, this time coming out as a cry that broke on a sob.

When I woke on the battered leather couch in Chris's office I couldn't remember anything that had happened after I left the park. I was covered in a thin blanket that was scratchy against the bare skin of my arm, and my head rested on my balled-up jacket. For a disorienting moment I couldn't remember where I was, but then I saw the neat rows of liquor bottles along the wall.

"Hey, kid," Chris said as I sat up and rubbed the back of my neck, which had knotted while I slept in an awkward position.

"Hey," I said quietly, my voice still thick with sleep. Chris sat behind his desk, a pair of reading glasses perched on his nose. He looked suddenly like an old man, though I usually thought of him as being not much older than I was.

"Man, you about scared the shit out of me," Chris said with a chuckle as he removed the glasses and tossed them on the desk. He rubbed at the hair on the back of his head, almost a parody of my own gesture. It was the first time I ever noticed that he and I had very similar mannerisms, looked an awful lot alike, in fact.

"You were going on about somebody you killed. Shit, I thought I was going to have to hide you from the cops," he said with a shake of his head. "Thought you had really killed someone."

"How do you know I didn't?" I asked.

"Because you're not half as tough as you think you are." He paused to let that sink in. Then he said, "And because Jordan stopped by, looking for you. He told me about Chick."

"Yeah?" I asked, and sat back on the couch as my gut started its familiar ache. "What did you tell Jordie?"

"Told him I hadn't seen you in a few days," Chris said.

I nodded but didn't thank him.

"You gonna tell me what the hell is going on?" he asked when it became obvious I wasn't going to volunteer anything else.

"Chick killed himself. Jordan told you."

"Yeah. He told me. You think it's somehow your fault?" he asked. "You said *you* killed him."

"Not just *my* fault," I mumbled, feeling self-conscious now that the initial tidal wave of emotion had passed. "Jordan and Mario's too. But yeah, we killed him, just as sure as if we had tied the rope and thrown it over the branch for him ourselves."

"Jaz, people don't do something like that unless they're sick. Sick in a way that there's nothing you could have done to help. Sick in a way maybe nobody can fix. It may seem like something you did made Chick really unhappy, but that's just a symptom." He paused but shifted uncomfortably in his seat, so I knew he had more to say. "I've been thinking, you know, about some of the things you said. About how things are between us. I'm lucky. Lucky that your mom stepped up to be a good parent to you while I was still fucking up in general. Your mom is a good person, but . . . well, she and I were already on the outs when she found out she was pregnant with you. I think maybe we both thought it would change things—having a baby, I mean. That it would somehow make us love each other. But it never did."

I couldn't escape his gaze as I looked around the room, refusing to meet his eye.

"So, I was thinking," he went on, looking more uncomfortable than I had ever seen him. "Maybe you'd . . . uh . . . want to come and stay with me for a while. I'm not promising anything," he said as he held up one hand, "but you can have my extra bedroom. I'm too old to change anything about my lifestyle so if you're expecting anything resembling a responsible male role model, you'll be shit out of luck."

"Wow," I said. "Well, when you put it like that, it sounds really appealing."

"Yeah, well," he said with a shrug but smiled.

"I'll think about it," I said. "I'm not sure I can leave Mom right now. Anyway, she's better now."

"The devil you know . . . ," Chris said with a nod as he fidgeted with his reading glasses, folding and turning them this way and that on the scarred wooden desk, cast off from some respectable office years ago.

"If I really had killed someone, is that what you would have done—hidden me from the cops?" I asked curiously.

"Yeah, sure," he said with another laugh. "See what I mean? Role model."

"Is it dinnertime?" I asked.

Chris shook his head. "Long past. Why don't you rest a little while longer? I'll get Carmen to fix us a couple of burgers."

"Yeah, okay," I said as I lay back on the jacket again, shoving it up under my head and shoulders to form a better pillow.

Chris stopped in the open doorway and turned back to me to say, "When you were crying earlier, you called me Dad, you know that? First time you called me Dad since you were a little bitty thing."

"Huh," I said as I stared at the exposed pipes in the ceiling.

CHAPTER THIRTY-FIVE

Chris drove me to Chick's wake at the funeral home. He hadn't come to Sylvia's funeral, because Mom would have freaked out if he had tried, but I was glad to have him with me, glad that I wouldn't have to face Chick's dad alone.

The service was held in a room with no chairs, no decoration other than a wooden cross on the wall, and Chick's casket, which was draped with his soccer jersey and seemed only big enough to hold a child.

Chris wore a sport coat with slacks and a tie and repeatedly ran his fingers inside the collar of his shirt, as if it choked him. It was the first time I had seen him in anything other than jeans and a T-shirt. I wore the funeral/cotillion suit again, deciding to myself as I stood there that I would burn it at the first opportunity.

Raine showed up at the funeral home in a simple black wool dress with pearls, her hair pulled into a knot at the nape of her neck. A tendril of hair strayed from the bun and curled against the side of her neck and I found myself feeling turned on as I looked at that lock of hair while she stood talking to Jordie and his mom. It was a strange sensation, being slightly aroused as I stood in the funeral home with Chick's corpse only a few feet from us. Maybe death had that effect on the living—somehow made you feel more alive.

Raine and I had hardly spoken at all since the news of Chick's death. Not that I didn't see her—just when I did, we said nothing, because there was nothing to say. I couldn't tell her how I felt, because I didn't know. My thoughts were so confused and twisted about, they paced the length of my brain like a man too angry or heartbroken to do anything but pull his hair and punch at walls.

When Raine finally broke away from her conversation with Jordie she came to stand beside me, her arm touching mine. I said hello to her and she didn't answer, just put her arms around me to give me a hug. After a few seconds, when it was clear she wasn't just going to give me a brief squeeze and step away, I put my arms around her and buried my face in her neck.

She told me she loved me, that she was worried about me, that I didn't have to say anything. I kept my face buried in her neck until the threat of tears passed and the lump in my throat shrank. After that, Raine didn't leave my side, kept her fingers twined through mine the whole time.

Chris stood against one wall, alone and talking to no one, his meaty wrists and large hands out of sync with his tweed sport coat, and I wondered if he had purchased the jacket new for the funeral.

A couple of teachers from school showed up at the funeral home. They looked uncomfortable and spoke only briefly to

Chick's dad, who was like a sleepwalker, his clothes disheveled and his hair standing up in places. Raine kept the few visitors in conversation until the forty-five minutes passed and it was time to move the casket to the graveyard. Chris, Jordie, Chick's dad, and I acted as pallbearers and carried Chick's casket from the wheeled carrier to the hearse. The casket was so light I probably could have carried it myself.

It still bothered me, this idea of carrying the weight of a dead body. But now that it wasn't Sylvia's body, I could handle it, not freak out entirely. And since I still felt somewhat responsible for Chick's death, this was a burden I didn't feel like I could leave to the care of someone else. Looking after Chick had been my responsibility.

Only four cars made up the caravan to the cemetery, and a slow drizzle started to fall on our way there. I drove Raine's car and she held my hand the whole time, squeezed it so that it almost hurt as we rolled through the rain.

"You okay?" she asked me. In answer I only nodded and slid my hand onto her thigh and gripped the flesh of the inside of her leg, just above her knee. She rubbed the back of my hand and wiped at her eyes as she stared out at the rain.

At the cemetery I recognized Mario's dad's car alone in the parking lot. As I put the car in park I watched Mario climb out of the driver's seat and stand at the side of his father's car.

"What the hell is he doing here?" I asked as I watched him in the rearview mirror.

"Just don't worry about it," Raine said as she rubbed my hand with more force. "Come on."

Gravel crunched under our shoes as we followed a path under the trees to where a tent had been raised beside a new scar in the earth. When I looked back over my shoulder, Mario was about a hundred yards behind us, walking with his head bent against the drizzle.

I stopped in my tracks, Raine tugging gently at my arm. The others were already clustered around the grave but I waited for Mario to catch up with us. His pace slowed but since his only other option was to turn back, he came on. When he was within a few feet of us I said, "You're not welcome here."

"I came to say good-bye to him. Same as you," Mario said, his chin thrust out defiantly, his words sounding rehearsed. "He was my friend too."

"You've got no friends here," I said, "dead or alive. You didn't care what happened to him."

"Jasz," Chris said as he came walking over to us. "Let it be." He came straight for me and gripped me by the upper arms, directing me away from Mario and the pathway.

"Get out of the way!" I yelled, but Chris just stood still, his face drawn and sad, and blocked me. Chris turned to look over his shoulder at Mario and Raine and said, "Go on. Both of you. We'll be there in a minute."

Raine and Mario turned and walked toward the small tent over the gravesite as Chris kept his hands on my arms, waiting until the others were out of earshot.

"We killed him," I said to Chris as I started to cry again. There was a seemingly endless supply of tears and snot in my head.

"I know," Chris said. "I know."

"Everybody leaves," I said, my voice a high whine as I tried to hold back the flood that was coming.

"I'm right here, man," Chris said as he put his arms around my shoulders. I cried for all the shame and embarrassment I had ever seen in Chick's eyes, for the sister I had lost without ever knowing what she had really meant to me, and for the friendship I had always imagined between Mario and Jordie and me that wasn't really there. I cried for the kid who had spent too many Saturday afternoons watching out the window and waiting for the dad who never came to see him, and for the boy who would be left behind when Raine went on with the rest of her life. All of these things that were latent under my skin, that filled my head with worry at night and haunted my walking dreams, I let them take over my body, rise to the surface like bubbles that broke on sobs.

It was a full five minutes before I pulled myself together enough to join the others at the grave. They were all waiting when Chris and I got there, he with one hand on my shoulder.

The priest didn't talk for very long. I got the sense he was a little uncomfortable. The only people there were Mario, Jordie, Raine, Chris, Chick's dad, and me. The priest called Chick Walter, so it wasn't even like he was really talking about the person we knew. I had never called him Walter in my life. Chick's dad stood with his hands clasped in front of him, swaying back and forth like he was rocking a baby in his arms. At first it didn't even really seem like he knew what was going on but when the priest picked up a handful of dirt to throw on the casket Chick's dad started to whimper, then sob.

We all kept our heads down and tried to let Chick's dad grieve privately, but Chris stepped over to him and put an arm around his shoulder. He whispered words of comfort we couldn't hear as Chick's dad wept openly, like a child, which, in a way, he was. Chris looked sick, like his stomach was tied up in knots and he might cry too.

When the priest finished he held his prayer book against

his chest and watched Chick's dad. I wanted to shout at the priest, ask him what he was there for if he couldn't even offer comfort. Instead I stepped up to Chick's casket and put a hand on the smooth wood, slick and cold from the rain. "See you around, Chick," I said, then turned and walked away.

Chris blocked my path and put both arms around me to hug me tight. I could feel him trembling and I had a sudden vision of my mom standing beside Sylvia's casket and was relieved to find that there was at least one other person, perhaps two counting Raine, who would weep at my funeral if it ever came to that.

"Come by and see me later," Chris said as I broke the hug first and walked away before anyone could see that my face was twisted with grief.

Raine caught up with me when I was almost to her car. "You okay?" she asked as she slid her arm under mine.

"I think I'm going to throw up," I said.

And then I did.

CHAPTER THIRTY-SIX

Raine dropped me at the apartment, but instead of going inside I walked down to the park, my hands crammed in my pockets for warmth. I was still wearing the funeral suit, and by the time I got to the hidden footpath through the woods wished I had changed into jeans and a hoodie. But I didn't feel like turning back. Didn't want to face the probing worry of Mom's glances, didn't want to see the reminders of Sylvia in the apartment.

When I reached the split in the stream I stepped across three rocks, the path to the island of boulders so familiar I could have done it in my sleep. There were a few beers stashed in the hiding place and I sat on the cold rock sipping a beer I didn't really want.

The movement of the water had lulled me into a trance as I sat and thought about Chick, him down at the park, cold and alone. His ghost still lingered in this place, probably would forever. It would have been dishonest to say that I really missed Chick. We hadn't paid much attention to him when he was around. But Chick represented something lost to all of us, and I wasn't sure we could get it back.

Mario came then, on his own, in a black leather jacket and a knit hat. He carried a brown paper bag under one arm, heavy enough that it upset his balance as he walked along the narrow path.

Mario finished the jump to our boulder and set the bag down behind me. I wanted to yell at him some more, but somehow the words didn't come. He busied himself with opening the bag, cracked a beer for each of us, then settled in to sit beside me. The space available on the boulder didn't leave him room to sit far away from me. We sat with our shoulders almost touching and I didn't pull away.

"It's cold as shit," Mario said to end the silence.

"He must have been cold," I said, my voice breaking on a tremble. "That's all I can think about. How cold he must have been."

"Stop thinking about it," Mario said. "He's not cold now."

"He came by the house," I said, determined to beat myself up. "Mom said he came by looking for me two days before he died. I was out with Raine. Maybe if I had been there. Maybe if I had stopped by to see him instead of just blowing it off."

"Don't go down that path," Mario said, almost angrily. "There's no point thinking how it could have been different. It will just make you crazy. Make me crazy too."

"I didn't think I could feel any more alone than I did after Sylvia died," I said as I blew out a sigh and shifted on my butt, now numb with cold. "I was wrong."

"You're not alone. You have Raine and Chris and me. Sort of. And Primo misses you," Mario said. "He always did like you better."

"That's because I'm not a fuckup like you," I said.

"Yeah, well," he said, letting the insult roll off him like rain, "you should come by and see them. Mama's worried about you."

Mario was looking at me but I was watching the trail, Jordie's familiar form approaching through the woods.

"Well, this ought to be awkward," Mario said under his breath.

And he was right.

We were all silent as Jordie made his way across the rocks to us. No one called out a hello or even looked at one another. Jordie stood above us on the edge of the boulder, hands in his pockets.

Mario took a cigarette from his jacket pocket and lit it, as if to give himself a distraction from the awkwardness.

"Hey, Jaz," Jordie said, his voice soft, like I might break if he greeted me too loudly. "Mario," Jordie said with a nod at him. "How've you been? I haven't seen you around in a while."

"Yeah, well, I've been by to see your mom when you weren't there," Mario said with a rueful smile, the smile that could usually get him out of just about any amount of trouble with his mama.

"Nice," Jordie said.

I wrapped my arms around my knees and rocked back on my tailbone. "Don't," I said suddenly, interrupting them. "No 'your mama' jokes. Chick wouldn't like it."

"Yeah," Mario said as he blew out a cloud of smoke and tossed his cigarette into the stream. "Yeah, you're right."

"I don't think he would mind so much now," Jordie said. "As long as he knew we were all down here together."

Jordie's comment surprised me. He wasn't usually very sensitive to other people's feelings, and I had thought him oblivious to how much it upset Chick that the rest of us weren't getting along.

"Maybe if we had been down here together more he wouldn't have done what he did," I said as I felt my throat start to fill with a familiar and unwelcome lump.

"You don't know that," Jordie said, and I responded instinctively with anger, because he wasn't willing to take any responsibility for Chick leaving. "It's not your fault, Jaz," Jordie said, his gaze on the middle distance instead of on me. That made me angry too. As if I had been asking him for some kind of forgiveness or absolution he didn't have the power to give. "You couldn't have done anything for him," Jordie continued, oblivious to my anger, "just the way you couldn't do anything for Sylvia. He was sick, like she was. Nothing you could do about it."

Chris had said the same thing, but coming from Jordie, it just pissed me off. Jordie had already rationalized the whole thing, absolved himself of all blame. "Who said anything about Sylvia?" I asked hotly. "I blew Chick off. Treated him like shit. We all did," I said as I turned my head to include Mario with an accusing look. "We were his friends. We were supposed to be there for him."

"Take it easy," Mario said quietly, and held out a hand as if to place it on my arm but then thought better of it and tucked his hands under his armpits for warmth instead. "You don't want to blame yourself, I get that," Mario said to Jordie. "But you can't let Jaz take it all on himself."

Jordie just shook his head and we settled into another silent stalemate.

"You think I don't feel bad about it?" Jordie asked, the first to break the silence. "This was our senior year. It was supposed to be the best time for us. Instead we've been fighting the whole time. We lost Chick. You know, he was the only one who ever really gave a shit about any of us. He loved us like we were his brothers." As he said this, his voice broke and he turned his back on us to hide his tears. "Shit." After another minute he regained his control and said, his voice hollow, "You want to know something really stupid? All I could think that night after we found out about . . . what he did . . . Chick never even got laid, man. I don't think he ever even kissed a girl."

"Stop," I said as I squeezed my eyes shut, still trying to banish the mental image of Chick cold and alone down at the park in the last minutes of his life. This thought, about Chick dying a virgin, hadn't even occurred to me before now. Now I had to add it to the list of worries that were already clogging my brain. Add it to the list of all the things Chick would never see or do.

"I loved him too," Jordie said, leveling a look of challenge on me. "You can blame yourself for being a shitty friend, Jaz. But you can't blame yourself for what he did. Chick wouldn't want that. He wouldn't want you to hate yourself because of something he did. If he knew how you were taking it, how we all felt, he never would have done what he did. The only thing we did wrong was not telling him how much we cared about him while he was here."

My gut ached and I realized suddenly I had to piss. I found it annoying, this need to go to the bathroom, such a trivial reminder of what it meant to be human and alive. It felt wrong somehow. To feel hungry or tired or like I had to take a piss when Chick would never feel those things again. But at the same time it was a reminder that life was going to keep going, even if after losing Sylvia or Chick it seemed like the whole world should just stop spinning. I knew that what Jordie was saying was right. That it wasn't my fault and Chick wouldn't want me to feel that it was.

"C'mon," Mario said after a minute, then stood and offered a hand to help me to my feet. "Let's head to the bar and see if Chris will feed us. We'll swing by the apartment first so you can change out of that suit," Mario said to me. "You look like an idiot."

"*Cállate*, motherfucker," I said, but without much conviction.

In a few months high school would be behind us, like a bad dream that I would conjure occasionally when I let myself think about it, but otherwise meaningless. Mario insulting Jordie's mom, telling me I looked like an idiot, was the closest thing to an apology any of us would offer.

Maybe it was enough.

9-23-15
2-10-22 — 1-22-20
4(LHQ)   8